GOING LONG

The Waiting Series Book 2

BY GINGER SCOTT

instead I wanted to make sure she knew that everything was because of me, not her. I wanted the blame, all of it.

And with that one small word from her breath, *yes,* I knew I was done. The sensation of her lips on mine was an addiction. The miles on my Jeep read 93,728, and all but 3,000 of those miles were treaded by my many drives from Tucson up to Phoenix, just to see the girl who rules my world. I knew she was worried when I first came to surprise her at her dorm room two years ago and begged her to give me one more chance. But I made a promise to her then, and I had every intention of keeping it.

I wanted her to know that she could count on me being there to greet her as soon as her classes were done on Thursday afternoons. I didn't give a shit that it meant I had to turn around and drive the same miles back to campus for light practices on Fridays and games on Saturdays—sometimes making several trips each week just to see her. And when games were done, I spent my nights with her, holding her close, and letting her call all the shots.

My freshman year, I took a lot of shit from the guys on the football team, who all expected me to head to the bars with them every night and rule the parties on fraternity row. But I wouldn't go unless Nolan was with me. Sometimes she would, and I spent most of those nights making sure strangers didn't try to ply her with liquor or hit on her.

She finally convinced me to go alone once, about halfway through our freshman season. She was stuck at ASU, working late on a midterm psychology paper, and couldn't make it for our game against Stanford. We were serious underdogs, but managed to pull out a win, and there was no getting around celebrating. The entire UofA campus was teeming with energy, and it was the first time in months I let myself get a little loaded. I drunk-dialed her that night —several times, so I was told. I was so sure I said something stupid, but she assured me I was nothing but sweet and romantic. I'm pretty sure I embarrassed myself, but she didn't tease.

I was careful not to drink too much now. That was another vow I made when I left home for college and signed to play for the Wildcats. Don't get me wrong, I'm still a college guy, and I can chug with the best of them. But I try not to let it get stupid, and usually Noles is there to keep me in line or tell me when it's time to go home.

I wasn't going to be my brother; I wouldn't be the *asshole*. Being the asshole was the easy way out. And I was fine with things not being easy. Jason was quickly becoming a business big shot with our father's company. He was good at business, sales and working a room full of important people into doing exactly what he wanted. People always wanted Jason to like them, even as adults. It stunned me that they couldn't see through his bullshit, but I guess, deep down, most of us want to be liked by the *in* crowd, even if the guy at the head of the table was a massive dick.

Now that Nolan and I were juniors, it was harder to sync our schedules. Nolan's schedule was pretty full. She was taking 21 hours to make sure she could graduate in four years with her specialty. And I was seriously considering entering the draft after this season. Our Rose Bowl win, and number four finish last year, put me in a pretty good position to be a top pick, and we were already ranked pretty high heading into this season. I didn't want to lose my chance to do this for a living. I loved the game, almost as much as I loved Nolan. But that's what made it all so damned hard. I knew I could end up on the other end of the country, and the thought of spending a year away from her tore up my insides.

We talked about it a few times, but Nolan always shut down. She was a planner, and when I brought up the possibility of her transferring, or doing her student teaching somewhere else, she just nodded and said she'd think about it. But it was the kind of nod that I knew meant she really wouldn't, and was instead hoping the possibility would just go away.

I didn't have to make my decision yet. But come December, I needed to have a pretty good idea of where I was headed. I had four months to work on her, but the whole thing was just making my stomach sick. And the fucking ring in my pocket was just making my stress shoot through the roof.

I wasn't going to ask her today. I probably wouldn't ask her this year. But I knew I'd ask her, and I just wanted to be ready. I had most of the day off and stopped by the house to talk to dad on my way up to see Nolan. He loved her like a daughter already, and when I brought up the idea of one day making her a permanent part of the family, he hugged me so hard that my feet left the ground. I didn't expect him to give me Grandma's ring; I just wanted his help picking something out. So when he disappeared upstairs, and came back down with the antique box, I knew I was making the right decision.

I shoved the stress back down in my body and reminded myself to stay in control the second I saw my girl round the corner of her building—just like she did every Thursday afternoon. She was looking for me, her heavy bag slumping down her shoulder and her hair knotted up on top of her head. Damn she was beautiful. And I was so lucky.

"Hey, gorgeous," I smiled at her, kicking off the wall I was sitting on and reaching for her bag to throw it over my shoulder so I could take her hand. She stood on her tiptoes and kissed me, reaching inside my arm to hug me tightly. I'd never get tired of this.

"Hey, I'm so happy to see you. I've had the crappiest day," she sounded exhausted.

"Let me guess, you just found out you have to take a test for a class you've never been to," I was teasing her. She'd had this dream several times. I heard it was a common dream, though I'd never had it. She smacked my chest with her palm when I started in on her. I caught her arm and wrapped her up in mine, kissing her for real this time.

"I'm kidding. Tell me about it," I followed her into her building and to the elevator. A few of the freshmen walking by us stopped and stared, one of the guys questioning who I was. We got this a lot. Both because it was strange for me to be at a rival campus, and because I was starting to get a bit of a celebrity following—at least, as far as the college sports world was concerned.

Noles had taken a job as a hall monitor this year when her best friend Sienna decided to move in with her boyfriend, Micah. She had to be available to students most nights, which made it even harder for us to find times to see each other, but it meant her room and board were covered, so it was a trade-off we both were willing to work around.

When we got to her door, she unlocked it and immediately walked to her bed flopping straight forward on her face, slowly sliding it sideways to look at me through her tired eyes.

I sat down next to her and pulled her hair from the band that was holding it up and started to brush it with my fingers. I knew she loved it when I did this.

"Mmmmmm, can you do that for the next six hours?" she giggled a little.

"Well, I can do it for the next four at least, then I have to hit the road," I just smiled down at her. "Tell me about this crappy day."

She rolled over on her side and propped her head up. "Uhg, group project," she rolled her eyes.

I laughed a little, knowing how Nolan felt about group projects —never mind that if it wasn't for a group project, we might not have ever gotten together. Nolan was the perfect student, but she also expected perfection from others. And when a group couldn't deliver that, it stressed her the hell out.

"Bad group?" I asked, already knowing.

"The worst," she let out a heavy breath, her lips quivering a little with it. "We have to perform practice IQ tests on each other, and the two other jackasses in my group started building towers with the blocks today, rather than lining up the colors for a pattern like you're supposed to do."

I laughed a little at her, but the look she shot me shut me up pretty quickly. "Sorry, it just doesn't sound sooooo bad," I said, stroking her hair again to make up for my gaffe. "I bet they pull it together for you."

She sat up then and looked me in the eyes with a serious expression. "You didn't let me finish. Then, they pulled out their *Angry Bird* stuffed animals and started catapulting them into the towers. This went on for 30 minutes; I prepped an *entire* test before they knocked over six blocks!"

Stifling the laughter was too difficult, and finally it broke free from me. Nolan just shoved her pillow in my face and leaned onto me roughly as she stood up. I couldn't help it though, the scene was just too much to handle.

"I'm sorry, Noles," I pulled myself together. "But you have to admit, it sounds pretty funny. I don't know what's better, the fact that they have stuffed animals in college, or that they came up with this idea."

The smirk on her face when she turned around let me know that she was starting to see the humor in it a little, too. "Well, thank goodness I have one more group member. He couldn't make it to today's meeting, but he's actually pretty smart, plus he runs the fifth floor, so I can work on the project with him at our building when we fail to get anything done with *Tweedle Dee* and *Tweedle Dum.*"

I didn't miss the *he* part of her statement. And I didn't really like the idea that this guy lived only two stories up from her, or that she thought he was *pretty smart*. But I kept that deep inside and put it in line with the other things I talk about—and probably swear about a little—to myself when I'm driving through the desert between our two schools. Instead, I just smiled at her, pulled her to my lap and went to work on her mouth. I had four hours with her today, and I was going to spend most of those minutes kissing her.

Chapter Two

Nolan

I NEVER GOT TIRED of seeing Reed waiting for me by my building. It made the day rush by, and I wanted to run to him every time I saw him sitting there waiting for me. It was only a hundred miles between our two schools, but it was still a hundred miles. I drove to his school a few times, mostly on game days. But he didn't like me driving through the desert, still a little shell-shocked from our accident.

Some days he was tired, and I could tell. But he made the trip anyhow. I knew he couldn't stay long today, and I knew he *desperately* wanted to have the conversation about me transferring schools if he went through with the draft, but I wasn't ready to have that talk yet.

I knew he loved me. Damn, he'd gone far to prove it. But the thought of uprooting things, just for him to find out that there were options in the big world—women out there, that were *better* still plagued my mind. It didn't help that his mother, Millie, never quite warmed to me. She got my name right when we were in each other's company now, but there was always an air of disdain in how she spoke to me. Reed always denied it, but it was there. I sensed it—my girlfriends sensed it. Hell, Reed's dad, Buck, even sensed it too, telling me more than once not to let her *bitchy streak* get to me.

But all of that didn't matter when I lay in his arms. I enjoyed the now. It calmed the constant churn of stress in my gut from my studies and the fear of blowing my scholarship—the one thing in my mind that edged out the worry over Reed's draft decision.

"You're still stressed about this project, aren't you?" Reed whispered in my ear, his breath sending chills through me. I just took a deep breath and turned on my side to face him, burying my face deep in his chest while he wrapped his massive arms around me.

"That transparent, huh?" I let out a big sigh.

"You were never very good at poker," he chuckled. "Can I help? Do you want to test my IQ? I mean, I'm a *genius*, so it will probably throw everything off, but I'm willing to play dumb if you need me to."

His damn smile and comforting humor always soothed me. His hair was shorter now, but still long enough for me to grab fistfuls, and his face was no longer the baby-skinned one I had first kissed years ago. It was rough, and almost always in need of a shave by the time I saw him. It was perfect. He was perfect. Kissing his stubbly chin, I looked up at him while I lay tucked tightly in his arms.

"You know, it's not fair that you're so smart and also so good looking," I said, for once giving him a compliment without backloading it with a joke. He just looked at me skeptically, and I couldn't resist. "Something had to give, though. I guess that's why your hairline's receding."

I held my serious face as long as I could without breaking. When I finally did, he just rolled on top of me and dug in with a breath-stealing tickle round. He finally let up, standing to look at the clock on my desk, his face souring a little because it was time for him to go.

I grabbed my keys and walked him down the hall to the stairs. I always hated this moment, but I knew I'd see him in two days for his game. We stood still just staring at each other for seconds, our fingers interlocking with one another, not willing to let go. I sensed the heaviness on his mind, seconds before his brow creased and he looked down, kicking at my feet a little.

"Spill it, Wildcat," I nudged him.

"We have to talk about the draft, Noles," he grimaced. I had made him afraid to bring the topic up, which I didn't like. But I also dreaded talking about it.

"I know," I sighed. "I just...I can't get my head there yet. Maybe, maybe in a week or two?" Why the hell did I throw that out there? Crap, I just gave myself a deadline.

Reed smiled a bit at my words, which solidified what I already knew, that it was right for us to talk about it, and I needed to come around. I just hoped that these next few weeks dragged more slowly than any before.

"Deal. We can talk about it during my bye week. Maybe we can get away for a bit, spend a little time together, alone?" he smirked.

"But we are alone," I said coyly.

"Yes, but...and no offense...your dorm bed is shit small. And this place always smells like burnt popcorn," he scrunched his nose a little.

I had to agree. And the thought of the two of us getting away did make the impending conversation a little more tolerable. I stood up on my tiptoes and kissed his cheek, holding his face in my hands and looking him in the eyes. "OKAY, two weeks then," I smiled, pulling out a damn fine poker face if I'd ever seen one.

———

It was amazing how much reading I had this early in the semester. Specializing in reading and writing disabilities was more challenging than I had anticipated, but every time I worked with a student in our resource center or at one of the local schools, I knew it was worth it. Seeing someone put together words, and read aloud, made my heart pump with pride.

I had been working on the poem project for a little more than a semester now. I had a dozen or so students that I met with on a regular basis, writing poetry. It was going to be part of my final portfolio, showing how teaching language through poetry helped with written and verbal communication skills. We were going to have a reading at the end of the semester at a local coffee shop where I spent most of my mornings and afternoons studying. Reed knew a little about the project, but I was keeping the reading a surprise. I wanted to invite him for a special evening.

Finally done with my homework for the night, I flipped out the light and kicked my feet into the giant comforter on my bed, breathing it in since it still smelled of Reed. My mind raced, "Two weeks. Two weeks until I gave him my blessing to enter the draft."

I knew I had to support Reed; I was being selfish. What I wasn't sure about was if I truly wanted to transfer. It wasn't so much that I minded moving to a different school, but I did worry about how I would pay for it. Reed always told me not to worry about the finances, but I didn't think I could let him help pay for my schooling. As ashamed as I was to even admit it to myself, I think part of my worry was that he'd end up breaking up with me and leave me stuck completely.

I also wasn't sure we could survive a full year being that far apart. I wasn't even sure what life after graduation meant for *us*. Reed always talked about me in his future, but he'd never really talked about kids or marriage. I think his own broken childhood colored his outlook on things like *forever* a little. Sure, we talked about living somewhere because of football. Buying a house thanks to football. Paying my tuition anywhere…with the help of football. But we were always careful not to cross that line into what that meant beyond football. Neither of us.

I wrestled with these thoughts for an hour, never coming up with answers and debating how our conversation about the draft would go. Sleep wasn't coming easy, and I blame that partly for the thought-stopping epiphany that hit my nerve endings with the jolt of a lightning bolt.

Sprinting from my bed, I flung my desk lamp on and flipped frantically through the pages of my day planner. I wrote everything down in that planner. Most people liked to keep their calendars on their phones or iPads, but I always had to have mine in writing.

Writing it down always helped me remember, or so I thought. I flipped to the current week and rubbed my eyes, hoping they weren't focusing. When a second and third look confirmed what I saw, I sunk to the floor, my heart beating at the speed of a hummingbird's wing.

I was four days late.

Chapter Three

Nolan

THE INTERNET IS a scary thing at 3 a.m. Like a fortuneteller, it tells you what you think you want to hear. Or, in my case, what I desperately wanted to prove wrong. I sat there for hours with my iPad, flipping through site after site about the signs of pregnancy, and how long before you could tell. I was pretty sure I could pee on a stick at this point and know for sure. But I also liked living in the 50/50. Peeing on the stick could mean 100-percent certainty. And I only wanted that if it meant I wasn't pregnant.

It's funny how your body and mind can operate on autopilot. I didn't move from that spot on the floor until the sun rose. I didn't sleep, and I was sliding my feet to the resource center in the middle of campus for a few morning sessions with some of my students. I didn't register a single word my students read during our sessions. I heard muffled sounds that resembled words, I smiled, I nodded and I encouraged. I was getting good at poker faces.

Autopilot took me to Sarah's apartment next. When I didn't see Calley's car in the parking lot, I pushed forward up the steps, knowing she'd likely gone to work, leaving my friend at home alone.

By the time she answered the door, I must have lost my ability to bluff, because the tears started to come, and words evaded me.

"Jesus, Nolan. What's wrong?" Sarah asked, pulling me inside and slamming the door behind me. She grabbed my hand and led me to the couch, pushing me down and kneeling in front of me with a truly confused look on her face.

I just shook my head back and forth, trying to form words with my lips but not even knowing where to begin.

"Okay, you're going to have to speak. Is it Reed? Did that asshole cheat on you?" she was grabbing my shoulders now, clearly going from her zero-to-sixty, friend-ready-to-defend-you mode.

I just shook my head no, fighting to slow my breathing down. After a few seconds, I slumped my shoulders, defeated, and looked up at her.

"I'm late," I said, twisting the side of my mouth to show her how helpless I felt.

She just blinked at me in return, taking her time to register what I'd said. Her eyes grew wider when it settled in. "You mean, like… late, late?" She kept a firm grip on my shoulders while she questioned me.

I nodded *yes* slowly, never blinking, and staring her in the eyes without really looking at anything.

"Oh…shit," Sarah said, not able to hide her emotions. I suppose that's why I came to her. I needed someone to freak out for me, to think quickly on her feet. Sienna was the practical one. But Sarah, she would go bat-shit crazy with me. And this revelation? Well, it called for bat-shit crazy.

"We need to go to the drug store, Noles. Like now. You have to know for sure," she said, pushing her feet into her shoes and rummaging around her kitchen counter for her purse and keys. I didn't move until she was standing right in front of me, my own feet dug deeply into the carpet and my legs unwilling to move.

"I…don't know if I want to know," I looked at her, my eyes pleading. Just then, my phone buzzed. Autopilot again, I pulled it from my purse and saw a text from Reed.

Miss you, baby. Have a late dinner tonight with family friend to talk about that thing we're going to talk about. Someone in the business. Call you after, K? Love you.

His message was short and sweet, but I took my time reading it, almost as if it was a full five-page essay. I didn't budge until I felt the weight of Sarah plop down next to me and felt her shove my arms down to get my phone screen out of my face.

"Noles, snap out of it. You HAVE to find out. You can't live in between," she said, standing and pulling at my armpit to lift me from the couch. She was right, but that didn't stop me from craving the blissful ignorance of *right now*.

The drugstore was only a block or two from Sarah's apartment. And unfortunately, our walk to get there didn't take us nearly as long as I would have liked. The rows were filled with appealing colors. I tried to drag us down the nail polish aisle, thinking maybe a new color on my toes would be nice. *Yank*. Sarah tugged my arm. I tried again for the candy aisle, thinking maybe a big bag of M&Ms would soothe me, but *YANK*. No such luck.

We stood there in front of the selection of various pregnancy tests in a section vividly labeled *Family Planning*. The entire thing was surreal. I heard words escape from Sarah's lips, but I wasn't listening. Everything sounded muted, and slow. She was throwing box after box in our small basket and soon was grabbing my hand to pull us to the register.

The judgmental look from the checkout lady was something I will never forget. If I hadn't been stunned and frozen with the constant stab of shock, I might have said something to her. I was getting better at sticking up for myself. But with this, being in this situation, I just let her judge. Who was I?

We walked back to Sarah's apartment with $60 in pregnancy tests. Sarah pulled them all out on the counter and went to work reading the directions immediately, first handing me a plastic wand and telling me to try to only pee a little so we could knock out a few tests. I just stood there holding the stick, staring at the small circle on the end that would give me my fate.

"Nolan, come on. You have to pee on it. Go!" She was chastising me. She left the bathroom for a few minutes to give me some privacy. I stood staring at the dry filter strip, considering briefly running it through the faucet and pretending I had taken the test. But fooling Sarah wouldn't do me any good in the long run.

I turned her sink faucet on to help me have to go and sat waiting —finally taking a deep breath and going a little on the tip of the test strip. Sarah was reading directions from the other side of the door, telling me that I needed to let the test sit on the counter for two minutes. But that wasn't necessary.

The colors were changing almost instantly, and when I saw the small *plus sign* start to appear, I wasn't surprised. But I *was* terrified.

"Are you done? I've got another one, tell me when you're ready," Sarah was leaning on the other side of the door.

"I don't need it," I said, faintly.

"What? Why?" she cracked open the door as I was pulling my shorts back into place, the stick dangling from my hand. "Nolan, you have to set it down and wait for two minutes. Didn't you listen to anything I said?"

I held it up in front of me, showing her the positive result. Sarah just looked at it with tightly closed lips, considering the best reaction.

"You don't know for sure, Nolan. Those things aren't always accurate. Come on, try one more," she was already pulling a new stick from the box and handing it to me.

"It's going to be the same," I said, shaking my head slowly. "I just know."

"No, you don't!" she said forcefully, putting the new test in my hand and pushing me back while she closed the door.

I humored Sarah and went through five of the tests—all positive —before she finally relented and slid down against the bathroom door to sit on the floor across from me. We didn't talk for about 20 minutes, just looking up at the row of tests every now and then and sighing, considering.

What was I going to do? How could this have happened? Well,

that's a stupid question; I know exactly how it happened. But we were always so very careful. This was going to ruin everything. I wouldn't be able to finish my degree, Reed might not be able to enter the draft, or worse, he might not want anything to do with me —or a baby.

Almost as if she was hearing my inner dialogue, Sarah interrupted my stream of thoughts. "You have to tell Reed," she said, abruptly.

"No," I shot back quickly. "I mean, not yet. I have to think this through. I should make sure, you know, with a doctor first."

I took another deep breath and pulled my knees up to my stomach, hugging them for comfort. My brain was searching for answers. I didn't know how I was going to deal with this. Suddenly, Sarah got to her feet and walked into her bedroom to grab her cell phone. She started dialing and I grabbed her hand.

"No, please. Don't call him," I tried to stop her.

She just stared at me and then kept dialing, finally speaking. "I'm not calling Reed, Nolan. That's your conversation to have. I'm calling the student health center to get you an appointment."

I watched as Sarah pretended to be me on the phone, answering the personal questions and looking to me for help with some, such as when was the last time I had intercourse. Things that I considered to be so private were instantly too public, and I wanted to bury myself and hide.

"Okay, Tuesday, in two weeks. Got it, thank you," Sarah said, hanging up and writing down a note on a scrap of paper for me. "Okay, you have an 8 a.m. appointment in two weeks. They said you need to be farther along before they can know anything for sure."

I just grabbed the paper from her hand and stuffed it in my front pocket. "Thanks," I said, attempting an appreciative smile that just curled my lip slightly to one side. I looked down at my lap, thinking about how my belly would grow soon. I knew what this all meant, but it also didn't seem real. It didn't feel like I had a baby, Reed's baby, growing inside me. But science, I suppose, begged to differ.

"What do you want to do?" Sarah said, instantly regretting it

17

and trying to fix it. "I mean, right now. Not, about…that. Sorry…" she just grimaced.

"It's okay, I know what you meant," I said, pulling myself to my feet and smoothing out my shorts. "I guess I'll go home. I have a ton of studying to do, and I have to get a huge paper out of the way before we head to Tucson tomorrow." In my mind, I conceded, that I might be in denial.

"Are you sure? You can stay here if you want, Calley doesn't mind," she was acting fragile toward me.

I shrugged a bit and let out a heavy breath. "No, it's okay. I promise," I lied. I was not okay.

Sarah walked me to the bottom of her steps, her face heavy with wanting to talk, but not knowing what to say. I could tell, and I loved her for it. But truthfully, there really weren't any words I wanted to hear right now. I wasn't used to this new starting line that life had thrown me, and I needed to get used to the new game board, figure it out and know what my rules were.

By the time I printed my final paper and proofed it, it was a little after 10 p.m. Reed would be home from his dinner soon, and I knew he'd be calling me. My mind was still pushing the new information to the back—the proof of that in the paper I had just finished writing, which was likely my best work to date.

I brought my phone into the bathroom and set it on the towel rack in case Reed called while I was showering. My body ached, and I just needed a little steam on my face to help me reset things, to think.

The hot water was like an eraser for my anxiety, my shoulders suddenly relaxing and my face almost smiling at the splash against my cheeks. I pumped a handful of body wash into my hand and smoothed it over my neck and shoulders, rubbing the smooth peach-scented wash over my chest and then stomach, my hands instantly stopping and holding protectively the spot around my belly button, instantly bringing me back to reality.

Looking down, I thought hard about what was inside me. For

the briefest moment, I thought to myself how I wished it never happened. I didn't want this. *I. Did. Not. Want. This. Baby.* Then I slid down to sit on the shower floor and cried harder than I ever had, ashamed of what I'd just thought and wanting to delete the words from existence.

I left the shower stall when the water turned cool. My skin was wrinkled from the soaking, and my hair hadn't really been washed, but I was too weak to finish the job. Wrapping my hair in a towel, I wrapped another around my body and picked up my phone, flopping myself on my bed to wait for Reed's call.

When the phone rang near 11 p.m., I forced myself to answer it. Somewhere between the time of my shower and now, I had decided I was going to pretend—at least for a little while.

"Hey you," I forced myself to be chipper.

"Ah that's a sound for…sore eyes? No, wait. That's not how that goes. Aw hell, you know what I mean," he chuckled. "Sorry I'm so late."

He sounded so good. Everything about his voice was everything I needed. Frozen a little with the fear of losing it all, I sat up strong and pushed everything deeper. "It's okay; I just finished my paper and took a shower. How was your dinner?"

"Hmmmm, well…" he was thinking.

"Was it bad?" I couldn't tell from his hedging.

"No, it's just…well. Are you sure you want to talk about this? It's sort of that topic that we took off the table until our weekend," he said carefully. I loved him for how much he respected me and my stupid worries. But suddenly, his entering the draft was the least of my worries. Never mind the fact that the news I was holding onto could ruin everything. For tonight, I wanted to pretend. And so I did.

"Yeah, it's okay. I want to know, talk to me. I like to hear your voice, and you seem excited," I said. His voice was animated, and I could tell that his mind was made up, if only I would get on board.

"Okay, if you're sure," he waited for a few seconds. "Well, I met with Brent Nichols. He's huge, Noles. He's repped so many amazing athletes. And of course, well, he's on the board for the children's foundation, the same one that my mom sits on. She sort of set this up, drove down here for dinner and everything."

I winced a little knowing Millie was involved and was instantly grateful Reed couldn't see my face. "Wow, that's amazing she has that connection. So, what'd he have to say?" I feigned enthusiasm, my acting skills surprisingly strong tonight.

Reed just sighed at first. Finally, when he spoke, he seemed careful. "Well, he thinks I need to really go this year. The options opening up are huge, and there's a great chance that I'll be picked up early and go somewhere really good. There's a huge quarterback need and the class coming out is only two or three guys deep."

I knew all of this, of course. The pundits had been talking Reed up a lot over the summer. He wouldn't be number one. There was a running back at the University of Texas who had that locked up, provided he stayed healthy. But Reed was in the mix for the top 10 for sure. Forcing myself to be supportive, I offered up my best. "Well, this gives you some good stuff to think about then, huh?"

"Yeah, it does," he let out a heavy sigh, but collected himself. "I still have some things to work through, though. I can't formally declare or sign with any representation, so I'm going to talk to Dylan Nichols. Brent said Dylan would give me a call. I think it's his son, and he's a little more off the radar. He can put feelers out, I guess, without it being front-page news."

"Ah, I see," I said, nodding and smiling as if he could see me. When I remembered that I was home alone under my covers, I let the frown reign again.

"You sound tired, do you want to go to sleep?" Reed asked in response to my silence. Suddenly, the thought of hanging up with him frightened me.

"No, no. I mean, yes, I'm tired, but… can I just keep you on the phone for a while? You know, maybe fall asleep with you near? Unless you have something to do."

"Why, are you asking me to talk dirty to you, Nolan?" Reed put on that deep, devilish voice that normally had my heart racing. But tonight that was the last thing I wanted.

"No," I giggled, hoping it sounded genuine. "I just miss you. Is that okay?"

"Of course. Get comfortable, and turn off the lights. I'll tell you a story, okay?" he said kindly. I knew what was coming. Sometimes, when I was really stressed, Reed would retell the story of our relationship, about the first time he danced with me, the first time he held my hand, when he wrote me a letter telling me he thought I was beautiful. He never retold any of the bad parts, about how his ex-girlfriend Tatum had bullied me and kept us apart. And normally, I didn't give thoughts of her the time of day. But tonight I was instantly zeroed in on my memories of Tatum, primarily her pregnancy scare...and how that almost ruined Reed's life.

I nestled into my covers and pushed my pillow up to my face, muffling the sounds of my crying while Reed spoke sweetly in my ear. So much for pretending.

Chapter Four

Reed

GAME DAY HAD ME PUMPED. Oregon was in town, and this game mattered more than most. Oregon was our biggest divisional competition.

Noles liked to pretend that the Devils would give us a run for our money, but not this year. I was glad, too, because the line last year really did a number on me. I was pretty sure I cracked a rib, though I'd never mentioned that to anyone. There was this unspoken rule about bringing up your injuries. If you said them aloud and a member of the coaching staff heard, they had to follow through with MRIs and doctors' opinions and shit. But if you never said them for anyone to hear, and no one asked, then those smaller injuries could sort of slide under the radar.

There were a lot of people that hated that side of the game, and I get it. But hell, I wanted to play, and if they had to tape my neck together just to hold my head on in order for me to do so, then I was fine with that. The lawyers, though? Well, not so much. So we kept our mouths shut, and played, no matter how much it hurt.

So far, I'd been lucky. No big hits to threaten my clear mind and strong arm. But I knew that *big hit* was always looming. I saw it in the eyes of every angry linebacker that looked right through me, every single game, sometimes even during practice. That's why my draft entry this year was so important. The longer I put it off, the bigger the risk that I would become damaged goods, unwanted in the only world I've ever really wanted to belong.

I had to make Nolan get that. I know deep down she understood, and I hated that I was making my priorities bigger than hers. *Selfish asshole.* That's how I felt. But whenever I tucked it to the back of my thoughts, it found a way back to the forefront with news about someone else's career-ending injury or some sad story about a washed up athlete working as a real-estate agent. Or my own damned brother and his pathetic, plastic life that I didn't want in the worst way.

But now it was time to clear my head. The walk from my dorm to the workout room was my favorite, especially on Saturdays. The campus was empty, so I slid by unnoticed. The truly dedicated academic sorts, filtering in and out of the main library on the weekends, couldn't give a shit who I was, and it was glorious.

September in Tucson was hot. Hell, October was hot, too. But September was downright brutal. Frankly, it gave us an edge when the West Coast teams came to town. When you practiced every day in the searing 100-plus degrees, playing a few hours during an evening game was no sweat, literally. The visitors were usually less fortunate, heat exhaustion quick to settle in.

The sun was lighting up the nearby desert hills, and the sky was on the brink of turning the most awesome orange. There was a faint and familiar smell of rain and dust in the air from the faraway thunderclouds. Everything about the desert was home to me, but I mostly loved taking it in because it reminded me of Nolan. I can't explain why, maybe it was all of the times I'd kissed her at sunset. But it did. And *this walk*…this time of the day? Well, it was just my favorite.

My phone rang as I opened the door to the workout room. I pulled it from my pocket, recognizing my dad's ringtone right away. Dad thought it was hysterical that I gave him ZZ Top's *Sharp Dressed*

Man. It was Nolan's idea because of the crazy-ass suits my pops always wears.

I dropped my bags by a bench just inside, and swiped my phone to answer. "Hey dad, what's up?" I said, sliding my feet from my shoes and getting my gear ready.

"Hey, Kid. You ready for tonight?" he asked, as excited as ever. No one would argue my pops was my number-one fan. He was my champion and rock, too.

"Hells yeah," I laughed a little, sitting down to try to pull at the laces on my cleats with my spare hand.

"Good, good," dad chuckled. "Noles is coming, yeah?"

"Of course! She doesn't miss a game," I smiled as I spoke.

"Good," Dad paused for a bit, which made me a little nervous.

"Why? What's up," I was suspicious now and stopped what I was doing.

"Nothing, nothing at all. It's just, well… Mom's coming tonight, too. She's got a lunch set up tomorrow for you to meet Dylan."

"Oh, okay, that's fine. Noles is okay with whatever, you know her," I relaxed a little.

"Yeah, I know she is. I just don't want Millie to get to her, that's all," Dad said, acknowledging the shitty attitude my mom always put out whenever Nolan was around. I didn't want to admit it, but she had never warmed to Nolan. I finally talked to my dad about it one night after an especially *Millie Johnson-Snyder* type of evening that sent Nolan home in tears I was sure. He just told me it was part of my mom's flawed personality and that I needed to write it off and tell Nolan to do the same. As much as I didn't want to think badly about my mom, I had to agree with him.

"Alright, I'll make sure I make Noles deliriously happy before she has to spend a second with Mom," I laughed a little, though I wasn't kidding, and I was already coming up with ways I could boost my girl's confidence before my mother tore it down.

"Okay, Kid. You're a good nut, you know?" Dad said.

"Yeah, yeah," I laughed. "You on your way?"

"Sure am. I'm going to pick up Dylan for the game. If I get

there early, we'll stop by, sound good?" he said, I heard a honking sound in the distance over the phone.

"Yeah, that works. Hey, though, Pops? Why don't you go focus on driving now, huh? I'm gonna let you go, okay?" I insisted. I had an irrational fear of car crashes; I knew this. But being careful wasn't the worst thing in the world.

"You got it; see you in a bit," Dad said, hanging up almost mid word. He was so awkward with his phone as it was; the thought of him pushing buttons while he cruised along the highway in his big-ass truck, going well over the speed limit, was about all my mind could take. That *stubborn ass* had a death wish, I swear! But not on my watch.

————

I'd been massaged, whirl-pooled, stretched, taped and wrapped. This was the part before the game where I sat on the training table with my legs dangling, listening to my favorite playlist; it was a new one Nolan had made for me. She sent me a new one every few games, always with some funny song that she said was the key to defeating my opponent. Colorado State had a John Denver tune, which was about as rockin' as on-hold music, but fuckin' funny nonetheless. The Cal game was a series of Beastie Boys songs—I kept that one around because it was just badass.

Lying back, I shut my eyes and readied myself for her latest masterpiece. The first one was some rancid song from the '90s; I think it was that chick that was married to Kurt Cobain? I couldn't even make it through the first verse without sending Nolan a text. I knew she was still in Coolidge.

Uh…grunge? What the hell?

I flipped to the next song, which was some old punk tune. Not half bad. This one I could take. I smiled as soon as my phone vibrated in my hand with her response.

Hey, first of all don't knock Hole. Vintage Courtney Love was the shit. Second, she grew up in Portland : -)

I laughed. It was a stretch, but she'd found an Oregon connection.

OK, good tie-in. But still, she's not helpin' me out here. I'm going to need to pull out my own stuff if this list doesn't get any better.

I waited for just a few seconds before she responded.

Song 11. Trust me. XXOO, leaving now. See you soon! I'm in section 111 with Sarah. I'll catch up with you and your dad after, ok?

I scrolled to song 11 before responding, and when I heard the familiar riffs of *Thunderstruck* start, I got a huge-ass grin and wrote her back immediately.

Ahhhh, now that's more like it. You do know me after all. Now, if I can just get you on board with Jay-Z and Kanye...

I waited, but there wasn't a response, so I knew she must have left. I tucked my phone into my bag and lay back, getting lost in Nolan's latest soundtrack, which, thankfully, got a lot better and rocked out for the remaining songs.

———

Dad showed up about an hour before the game, just like he always did. Buck Johnson had a special pass, and he got to wherever he wanted in the building—probably *any* building, I thought—on campus. His name was on more than a few gold donation plates throughout the athlete quarters, and most of the coaches knew him by first name. Hell, Coach Toms, my quarterback coach, had bought every family automobile from Johnson Buick in Tucson since the late '90s. To say my dad was tight with the staff around here was putting it mildly. They were family.

Manly hugs and pats on the back were being passed around. I just watched, leaning on the table. My dad could work a room. I hoped that one day I'd have a tenth of his charisma. The love fest was soon broken up by a series of whistles and catcalls. I watched my roommate, Trig, jump up on one of the benches and cover his mouth, waving his hand like he'd just bit into a hot pepper. He was starting to laugh a bit with surprise when he locked eyes with me, almost as if he was trying to give me a warning telepathically. His message, however, hit me too late. I was suddenly in the presence of a five-foot-ten-at-the-very-least blonde with legs that could make even the most faithful of boyfriends turn flirtatious and stupid.

My elbow slid from the table, making it impossible to hide my gawking. I hadn't even pushed my eyes upward to take in her face yet, but I knew from everything I'd seen so far that she was hot… like…supermodel hot. I saw my dad put his hand flat against her back and lead her closer to me, and for a moment, I understood. "Ah, I bet this is his latest girlfriend," I thought.

"Hey, Kid. You said you were ready. You don't look it to me, you look lazy," my dad kidded, but with a bite of truth. "Do I need to have a talk with Toms? Is he letting you slack off?"

My dad's belly laugh was iconic. I watched him nod to Coach Toms across the room, who acknowledged my game-readiness with a smile and thumbs up. "Kid's always ready, Buck. Born ready," he yelled over his shoulder as he headed into the front office to choke down some dinner.

"Yeah, he sure was," my dad said, reaching over to give me a hug now. My eyes finally found the spectacle standing behind him—her blue eyes crystal and perfect, not a hair out of place. Her silk blouse was so tight over her chest, leaving little to my imagination, though what my imagination was doing needed to be stopped, immediately. This was difficult because she was smiling now, and it was the kind of smile that reeked of whatever that thing was that kept heroin addicts coming back for more. *Trouble.* It was trouble.

"Dylan Nichols," she said, holding her perfectly manicured fingers out for me to touch, her eyes drilling into mine, and her shiny lips stretching into a smile that showed off her very expensive teeth. Shit! This…is Dylan?

I reached out and shook her hand, removing the grin from my face and pulling out my best indifference despite the worry that now consumed the pit of my stomach. "Nice to meet you," I said—friendly, but nothing more.

"We made good time," my dad piped in. "Thought I'd get the introductions out of the way, before we meet up with your mom tomorrow."

Mom. That's what it was about Dylan. She was, in so very many ways, Millie Johnson-Snyder. No wonder my mom liked the Nichols family so much.

"My dad's told me a lot about you, Reed. He's a big fan," she said with a certain air of confidence.

Okay, flattering, but she wasn't flirting. This was good.

"Your numbers look good—impressive, in fact. You could go higher than Patricks did last year, but only if the timing's right."

Dylan Nichols knew her way around the business of football. "Thanks," I said. One-word answers were safe.

"We'll talk more tomorrow, sorry. I didn't mean to let business creep in before your game. Habit, blame my dad," she giggled, but not in a girly way. She *was* Millie…and Nolan was going to *flip the fuck out* at lunch tomorrow.

"I gotta go get ready," I said, slinging my jersey over my shoulder to take her hand one more time in a business-like shake. "It was nice to meet you, Dylan. My girlfriend's excited to meet you, too," I said, forcing the words from my mouth and putting them where they didn't belong, but wanting to make my relationship clear —probably wanting to clear my own conscience a bit, too. The part about Nolan being excited, however, was overkill. All I had going for me now was playing up the humor in the misunderstanding of gender-neutral names, something Nolan could relate to. But I knew even that wouldn't soothe the discomfort she was sure to feel when she was sandwiched at a table between the young and seasoned versions of my mother.

———

Dylan left my mind the second I stepped through the tunnel. Truth was there wasn't much room for anything other than winning when I was on the field. I always had the gift of concentration. It was my edge, and it'd taken me pretty far.

We ended up defeating Oregon 14-21. Their defense was everything I'd expected it to be, punishing, tough, brutal and strong. But they didn't break me. I'd made it through one more game with my wits still with me.

"You comin' out with us tonight, Johnson?" Trig said as he walked by on his way to the showers, smacking my head with his rolled-up towel, "Or your girlfriend got you on a leash tonight?"

I knew he was only teasing, but it pissed me off. "Fuck off," I said, shoving him a little.

"Shit, man. I was kidding. Noles is my girl, you know that," he looked offended.

"Sorry, just a little stressed..." I said, my mind bouncing between wanting to talk to Nolan about the draft, warn her about Dylan and then...*Dylan*. "Yeah, we'll probably come out with you guys. Where you headed first?"

"Cooler's, I guess. They never charge," Trig said, flipping on the water to his shower.

"Okay, we'll meet you there," I said, turning to the hot water now streaming at my face.

I lucked out when I hooked up with Trig. He came to Arizona

from New Mexico, and the man was a quarterback's dream. If I put the ball anywhere near his shadow, he was catching it. We were both Johnsons, which had become the favorite headline for the campus paper. 'Johnson & Johnson.'

Trig came from a big family, and he was the youngest. He had four brothers who all played college ball. His oldest brother, Miles, was a left tackle for the Cardinals, and we got some pretty sweet seats to some of the games thanks to that little connection. Trig understood my pressure better than anyone else on the team, and he'd been there to talk through a lot of the draft shit when I wasn't ready to bring it up to Nolan. And after, when it freaked her out, he was there for that, too. His girlfriend went to UofA with us, and they'd been dating about as long as Noles and I had. Trig was looking to enter the draft this year, too. But his girlfriend, Amy, was all for it. And I envied him for it.

———

Nolan and Sarah were waiting on the leather sofa at the main entrance to the athlete quarters, their feet folded up in their laps. The girls had grown closer in college and even more so when Sienna moved in with her boyfriend. I was glad that Nolan had someone like Sarah to look after her. She'd told me off a time or two, and I'll be honest, it made me nervous. I wanted that same toughness at Nolan's side when I wasn't around.

"Well, how'd I do?" I asked, kicking at Nolan's folded legs a little.

She stood up, pulling her shirt down over the top of her shorts, always modest and still so damned unsure of her beauty. Chewing at the inside of her cheek a little, she put her thumb to her lip like she was considering something. "Hmmmm, I don't know, Johnson. I'd put you at about eighty percent," she nodded, acting with disappointment.

"Eighty percent, huh?" I said, rushing her a little and swinging her over my shoulder to carry her through the doors. Her giggling started then, the best sound in the whole damn world. "Eighty percent?"

I took off running, leaving Sarah behind. Nolan knew exactly where I was going as she started slapping at my back and threatening me that I'd *better not*. When we got to the main fountain at the center of campus, I pulled her back over my shoulder and held her in my arms as I pulled off my shoes with my feet.

"Reed Johnson, don't you dare!" she screamed as I stepped over the concrete edge and waded in the water, sliding closer and closer to the main spray. Her screams and giggles only egged me on.

"You want to rethink that *B minus*, Noles? Eighty percent? You sure about that?" I said, freezing in place, just one more step away from the full effects of the waterfall. I looked her in the eyes and watched as she flinched, just for a minute, and then finally did it.

"Okay, maybe I was being a bit unfair. You were really more of an eighty-two," she said, baiting me.

Our eyes locked, I pushed my lips tight into a disapproving grin and shook my head. "Oh, now you've done it," I said, stepping forward and stopping us underneath the force of the fountain's shower. Nolan wasn't mad. Sure, she screamed and smacked at my chest as the freezing water poured over us. But my playfulness never rattled her. If anything, it had the opposite effect, which I was counting on as she reached around my neck and pulled my head to hers for a forceful kiss. Her hands grabbed at my soaked T-shirt, pulling me closer. I let her body slide from my arms so I could wrap my fingers through her hair. It was a good thing Trig and Sarah reminded us we were in public.

"God, you two. It's bad enough that I don't have a boyfriend, but do I really have to be the uncomfortable third wheel on our way to the bars, too?" Sarah broke us up.

"Sorry, Sar. I get carried away, what can I say," I said, grinning.

"Yeah, yeah," she said, reaching for Nolan's hand to help her climb over the edge of the fountain. But I wasn't about to let her go. I grabbed her back in my arms and dunked her once more, pushing my forehead to hers as she slid her hair back out of her eyes and blinked the beaded water from her lashes, laughing. I swung her back and forth in my arms as I carried her back to the dry side, the tips of our noses touching and my lips tingling just watching her bite her lower lip. Unable to take it, I had to kiss her once more, the soft and slow kind I did when I forgot others were watching—or when I wanted everyone to know she was mine. And she was…she had my entire heart.

———

We dripped dry during the rest of our walk to the dorms. Sarah and Noles changed in our bathroom while Trig and I got ready in our room. I hung our wet clothes over the backs of our desk chairs as Trig answered the door to let Amy in. He grabbed his wallet, and then the two of them headed out. I promised to catch up with them later.

Sarah and Nolan finally left the bathroom after about 25 minutes. I couldn't tell for sure, but something seemed off—more than once tonight I had noticed the two of them glaring at one another, almost as if Sarah was urging Nolan to do something. I was pretty sure Sarah knew about my draft decision, and I sort of figured Nolan would talk to her about it. But something told me *this* was more than just the draft.

I shook it from my mind when Nolan stepped out in a pair of strappy red heels, faded jeans and a tight red top—clearly an outfit of Sarah's design, but one I was deeply thankful for.

"Uhhhh, dammnnnnn," I said, reaching for her back pocket and pulling her close to claim her right away.

Her giggle was nervous. As I wrapped my arms around her and kissed at her neck, I felt her tense a little. It was almost…hesitation? Something was definitely off. But I needed to wait for Sarah to be out of the picture for that talk. So in the meantime, I'd just enjoy the damn sexy view.

Chapter Five

Nolan

SO, it turns out there really isn't an easy segue into a conversation with your boyfriend about being knocked up. I spent the entire drive to Tucson listening to Sarah preach to me about what I needed to do. "You HAVE to tell him," she said, a million times, in a million ways.

But why did I *have* to tell him now? I mean, I know. I have to tell him. But it didn't have to be tonight. I just wanted to enjoy our blissful innocence for a little bit longer. And I didn't want to yank everything out from under him yet, either. I wanted to wait, just to make sure. Wait for my appointment, perhaps. I'd spent the last 24 hours sick and bouncing between reality and my make-believe world where my problems went away. And now I was consumed with finding a way to hide the anxiety on my face. The last thing I needed was Sarah's constant bringing-it-back-to-the-forefront.

Reed pulled me away from my thoughts as he grabbed my hand and led me out to the dance floor at Cooler's. The place was really a dive bar, but it had such a huge following and was always packed. The dance floor was a giant stretch of polished concrete; the graffiti that decorated it had been sealed in place by the glaze on the floor. I wondered if you would actually reach anyone if you dialed the 1980s phone numbers that were barely legible but still there.

Sarah started dancing the moment we entered the bar, already snuggled up against some tall frat guy that Reed nodded an *okay* to —just to let Sarah know he was *safe*. Reed wasn't much of a dancer, but he liked the slow songs. So did I. Slowly swaying in his arms, with my ear pressed against his heart, was the best place in the world. We stayed like that for two or three songs in a row before Reed kissed my head and led me back to a table so he could hit the restrooms.

I caught a glimpse of Sarah out on the dance floor with Amy. The two of them looked like professionals, twisting and grinding in sync. With their curves and exposed skin, it was no wonder that they drew the eyes of most of the males at the bar when they danced together. And it wasn't a surprise when Trig had to step in, and, on occasion, throw a punch or two to get Amy back to himself. Sarah thrived under the attention, and I was constantly worried about her getting in over her head. She had a knack for going home with the wrong guy.

"So, you tell him yet?" Sarah said, a little too loudly, as she slid into the chair next to me and reached for her beer.

"Uh, no...and I won't need to if you keep shouting shit out loud like that," I scolded her.

"Pfft," she took a big drink, set the bottle down hard and leaned in to me. "I'm sorry to be tough here, Nolan, but you can't be a chicken about this. It's a sucky situation. But it's not just going to fix itself. And it's not just about you."

I knew everything she was saying. And I knew she was just dishing out her own brand of *tough love*. It was the only kind of love the Perez sisters knew how to serve. But add that to the fact that she was working on a pretty good buzz, and it was starting to get obnoxious.

"Yeah, I hear you," I said forcefully, hoping she'd get the point and drop it.

She stood and pushed her empty bottle at me. I tensed a little as

I saw Reed walking up behind her. "Sure you do, Nolan; you hear me," she said, slamming her chair back into the table and taking off for the dance floor.

"What's her deal?" Reed asked.

"Who knows; some guy's not paying attention to her or something, whatever," I was flippant and lying. It made my stomach hurt, because deep down I knew Sarah was right. But I kept up my façade anyhow.

I didn't feel much up for dancing after my tiff with Sarah, and I was pretty sure she was done with me for the night when she came up to the table to grab her purse and told us she'd just meet me back at home to drive back to campus Sunday. I watched her leave with Mr. Tall Frat Boy, admonishing her a little in my mind for giving it up so easily. "Hypocrite," I thought to myself.

"Hey, where you at tonight?" Reed asked, pulling my hand to his lap and rubbing my palm with his thumbs.

"Sorry, I feel bad that I was grumpy with Sarah, that's all," I said, a half-truth.

"You wanna call it a night?" Reed said, standing and stretching. His beautiful broad body doubled my size, and when we were out and he was dressed in his snug jeans and tight, black T-shirt I felt defensive, ready to fend off the dozens of college co-eds drooling and begging for a chance to take him home.

"Yeah, I think so. Trig okay with us leaving him?" I asked, looking over to where he was dancing with Amy, his hands roaming her body for the world to see.

"Uhm, I'm pretty sure Trig couldn't care less where we go," Reed laughed.

———

The drive back to Reed's was quiet. I knew why I wasn't talking, and I had a guess what was on Reed's mind, too. He was really battling not to bring up his draft options with me before we had a chance to really talk about things. I felt like such a terrible person. Here he was, pausing his own dreaming just to make me happy, and all I could do is think about how I was going to ruin it all anyway.

Reed cracked open the window in his dorm room when we got there to let a little bit of the breeze in. It was still warm at night, but the desert air smelled sweet, and it made the concrete walls Reed was living in seem a little less cold and stuffy. Reed turned the lights off and slowly walked to me. He reached for the bottom of my shirt as he pulled me closer, until I crashed into him a bit, and he fell back, sitting on his bed with me on his lap.

"Those shoes have to be killing you, if I know you at all," he smirked, pulling at the straps on my feet to relieve their misery. He did know me so well. I couldn't wait to be barefoot.

He started rubbing the arches of my feet as I snuggled into him. "Oh my god, you have no idea how good that feels," I said. Reed laughed in response, a little sinisterly. I poked him in the ribs for his dirty mind.

"Sorry, it's just…anyone walking by wouldn't think I'm rubbing your feet," he said, walking his fingers up my leg and tummy a little, flirting with the edge of my shirt. Suddenly, I stiffened. I know Reed could sense my hesitation from his touch, and I was a little surprised by it, too. I tried to play it off, sliding from his lap to lie back on his pillow. He quickly pulled his shoes off and slid next to me, propping his head up on one hand while his other stroked my hair behind my ears.

He was looking just above my eyes, his gaze a little distant. He was thinking, and I recognized his *I want to talk* expression. "You want to say something, I can tell," I said, scrunching my nose because I knew what he wanted to talk about.

Reed let out a deep breath. "I do. It's the draft," he locked his eyes with mine. "I know we were going to wait to talk about it, but my mom's in town, and she set up a lunch tomorrow with Dylan and…"

All I heard was Millie was in town. I always had an adverse reaction to Reed's mother, but for some reason it made me shiver tonight. Like a child, I rolled to my side, looking away from him and cutting him off mid-sentence.

"I know, I know. I wanted to just spend the day me-and-you, too…but I don't have a lot of time, and I need to talk with Dylan because I can't talk with Brent, legally. And…" Reed was pleading with me. I wanted to be open to his needs, but the weight of my secret and the thought of having to make decisions and bring my news out for his mother's judgment repulsed me. It made me irrational, and I was being a bitch. I couldn't stop, though.

"It's fine," I cut him off. "Seriously, whatever. We'll go to lunch with your mom, and talk about it tomorrow. Just not tonight, okay?"

Reed took a slow long breath, his arms falling away from me as he rolled to lie on his back next to me. I couldn't turn to face him. I wasn't sure my face could continue to bluff. "I'm sorry, I'm just really tired," I forced out the words.

Reed rubbed my back a bit and then leaned over to whisper in my ear as he reached his arm around me to pull me close. "It's okay," he said, kissing my neck a little. "You go to sleep."

Within an hour, I heard Reed's breathing start to steady, and I knew he was fast asleep. I, on the other hand, was probably looking at pulling an all-nighter with my own thoughts. Again.

Chapter Six

Reed

I PROBABLY COULD HAVE BEEN SMOOTHER when I brought up lunch with my mother. I knew Nolan had strong feelings about my mom and how she treated her. But I wasn't expecting her to completely shut down like she did tonight. And I didn't get to explain who Dylan was, either. There wasn't really a good time to squeeze in "Oh, by the way, Dylan is a really hot 24-year-old blonde, and she's going to be spending a lot of time with me until I can sign with her dad, hope you're cool with that."

We were walking into the golf resort restaurant my mom had selected, and I had Nolan's hand firmly grasped in mine, hoping like hell she'd let me hold onto it after she met Dylan. I saw my dad sitting in the distance at a table near the giant panoramic window, and as we rounded the corner, the two blondes with him came into view. I forced myself to remain calm, not show any emotion or worry.

As we got to the table, everyone stood, and I noticed Nolan's eyes were just a little wider than normal. Her mind was putting this together, and I was anticipating the moment it all hit her. Making things worse, Dylan stood up from her seat and walked around my seated mother to me, her legs exposed in a short mini skirt and her breasts out on display in a tiny tank top, ready to close the deal.

"Reed, so good to see you again," she smiled, leaning into me for a hug and then giving me a small kiss on the cheek. Fuck!

Nolan's hand dropped from mine immediately. I tried to get her to look at me, but she kept her eyes focused on the table in front of us. She was reaching to pull out her own chair when Dylan spun around and flashed her trademarked perfect smile. "And you must be the girlfriend?" she said, in a tone that was, I swear, a carbon copy of my mother's. She reached out her hand and, by some small miracle, Nolan shook it rather than punching her in the face.

My dad took over the conversation during lunch. I tried to force myself to pay attention, answer questions and be engaged, but most of me was preoccupied with trying to fix the fantastic fuck-up I was pretty sure was left in the wake of Dylan's touchy behavior towards me. Seriously, what the fuck *was* that!?

I tried to reach for Nolan's hand under the table more than once, but she always kept it at a distance. She was pleasant and smiled fondly at my dad when he spoke; she tolerated my mother, who never once even acknowledged her, and she conversed with Dylan about her classes and working in special education. But I was clearly cut out, and that was made extremely clear as soon as we left the restaurant, said our goodbyes and climbed back into the car for me to drive her back to Coolidge.

"Noles, I'm so sorry to spring that on you like that, let me explain…" I started before she turned to look at me and clicked her seatbelt, her teeth gritted and mouth shut tight.

"Nothing to explain, Reed," she said flatly, almost removed from the conversation. She just turned to face forward again, pulled her purse to her lap and began looking through it, avoiding me.

I reached over to stop her, and she jerked to the side. "It's fine, really," she said, still looking through her purse.

"Nolan, come on," I grabbed at her wrist now.

"What do you want me to say, Reed?" she was yelling now. Yelling is better than avoiding, so this was progress. "Do you want me to say that Dylan is awesome? That I like her a lot, and that I'm super excited she's going to make your life decisions with you, because she's born into some fancy privileged family and came out of the womb with a CEO title stamped on her fucking forehead and is just waiting for her time to run her daddy's millions?"

"Woah," she needed to slow down. "Noles, that's a little unfair…"

She stopped me again, holding a flat hand to my face. "Don't you fucking dare, Reed. Fair? I'm being unfair? I show up for my weekend with my boyfriend, and then I spend it watching some status-hungry woman gush over you, drape her body on you, and then treat me like I'm a kid getting to sit at the grown-ups' table during lunch with Millie. Oh, and Millie…that's just the icing on the cake. I was fucking invisible to her, which—don't get me wrong—is usually preferable. But not when she's busy fawning over the daughter-in-law she's *clearly* hoping to have in front of me? My replacement she's brought in, the one she approves of? Uhhhhg…" Nolan let it all out in one breath. She finally turned her face to look back out her window.

We drove the rest of the way to Coolidge in silence. It took almost an hour. Nolan didn't make a single sound. She didn't turn her head my way once, and the only movement she made was to check the time on her phone and to pull some ChapStick from her purse. I started to panic when I turned to drive down her parents' street. We'd fought before. Hell, we were good at fighting. But since high school we never let a fight go without closure. Today gave me a bad feeling, though.

I pulled into her driveway and put my Jeep into park, half expecting her to bolt from my car and slam her door closed in my face. But she didn't. She just sat there. I let my seatbelt go and turned my body to face her, my face resting on the headrest. She was just staring straight in front of her, looking lost. *Damn it, I've done it.*

"I'm sorry, Noles," I was whispering, pleading now. "I didn't want it to hit you all at once, and I sure as hell didn't expect Dylan to be…well, who she is, or do whatever the hell it was she did. I just met her, and she made *a lot* of assumptions about how friendly we were. Fuck, I'm sorry."

I reached for her hand, and she let me hold it this time, giving me hope. She let her head flop to the side so she could look me in the eyes now, and the damn water building in them was breaking my heart. I reached up to wipe away a tear just as it fell and then brought her hand to my lips to kiss it.

She finally took in a deep breath and bit her lip a little, readying herself to speak. "It's not Dylan. Not really," she just stopped. I reached up to wipe another tear, waiting for her to continue. I waited for minutes, just searching her eyes, which weren't giving me anything. Unable to take it, I started.

"It's the draft, I know. Nolan, what do you want me to do? I mean it. What do you want?" I couldn't believe I was putting it out there like that, but I was scared. I was gambling that she'd give in, but was I really willing to wait if she asked me to? She took in a sharp breath and looked away again.

"It's fine. You have to do this, and I understand," she was gone again.

"Nolan, I mean it. Tell me what you want," I asked urgently as she opened her door and slid from her seat. She pulled her purse strap and backpack over her shoulder and looked at me one more time.

"That's just it. I don't know. I…I need to figure some things out, Reed," she said, turning away and then stopping again. "Please don't feel bad. You didn't do anything. Really. I'll…I'll just call you when I get back to school, okay?"

She was already inside when I sent her a text that read: *I love you.* I drove back to Tucson, and when I got into my room, I checked my phone—and she hadn't texted back. For the first time in months, I wanted to drink. No, fuck that. I wanted to get ripped and forget fucking everything.

I picked up my phone and called Trig. "Hey, where you at?" I asked, putting a hat on my head and shoving my wallet and keys back in my pocket.

"We're at Cooler's, just shooting pool. You wanna come?" he asked, half surprised.

"Yeah, I'll be there in ten. Then we're drinking. A lot," I said and just hung up.

Chapter Seven

Nolan

I DON'T KNOW what I was thinking. I guess that was part of the problem. I didn't know what to think, about anything. I actually wanted just to *not* think, which was impossible!

By the time Sarah picked me up from my parents to drive back to campus Sunday morning, I was a mess. Thankfully, the yin to the yang that was Sarah's spitfire temper was that she was also quick to forgive. I filled her in on everything, and she agreed that I was right to freak out over the close and personal touching by Dylan. She also defended Reed, telling me it wasn't fair that I was mad at him for trying to include me in his decision about the draft when I was hiding such an enormous secret from him.

Sarah was right. And when we went out to dinner with Sienna that night back at campus, and I filled her in on everything—after breaking down to cry every 30 seconds—she agreed, too.

I hadn't talked to Reed since I walked away from him Saturday afternoon. It had been almost 24 hours since I'd heard from him. I couldn't imagine what he was thinking after the way I'd left him. With the girls' help, I drafted a text to send to him from our table.

I'm sorry I walked away from you. You're only trying to include me, and I love you because of it. Maybe we can get together and really talk about everything sooner? I promise to have an open mind.

I didn't think a text was a good place to elude about having to talk about *other things*, so I just left it at that. It took three of us to perfect the pathetic four sentences I did send.

We finished eating, and I walked back to my dorm from the café where we met. It had been an hour since I sent my text, and I still hadn't heard from Reed. I was getting a little anxious on top of the heavy worry that had already permanently moved into my conscience.

To distract myself, I pulled out the latest spreadsheets from the testing trials for the IQ project. I loaded a few of them up on my computer and then went through my emails to see the others that my group members had sent, which only made my stress shoot through the roof. *Nothing* was right!

Exasperated, I flopped back on my bed and stared at the ceiling. It was going to take me hours to sort through the results and put things in the right order just so I could merge everything together. "I HATE GROUP PROJECTS!" I thought.

I rolled sideways to glance at my phone once again and there still was no message from Reed. Happy to have something new to worry about—something I at least had some power over—I pulled my laptop cord from the wall, gathered up my pages of notes, stuffed a pencil in my hair and grabbed my keys to go upstairs.

When I knocked on Gavin's door, one floor up, it slowly slid open since it wasn't really latched. Gavin was sitting on his floor in front of his laptop with notes spread all around and his hands on top of his head. I started to giggle, realizing he was probably coming to the same conclusion I just had.

I could tell he had headphones in and I didn't want to scare him, so I reached over and knocked a little louder on his now-open door. He turned around quickly and pulled an ear bud from one of his ears.

"Nolan! Thank God!" he sprang to his feet, carefully stepping through his maze of papers and Monster Drink cans. He was trying to clean up a little as I walked all the way into his room.

"Hey," I just smiled, sitting at his desk chair and putting my computer down. "So, I take it you saw the data from the dingle twins?"

Gavin started laughing, putting his hands on his hips and nodding a little. He had given them that nickname during our last class when they had completely blown an IQ test attempt. "Seriously, what is wrong with those two?" he asked, grabbing a hat from his bed and sliding it over his chin-length hair.

Gavin was the complete opposite of Reed—artistic, tall and thin. He had black-rimmed glasses that he wore all of the time and longer hair that he usually kept pulled back or hidden under a hat. Both of his arms were covered in tattoos, and his wardrobe consisted of nothing but old concert T-shirts—most of them from shows he'd actually seen. Like Reed, though, Gavin was smart, ridiculously smart. We'd talked about the stress of attending school on scholarships during our classes, and I'd found out Gavin was a Mensa Scholar. He was a bona fide genius, which was good, because I was going to need one to survive the *dingle twins*.

"I think we can fix it, but it's going to take us a few hours," I said, blowing the loose hairs from my face.

Gavin just stood at his doorway and put his hands in his pockets, shrugging his shoulders. "I got nowhere else to be, so let's do it," he said, scooping up his papers and sitting down on the floor with his legs stretched out to hold up his laptop.

———

My estimate wasn't even close. Gavin and I worked until midnight finishing up the data and running our results. It was worth it, though, because not only did we come up with some killer findings and draw some great conclusions for our report, but also I was able to forget about everything else in my life for most of the night.

We ordered pizza, made fun of our lab partners and swapped stories about growing up with rich kids. Gavin came to ASU from Compton. I laughed at first when he told me, because I didn't think anyone actually came from Compton, but he assured me they did. He said his neighborhood was full of families that had lived there for years, but that it made him sad to see people afraid to go out at night. He took a bus to a private school that he was able to go to on a scholarship. And I thought I had it hard.

I'd also learned that Gavin came to ASU because of a girl, but after their freshman year, they broke up; his ex, Maya, moved back to California, but Gavin decided to stay. This part of the conversation started to make me a little uncomfortable, partly because I didn't want to go into my relationship with Reed and the drama that had descended on my life as of late, and partly because it felt a little as if Gavin was flirting with me.

When we were eating, he reached over twice to dab my cheek with a napkin; I kept one in my hand to take care of my own face after that. Then, when I was typing up our final results, he stood behind me and massaged my shoulders a little, sometimes his touch lingering just a little too long.

Gavin was incredibly good looking. He was the kind of guy who played the guitar with random bands for fun and rolled to class on a skateboard. His intelligence was a sexy contrast with his entire bad-boy image. When I was packing up my things and getting ready to leave, I felt a rush of heat hit my nerves as Gavin put his hand on the center of my back as he walked me to the door. And when he reached over to give me a friendly hug—one that suddenly felt not-so-friendly—I panicked.

"I have a boyfriend," I just laid it out there, just like that. No preface, no real reason to add it to the conversation, other than the massive blood-rush hitting my eardrums and making me feel as if I might soon pass out. I had nothing left other than to give Gavin the stupidest of smiles.

"Oh, uh…okay?" he said, once again shoving his hands in his

pockets, seeming to try to make himself appear less threatening. "I didn't mean anything. I just...boy, I'm not really sure what to say here."

He stood there rubbing the back of his neck and chuckling nervously. I had just made this *extremely* awkward.

"Sorry," I said, trying to fix things. "I just... I realized that we talked a lot about you, and I hadn't shared much. I thought it was one of those things that were good to know."

He just smiled at me, his lips forming the most adorable grin, forcing his eyes to scrunch a bit. "It's okay. Yeah, that...the boyfriend...it's good to know," he said, nodding and reaching out his hand in a fist to give me a pound. I just pounded back and laughed a little.

"Thanks," I said. "Sorry, I didn't mean to get all weird. I think I just need to go home and get some sleep."

"That sounds like a good plan," he said, opening his door for me and leaning against the frame as I walked out backwards, making my way to the stairs. "Sweet dreams, you."

He watched as I walked all the way to the stairway door, and then he closed his. I may have not had much dating experience, and I may have only been with Reed, but I was pretty sure Gavin was hitting on me, ever so slightly. And I didn't hate it. But the guilt it left behind as I made my way back into my room and dumped my pile of papers and computer on my desk was certainly not worth the small little rush of being found attractive by someone who wasn't Reed. And when I forced my mind back to Reed, I started to cry. Hard.

Reed had sent me a couple of texts while I was working on my project with Gavin: one apologizing for missing my call, and the second one—a longer one that came a few hours later—explaining that he'd slept most of the day away, hung-over from a really rough night.

I cringed a little thinking about a pissed off Reed doing shots at some bar in Tucson, cursing my name. I knew I had driven him to it, and I knew what he was like when he was drunk. The fact that he had slept an entire day away in recovery led me to believe he'd probably had *a lot* to drink, and that made me nervous. His texts were very formal, almost as if he was apologizing for missing some tutoring appointment we'd had. And they were without any mention of love or X or O. I was probably reading into things, but with the vague way I'd left things with him in front of my parents' house, I couldn't block my imagination from pairing him with some strange woman.

I knew it was late, nearly 1 a.m. But I took a chance and sent him a text back.

Sorry, I was upstairs working on a project all night. It was a mess and it's worth most of our grade. I miss you.

I put that last bit in hoping he'd bite, and when my phone rang seconds later, my eyes teared up again, this time with relief. I answered almost immediately.

"You're awake!" I was a little too excited.

"Yeah, Noles. I'm awake," Reed's tone was less happy to hear me. We both sat there listening to silence for more than a few seconds when finally he spoke, first letting out a huge sigh that put my mind on edge. "Nolan, I did something stupid."

Oh my god. This is the second time my body went into shock in less than two weeks. I shut my eyes tightly, trying to battle the images of Reed and some girl he met at the bar last night rolling around with one another. It was impossible, though, since in the nanoseconds after he uttered that single sentence I had already visualized his hands touching someone else's face, his lips biting at some stranger's shoulder and his bare chest pressed up against hers, whoever *she* was—hoping she wasn't Dylan. Unable to speak, I let my mouth fall open and somehow squeaked out a pained "Oh."

"Shit, no," Reed yelled into the phone, almost angry and frustrated. "God, Nolan, no! Not that...shit. I'm sorry, I didn't mean anything that you're thinking. I swear...I would never. Ever!"

I was still frozen. I was having a hard time bringing my mind back from the dark place it was. I was able to muster an "Okay," just so he could continue.

"Noles, it's the draft. I made a verbal commitment to work with Dylan and her dad," he waited a minute, letting me take this much in.

"Can you even do that, Reed?" I was new to a lot of this draft business, but I was pretty sure committing to an agent took away Reed's amateur status.

He just let out another huge sigh. "Noles, I fucked up. Thankfully the Nichols are family friends, and they are keeping a tight lid on everything."

"How did you get to this?" I asked, a little taken aback from his instant decision and the fact that he did something he knew better than to do.

"I was fucking drunk, Nolan," he exasperated. "I was so pissed after I dropped you off. I know, I know. But I haven't done anything like that in a really long time, so spare me the lecture, okay?"

He sounded pissed, and I was still trying to sort through everything in my mind, so I just kept an even tone. "I'm not lecturing, Reed. Just trying to understand what this all means," I said.

"I know, I'm sorry," he continued. "I was drinking with Trig and got worked up about not being able to make a decision, not understanding our fight and then everything just got all crossed and messed up. I called Brent, and Dylan answered the line. She put me on speaker, and then the next thing I know I was making a verbal commitment to work with them. They told me some shit about me missing out on important opportunities, *tying their hands* when every other quarterback looking at the market was already working with someone. It was all a little fuzzy, but Dylan brought over a file with paperwork tonight, which made it all way too real. She saw the panic in my eyes and talked me down. She said she and her dad work with a lot of people under the radar and that they will be very discrete and will work with me on a press conference as soon as our last game is finished."

The phone went silent after that, and Reed and I sat there listening to one another breathe—for minutes. Actual minutes.

"Tell me what you're thinking," he finally said. I could sense the fear in his voice.

I waited a little longer before finally answering. "I guess, I'm thinking I'm really glad you didn't sleep with someone," I said, laughing nervously, but also masking the gut-twisting hurt I was experiencing from this new turn in things.

"Oh my god, Nolan, I'm so happy to hear you say that. I mean… I'm not happy you thought for that second that I did *that*. I love you so fucking much. I would never do that to you. Not in a million years," Reed sounded so full of hope. I couldn't dash it. Not again.

"We'll figure it out. The draft, huh?" I said, letting the new facts of my life align with the other ones.

"Yeah, the draft," he sounded happy for the first time since before I came face-to-face with Dylan Nichols. "And I want you to be involved. In everything."

I just nodded to myself, resolving myself to tell him the other surprising news that was going to hammer away at his life. "Okay," I said, gathering up the courage to start when Reed cut me off.

"Hey, my other line's buzzing. It's Jason. That's really weird for him to call this late. I've gotta get this. We'll talk tomorrow, though, okay? I love you. So much."

He was gone before I was able to get out, "Me, too."

Chapter Eight

Nolan

I USED TO LOVE FRIDAYS. I spent most of my time in lab working on my projects, tutoring students and finishing up homework. The rest of the day and weekend was reserved for Reed and me—not a care in the world, like we were both locked in our own little time capsule. But I was dreading this Friday.

My appointment at the health center was just a few days away, and I had finally come to terms with the fact that Reed needed to know what was happening. My moods had been unmanageable, and I feared that holding in the secret was starting to chip away at my insides. Sleep was sporadic, and my grades were starting to suffer from my lack of concentration. Thankfully, I was able to draft a bit off Gavin in our psych class, though I was careful not to get too close with him after our last study session.

It was Reed's bye week, so he was spending some extra time in Coolidge. He had several practices, but there were at least two almost full days where we would be able to get away. Reed wanted to camp again so he wouldn't be too far from school or home. Buck had broken a leg while attempting to water ski in Mexico. Jason was staying at the house, running things while Buck was out of commission, but Reed's brother wasn't the most caring man in the world, and he made it very clear that he wouldn't be playing nurse while his dad was laid up with his leg.

Reed called Thursday night after practice, during his drive to his dad's, and spent most of our conversation venting.

"I just don't get how Jason and I are related. I mean, how hard is it to drive dad to a few appointments, make him dinner? Hell, all he has to do is heat the shit up, Rose does the actual cooking," Reed said, his stereo blasting in the background and the wind whipping in the phone from the open windows of his Jeep. "Sorry, I know I've been complaining for like 10 minutes, but I just don't get my douche bag brother. Everyone loves him, and it disgusts me."

I mostly listened. I had only met Jason once or twice in passing introductions. He'd spent most of his time in New Mexico. I was actually a little nervous about spending more time with him over the weekend, fearful that if Reed found him so deplorable, I would find him downright threatening. I got the distinct impression that when the gene pool divided between the two Johnson brothers, Jason was mostly Millie, and Reed was a lot more Buck.

"I'm sorry, I've been yapping this whole time. You haven't even had a chance to tell me about your day," Reed asked. My day was honestly uneventful, and the only thing on my mind was how I was going to open up to him about this pregnancy, my emotions still not ready to face the questions that came barreling at me once that little fact was out in the open. And this conversation certainly wasn't going to happen over the phone.

Suck it up, Nolan. Keep pretending. "It's okay, you're allowed to be irritated, and I'm glad you can talk to me about your frustrations. My day was pretty boring, so you're not missing much."

"Noles, every day I'm not with you, I'm missing a lot," he was sincere, and when he said things like that, it made my heart race. I believed him. I just hoped he'd still feel the same and say those same words after we talked this weekend.

Reed talked a little more about Jason and his dad's leg. He said his father would be in the cast until the holidays, but that he should start to be able to get around after that. Rose was coming to stay at the house to help out, too, and Reed was hopeful that Jason wouldn't stay the entire time. I didn't want to tell him, but I was pretty sure Jason loved being in charge, and I wouldn't put it past him to break his father's other leg just to hold onto the job a little longer.

I let Reed go as the sun was setting, promising to call him before I left to come home in the morning. Most of my dorm residents were out partying at the nearby apartment complex—where the campus rules didn't apply. Thursdays were more like Fridays around here, with most of the classes wrapping on Thursday afternoons.

I took advantage of the peace and solitude and hauled my bag of laundry down the hall so I'd have clean clothes for the weekend. I kicked back in the laundry room for about three hours while I put two loads through wash and dry cycles. I was able to finish my poetry reading and even made my notes for our class discussion on Monday. I was determined to pull my Bs back up to As—even if my grades didn't matter after this semester. "Push those thoughts back down, Nolan," I told myself.

It was close to 11 p.m. by the time I finally got everything folded and packed and was settled in my bed for the night. I checked my phone one last time and found a short text from Reed.

See you tomorrow, Princess.

That was it, but it was enough. I closed my eyes and fell asleep quickly for the first time in days.

The clock read 3 a.m. when my eyes flashed open. I was suddenly and completely alert, but I had no idea why. My pulse was pounding, and I stilled my breathing, listening for a noise. Something must have startled me. I watched the small line of light that marked where my door met the floor, studying it for foot traffic or a shadow, but there was no one outside. Deciding it must have been a dream, I threw my covers off and slid sideways from my bed. That's when I noticed the blood.

My pajama bottoms were soaked, and I could feel dampness on my sheets. Fully awake with adrenaline, I flipped on the light next to my bed to understand. I was bleeding, and badly. I raced to the bathroom and pulled my clothes off, still trying to understand. *How could I be bleeding?* I checked for more blood, and it was heavy.

No, no, no. I was so scared something was wrong. I was now more than two weeks late, so something had to be wrong with me. I wrapped a towel around my body and went to my desk to grab my phone. I needed Sarah.

I dialed, not even thinking what time it was. When she answered, I realized. "Hello? Nolan?" she whispered groggily. "What the fu…"

"Sarah, please come. Come right now. I need you, something's wrong!" I was shaking and crying hysterically. "Hurry, please."

"Okay, okay, calm down. I'll be right there," she said, hanging up before I could fill her in any more. I slid down to the floor, pulled my knees to my chest and just rocked myself back and forth.

My thoughts raced, "I didn't want this, but I didn't want *this*. This is my fault." I couldn't stop the voice in my head. I tortured myself with fear and guilt until I heard the ding of the elevator down the hall. I went to the door to unlock it and let Sarah in.

"Nolan, what's wro…" she took one look at me, and suddenly she knew. My lips were quivering now, and I was shivering uncontrollably. "Nolan, it's okay. Come here. It's okay."

Sarah was talking softly now. In an instant, I became a scared child, fragile and broken. She pulled me into her arms and cradled me, stroking my hair back behind my ears and holding my head to her shoulder. We stayed like that for several minutes, light sobs coming from me unexpectedly, and each time Sarah just squeezed me tighter and whispered softly in my ear. "Shhhhh, it's okay. It's going to be okay," she said, knowing it wouldn't, but also knowing that those were the only words she could say right now.

Over the next hour, Sarah helped get me in the shower while

she discarded my clothes and changed my bed sheets. I lay awake with my head resting in her lap until the sun started to brighten my curtains. Sarah didn't sleep either, but instead sat awake with me, just stroking my hair and whispering whatever I needed to hear in my ear. When my alarm clicked on at 6 a.m., the time I usually got up to head to the gym, I reached over and slapped it off.

I rolled my head to look up at Sarah through my puffy eyes. She was a mirror of me. "I have to go see Reed," I was matter-of-fact. "He's the only one that can make this okay."

I started to cry again a little, but sucked back the tears long enough to push myself up from the bed and walk to my dresser.

"Are you sure that's a good idea?" Sarah said, her voice careful and full of caution.

I just looked down into my open drawer and stared endlessly at my socks and running shorts and sports bras. My drawer was full of youth. Isn't this what I wanted? We weren't ready for this. But…this way? The guilt was pounding away at my heart, and each time it did, I fought to not break down in tears again.

"I need to see him. I just do," I said to Sarah, turning and shaking my head, biting my lip a little to help hold myself together.

"I get it," she said, standing and bending to pick up my running shoes to hand them to me. "Let me help you get ready."

Sarah walked me all the way to my car and offered several times to drive me. But I didn't want her there for any of this. I didn't know how long it would take to be brave enough to tell Reed everything. There was a chance I would stay parked in the middle of the desert for hours before heading the rest of the way to his house.

I drove extra slow. In fact, I was a little surprised when a cop parked on the side of the main highway just let me pass without an inquisition; I was sure I was going at least 15 miles under the speed limit. I powered through my doubts and pushed myself to drive all the way to Reed's house without stopping. I noticed the additional giant, lifted four-wheel-drive pick up parked right in front of the main entrance. The license plate read *J-DAWG*, confirming my suspicion that Jason was still staying at the house.

Somehow, I managed to park and get to my feet. I walked up to the front door three times, turning away with each approach to head back to my car. My fourth attempt was successful and I rang the bell. I didn't hear anyone stirring for the first several seconds, so I pressed my face to the obscured glass insert in the door. Finally, I saw some movement coming towards me. When it cracked open, I was met with the last face I expected to see. Dylan was standing there in a gray T-shirt, Reed's T-shirt, and nothing else. Her hair was messy, and her face was smeared with last-night's makeup.

"Can I help you?" she said with a bit of a southern accent.

"I…uh…I need to talk to Reed?" I was questioning myself, like I had no right to be there. I was so thrown by her presence and her lack of familiarity with me—even though we'd met just a few days ago. "I'm Nolan?"

I felt stupid and out of place, instantly. It was the first time I'd felt that way in months.

"Oh, right. Nolan," she said with a faint smile. I couldn't tell if it was smugness or politeness, but something told me it was the former. I was trying to look inside the house over her shoulder when she leaned sideways to move her eyes in front of mine. "He's still sleeping."

She just stopped short there, waiting for me to either continue to act the part of the asshole or get what was going on.

"We had a late night," she offered more, biting her lip a little like she was both proud and ashamed at once. And that was enough. She was here because of Reed, wearing his shirt. And I was pretty sure that smile was arrogance and not friendly in the least. "Want me to tell him you stopped by?" she said, feigning manners now.

My heart was pounding with anger, and I was forming fists at my sides, digging my nails into my palms to try to stave off slapping her. "No need. Thank you very much," I said, turning and marching back to my car, like a kid who was angry he didn't get picked on a dodge ball team.

I heard the front door close behind me as I opened my car door. I quickly got in and drove all the way back to campus. I was completely numb, not able to feel, and I couldn't recall whether or not I stopped at a single stoplight or what exit I took from the freeway. But somehow, somehow I'd made it to my parking lot at school. I leapt up the stairs to my dorm room and threw my running clothes on. I was so angry, and my rage was directed at everyone. I picked up my phone and typed out a text to Reed.

So much for never.

I paced my room, debating writing more, but ultimately decided to leave it short and sweet. My emotions weren't right, and I couldn't tell if I wanted to cry or scream obscenities and punch something. If I didn't do something to center myself, I was going to get into trouble. I grabbed my gym bag and threw my phone, wallet, towel and iPod inside.

It wasn't quite 10 a.m. on a Friday morning; campus was blissfully quiet, and the gym was empty. As I walked with purpose down the long trail that led to the recreation center, my stomach rolled with stress and rage more than a few times. "Push it down, Nolan. Push it down." My mantra was the only thing holding me together, not ready to fully download all that I'd lost over the last 24 hours.

I climbed onto the treadmill and wrapped my iPod armband tightly around my bicep, pushing my favorite playlist and pounding my feet into the machine. I'd gone through all of the songs once, letting me know I must have been running for at least 45 minutes, before I slowed down to a brisk walk. As soon as my steps slowed, though, my mind went back into action, my eyes flashing back to Dylan in that damned familiar shirt. Then I started to think about last night, and before reality set in, I pushed the up arrows on the treadmill and roared it back to a steady running pace.

My playlist went through once again, and I was panting heavily. My eyes were wide and focused on the window in front of me, and I barely registered the blurs of color passing through the reflection. People were here, in the gym with me. I pulled one ear bud from my ear, and I heard the clanking of weights and the smashing of

57

racquetballs behind me. It must have been near lunchtime. "I should stop."

I was about to attempt a walking speed again when things turned yellow—then black. The funny thing about exhaustion is you don't really see it coming. There aren't any warning signs, at least not when your head is as messed up as mine was. I remember my surroundings went bright, a golden yellow like I was suddenly thrust under a heat lamp. My balance was thrown, and I stepped to the side in an attempt to regain it. That's when I felt the zip of my other foot whirl by my now stationary one and felt the smack of my face hitting the conveyer belt, my legs twisting and my vision suddenly fading to black.

I awoke to the sting of an ice pack on my forehead. I was laying flat on my back and the room was spinning above me, the air conditioning was making a whooshing sound over my eardrums.

"Hey you," a voice was calling to me, but my eyes couldn't yet focus. When I was finally able to make out the soft white towel being pressed to my face and recognized what it was, I let my vision focus on everything else. Suddenly Gavin was there. "Ah, there she is," he said, his mouth forming a stretched smile, pushing dimples into each of his cheeks.

"Wha…happened?" I was still pretty woozy, and suddenly I felt like vomiting. I grabbed hard onto Gavin's arm and pulled myself into a sitting position, slapping my other hand over my mouth and gesturing to him that I thought I might be sick.

"Oh, got it. Let's get you somewhere. Here, hold onto me," he lifted me to his side and supported my weight as he walked me from the circle of people who had gathered around us to the lobby of benches near the drinking fountain. The women's locker room was really close, and I was pretty sure I needed to go in there. I looked over at the door. Gavin understood what I was saying and leaned against it, yelling inside to see if anyone was in there.

"Free and clear. Come on, let's go," he said, sliding over a maintenance sign so he could walk me into the ladies locker room. Once I got to the sink and splashed some water on my face, the nausea I was fighting against started to fade. I gripped the counter by the sink and turned my head up to take in my reflection. I was ghost white and my hair was drenched with sweat. I couldn't tell if it was from the running or my fainting spell.

"Are you feeling okay?" Gavin asked, reaching over to steady me as he walked me back through the main door. A few women were waiting outside and gave him a skeptical look when he removed the maintenance sign and smiled at them as we walked by. I started to lose my balance a bit again and caught myself on the nearby bench.

"Okay, that's it. You're going to get checked out by someone," Gavin said as he started to walk to the main front desk.

"No, I'm fine. Really. I just overdid it," I tried to stop him.

He paused for a moment and pulled one side of his mouth up to consider what I was telling him. Then he shook his head *no* quickly and continued to the front desk where the girl working there ogled him as he leaned over the counter and pointed toward me. Her flirtatious smile soon faded into a frown as she looked at me. She got up and walked into the back offices and came out with one of the sports trainers and the three of them approached me.

"She was running and then I looked over and saw her completely go limp on the treadmill. She hit her head pretty hard, and she was out for several seconds," Gavin explained to the man who was now kneeling in front of me with a medic box filled with gauze and ointments, none of which could do anything to solve what was wrong with me.

"Hmmmm," the man considered for a moment. "Do you mind going into our back office and grabbing one of the big water bottles for me?" Gavin just nodded and jogged to the back rooms immediately. When he was gone, I just brought my pathetic and embarrassed gaze up to meet Mr. Trainer's.

He smiled at me softly and reached up to grab my wrist to test my pulse. "I'm Chris. Can you tell me your name?" he said, watching the seconds on his watch and staring at my eyes to follow their movement.

"I'm Nolan," I said, quiet and mortified.

"Nolan, nice to meet you," he smiled again, that fake smile someone gives when they're suspicious of you and trying to unravel your mystery. "Your pulse seems okay. Can you tell me, have you ever fallen like this before? Do you know how much water you've had today? Were you feeling dizzy before you started your workout? Did you trip? Do you feel nauseous…?" Chris was hitting me with question after question before I could even answer. My head was bobbing back and forth, like I was watching a tennis match just trying to respond and keep up with him. I was hearing his words echo, and my heart rate was racing again when I had a sudden break.

"I just had a miscarriage," I said, slapping my hand over my mouth and closing my eyes tight trying to force the reality back into hiding.

I felt Chris's hands on my wrist again, pulling my hand from my face and forcing me to look at him. "Okay. That's definitely what led to you passing out. And it's okay, Nolan. Do you hear me? It's okay. You probably shouldn't be working out now, though. You are likely extremely dehydrated, and your body is exhausted. Do you…I mean have you…talked to anyone?" Chris was being careful with me. I didn't like feeling so weak, so I straightened my posture and shook my head with my last vestiges of confidence.

"No, I'm fine," I said, forcing myself to stand and dry my tears. My legs still felt wobbly, but I wasn't going to let anyone here see that.

"Okay, well…you really need to see someone. It can help. What happened…it's not something that's uncommon. But it's also not something that is easy to deal with always," Chris seemed uncomfortable. So was I.

"I'm fine, really," I forced again, giving him a flat smile and willing him to drop it.

"All right, I hear you. I'd just feel better if you at least met with one of the physicians at the health center today. Hmmmm?" Chris nodded at me, begging me to consider.

"I have an appointment Tuesday," I was defensive now, even my false pleasantries gone.

He just stared at me in silence for a few seconds, considering his move. "I'm not trying to be intrusive. I'm only looking out for your health here. You shouldn't wait until Tuesday. Maybe just drop by for an urgent care visit, huh?" he was really trying. I gave in and nodded.

I saw Gavin walking up with the bottle of water, and I reached out to shake Chris's hand. "Thanks. I appreciate your advice," I forced a closed mouth smile then grabbed the bottle of water from Gavin. "Can you walk me to the Health Center, and then home? It seems I'm dehydrated and need some rest."

"Sure," Gavin said, pulling my arm over his shoulder once again, letting me lean most of my weight on him. "Let's go. Thanks for looking her over."

Chris the trainer just smiled tightly, nodding, and packed up his small, useless box. I made eye contact with him and could tell he had thought he'd put my puzzle together. But he wasn't even close.

Chapter Nine

Reed

I'D MANAGED to sleep hard last night after going a few rounds with Jason. He was already bitching about having to take my dad to an appointment next week in Tucson, like it was some major inconvenience—never mind the fact that he'd be driving into town to take care of business at the Tucson dealerships anyhow.

Sometime over the past year, I'd started challenging my brother. I don't know if it was something that changed inside of me, maturity perhaps, or if my brother had just managed to become yet an even bigger asshole.

Dylan stopped by my pop's house on her way from Tucson to Phoenix to run through a few scenarios with me and to pass along some messages from her father. We sat at the counter and went over some things and Jason—not to miss out on the attention from a hot blonde—pulled up a seat to join us, quickly taking over the conversation. Dylan seemed to be annoyed by his presence at first. But when I mentioned some of my hesitation over everything and how it was going to affect Nolan, she was suddenly won over by my dickhead brother's insensitivity.

"You're such a pussy over that girl. When you go big time, you're going to have chicks throwing themselves at you. You'll be so over your cute, little high school fuck. Don't make life decisions because of it," he said. What a dickhead. I hated him.

I just stood at his words, looked at Dylan, who was smirking at my brother's comments, and told her I was done for the night and would call her next week. I shoved my brother from his barstool so hard that he fell to the floor, and I went upstairs. To think there was actually a time in my life when I looked up to that prick.

I was starving by the time I woke up for breakfast. It had been months since I'd been able to sleep in past 8 a.m., let alone until 10. I threw on a pair of shorts and my old high school championship shirt and jogged down the stairs only to find Jason sitting at the breakfast bar, sheets of his newspaper spread out across every inch of surface and a plate of waffles stacked in front of him.

"Mornin' shithead," he said, raising his cup of coffee and not looking up from his paper.

"Fuck off," I said right back at him.

When I realized Rose was there, finishing up a plate for me and prepping a breakfast tray to take upstairs to dad, I instantly felt embarrassed and guilty for using those words in front of her. Rose had known me almost as long as my parents and was, in many ways, like an aunt to me. She'd lost her husband years ago and had two grown sons that were both in the military, *lifers* she always said. I think it made her lonely, which is probably why she didn't mind spending so much time with my pops.

"Sorry, Rosie," I said, leaning over to kiss her cheek, which she had extended out for me.

"It's okay, mijo...," she urged me to come in close, then whispered, "he deserved it." She gave me a wink and then slid my plate on the counter and retreated upstairs with a full breakfast spread for my dad.

I picked at my plate a bit before diving in, my stomach rolling with hunger pangs, but also conflicted with anger at my brother and what he said about Nolan. I was pretty sure he knew how pissed off I was because he had buried his face in the business section and refused to even glance my way. I just stared at him while I drenched my waffles in syrup, fighting the urge to send my fist through his jaw. "You're such a dick," I said a little under my breath. I bowed my head and took a bite but could tell he had glanced up when I said it, tilting his paper down for a second, and then raising it back up.

"Whatever," he wasn't even phased.

Stuffed on Rosie's amazing breakfast, I brought my plate to the sink and was rinsing it when I heard feet sliding down the stairs. I did a double take when I looked up, and it took a few seconds for my eyes to finally focus and relay the message to my brain of what I was seeing.

"Good morning," Dylan said as she passed me and went to the fridge to pull out the carton of orange juice. She turned around while she was shaking it. "Glasses?"

I just stood there dumbstruck, my brain unwilling to make the connections of what likely had happened last night. I motioned to the cabinet next to the fridge, and Dylan just nodded and turned to get her glass. While she was pouring her juice, I looked over at Jason who still had his fucking nose in the newspaper. I pushed the pages from his hands flat to the counter and mouthed, "What the fuck?" to him. He just smiled and shrugged, then picked the paper back up.

Dylan slid a stool over next to him and turned sideways to swing her legs over his lap, which was maybe the only thing that finally got him to put his paper down. When he leaned over and kissed her and smiled as she nestled into his neck, I was floored.

"Okay, what the hell is going on?" I couldn't stand it anymore.

"What does it look like?" Jason said, sliding his coffee cup over to me and motioning for me to fill it up. "You mind?"

I just shook my head, my eyes bulging from my face, I was sure. I grabbed his mug and filled it with what was left of the morning's brew. I slid it back to him and then looked again at Dylan, who was now hiding her face a little from me, perhaps a little embarrassed.

"Reed, I hope you don't mind, but I borrowed one of your shirts," she said, pulling up the collar a bit to show me.

I just stared, speechless, and turned for the living room. I flopped on the couch and put on Sports Center to take my mind away from the soap opera that was no doubt unfolding in the kitchen, somehow my future tangled up with it, too. "Fucking Jason," I thought.

I zoned out for about 45 minutes before I heard the sound of the breakfast stools skid on the floor and turned to see Dylan cleaning up the counter, her bare legs barely covered in my long shirt. I had to admit, I understood why Jason couldn't help himself. But I would never quite understand what was in it for her. I turned back to the TV and then glanced down at my watch.

"Is it seriously 11 already?" I asked, stretching and getting to my feet.

"Yeah, you slept most of the morning away," Jason said, folding up his paper and pushing it into the recycle bin. "You get a day off, and you waste it." His tone was condescending.

My jaw clenched and I held my response in. "I'm just waiting for Nolan," I said, realizing she probably should have been here by now.

"Oh! I totally forgot," Dylan said, wiping down the counter and not really paying attention to me. "She came by this morning. Early."

I was waiting for her to tell me more, and when I realized she wasn't going to, I urged her on. "Uh, yeah? What did she say?" I had my hands held out to my sides, waiting.

"Nothing. It was really early. I was the only one up, so I told her you were still sleeping," she started toward the stairs. Suddenly, a suspicion flared inside me.

"Hey, Dylan? Were you in my shirt when you went to the door?" I asked, already knowing but hoping nonetheless.

"Uh, yeah," she rolled her eyes at me and darted up the stairs.

"Shit!" I pulled my phone from my pocket and saw a text from Nolan.

So much for never.

"Goddamn it!" I grabbed my keys from the counter and rushed to the door, sliding into a pair of flip-flops. Jason had put it together, too, and just started bellowing with laughter, like it was the fucking funniest thing he'd ever seen. I really did hate him.

Chapter Ten

Reed

I MUST HAVE DIALED Nolan's phone 20 times during my drive to her dorm, each time it clicked right to voicemail. I knew it would. Why I kept hoping for a different result each time I pressed her number, I don't know.

Two girls were working at the front desk in her dorm, and thankfully, they were too distracted by their own conversation to pay much attention to me when I blew right past them and charged up the stairs. I got to her room and knocked lightly at first; I could hear the light murmuring of her television so I knew she was there. I waited for a few long seconds and didn't hear any movement so I knocked louder. When I still heard nothing, I reached for the handle and started to turn it when suddenly the door flew open, making me stumble.

The tall, skinny tattooed guy staring back at me was not what I expected, and I had to shake my head a little, worried that perhaps somehow I'd barged into the wrong room. When I heard Nolan call my name, I was even more confused. I sucked my top lip in a bit and let my vision bounce between Nolan and the strange guy who was in her room…in his socks? He looked waaaayyy too comfortable to be in here.

"Uh, and you are?" I folded my arms in front of me and stared him down. Unfazed, he just reached out a hand for me to shake it.

"Hi, I'm Gavin. I live upstairs," he said, like everything here was normal. I didn't shake his hand and instead just pushed by him and made my way to Noles who was lying on her bed, her head propped up with pillows and her favorite blanket wrapped around her feet.

"What the hell?" I said, forgetting for a second why I'd come. I pointed over my shoulder to the strange dude who I did not like *feeling so at home* in Nolan's room.

Nolan just rolled her eyes at my gesture, and I would have taken her bait if the cold stare that followed didn't jolt me back to the entire reason I'd driven here. "Noles, you are soooo off on this one," I started, but she was quick to cut me off.

"What are you doing here, Reed? Just leave," she was pale and looked ill. I'd hurt her, and it was killing me.

"I'm not going anywhere," I said, probably a little too defensively, but I was still worked up. When Gavin interrupted us and reached for my arm it didn't help things.

"Reed, right? Why don't we go take a walk or something, hey? She's had a bit of a day…" he was trying to explain things to me, like he had any part in our lives. It was pissing me off.

"Gavin, right?" I said, mocking his words. "Why don't you take a walk?" I stood right in his face, our chests inches apart. I was pretty sure if I had to I could break him in half, and part of me wanted to.

Looking for a lifeline, Gavin peered over at Nolan who just rolled her eyes and told him to give us a few minutes. A few minutes? What the fuck was going on?

Gavin left, letting her know he'd just be upstairs if she needed anything. I did not like this guy. When the door closed, I turned back to Nolan who was sitting up taller on her bed now and pulling her blanket up to her chest. Something was definitely wrong with her; she was sick, maybe? I just wanted to pick her up and put her in my lap and stroke her hair until she fell asleep. But I had to fix the mess my brother made for me first.

"What are you doing here, Reed? Shouldn't you be somewhere with Dylan?" her words had bite to them, but she also seemed distant and detached. I hated Jason for this chain reaction he'd started, but even more so because he found it all so damned amusing.

"Nolan, Dylan wasn't there for me. She was there for Jason," I said, sitting down next to her. She flinched a little at my nearness, and it broke my heart. She was wary of me. "I told you never, Nolan, and I meant it. *Never.*"

I could tell that the truth was starting to creep into her fortress a little, her eyes pooling a little. She was staring me in the eyes, wordless. I slowly inched closer to her until our legs were touching, and then I placed my hand to her cheek and she shut her eyes, leaning into it a little. The tear that had been threatening to fall finally slid down the side of her face. When she finally looked up at me, she seemed like there was so much she wanted to say, but her mouth would only open and shut, like she was struggling for where to begin. I didn't need to hear any words, and she didn't need to say sorry.

"Don't, just shhhhhh," I said pulling her close to me and cradling her, kissing her ear and holding her tightly while I rocked her back and forth a little. "It's okay, baby. It's okay. It was just a really messed up misunderstanding. It's okay. We're okay."

I held her like that for the next hour, waiting for her to fall asleep, but she never did. When a smile finally tugged at her lips, I felt like we were back on even ground. I lay back with her and clung her to my chest so I could play with the long wisps of hair that were sweeping over her shoulders.

Unable to help myself, I broached the other topic that had been rattling in my head. "So, Gavin's…nice?" I said, so obviously not a fan.

"Stop, Reed. He's just a friend, from class. He lives upstairs," she explained him easily, but I still didn't like how familiar he was with her.

"Okay, I trust you. But that guy's a little too comfortable with you," I pursed my lips and shook my head a bit.

"You're cute when you're jealous, you know that?" she poked at my nose, and I bit at her finger teasingly.

"Well, I'm glad you think so…" I trailed off, just staring into her eyes. "So, why was he here?"

She blew the loose hairs in her eyes up with a fast breath and then sent me a sideways grin. "I had a little accident," she grimaced, almost embarrassed. "I got a little overzealous with my running when I came home. I was a little angry, in my defense. Anyhow, I sort of fainted."

She was shadowing her face with her hand a little, hiding her embarrassment. I didn't like that she'd fainted. It wasn't anything for her to be embarrassed about, but it was something to worry about. I just threaded my fingers through hers and pulled her hand to our sides then leaned forward to press my lips to her forehead, mostly to see if she was running a temperature. Instead, she was extremely cold.

"You probably got dehydrated," I decided, standing up and walking into her bathroom to fill a cup with water. "You're still really clammy; you should drink more liquid, okay?" I handed her the cup, and she sat up to drink it, giving me her trademark salute, a cute gesture she'd been doing since we first started dating in high school.

"And Gavin?" I said, biting my lip, not wanting to seem overly suspicious, but still wanting answers.

She put the cup on her night table and nestled back into her blanket and pillow. "He saw me go down. I hit my head pretty hard, and he helped me get back home," she rubbed at her forehead a bit, and I could see a small bump forming.

"Noles, did you have someone look at this?" I asked.

"Yeah, we made a stop at the Health Center. I'm fine. Just need to take it easy today, that's all," she shrugged her shoulders like she felt bad for ruining our plans somehow. Truth was, there was no place I'd rather be.

"Sounds like a plan," I said, scooting her back over and getting under the blanket with her, tickling her feet with my toes. "So, what are we watching?"

Her face lit up for the first time since I'd entered her room. "*Happy Gilmore*," she said, reaching for the remote to turn the television back on. She sank down into me, and I spent the next four hours—two movies—not moving an inch, trying not to think about the douche bag who lived upstairs.

Chapter Eleven

Nolan

IT WAS like half of my heart healed the instant Reed showed up. I knew when I saw him that he never slept with Dylan. I felt rather foolish even thinking it. But my emotions were still so tangled; it took me a little while to get my heart back where my head was. I was holding on to so much, my guts twisted with grief and confusion and the secret that was burning a hole in me.

The doctor at the Health Center had the bedside manner of a UPS truck driver, more interested in checking off the list of questions on his iPad questionnaire rather than actually talking to me. After a short and impersonal exam, he confirmed that I likely had a miscarriage. He told me it was incredibly common and that most women had at least one in their lifetime. He gave me a packet of brochures and a condom with a rehearsed lecture about safe sex and then sent me on my way.

I tossed the paperwork in the trashcan just outside his office and shoved the condom in my pocket, not sure why I even kept it. The entire visit only made me feel emptier, guiltier. Gavin never asked any questions after I told him everything checked out fine and just went about getting me comfortable in my room.

Not wanting to be alone, I asked Gavin to stick around to watch movies with me. And when he sat next to me, our sides touching a little, I felt a rush of nerves. It wasn't the same tingles I got when Reed touched me. These were the curious kind, and they made me nervous. When I heard the pounding on my door, my heart began to race, because I knew it was Reed. And I didn't want him to see Gavin anywhere near me, let alone in my room. I was grateful when Gavin got up from my bed, even if it meant he'd be face-to-face with Reed at the door.

Once our misunderstandings were behind us, Reed ended up staying with me through the night. I still had a few things to pick up from my parents, so we both drove back to Coolidge separately on Saturday morning and spent the rest of the day bouncing between visits with Buck and my parents. That night, we drove out to the desert camp and sat on the hood of Reed's Jeep, just looking at the stars. The big talk about our future plans never really happened, but that was okay. I'd come to terms with the fact that I was going to have to face change, and I might have to make a choice between following Reed to whatever city he landed in or trusting the strength of our relationship and staying at ASU. And that wasn't something talking would help; I'd have to figure that out all on my own.

———

Two weeks had passed, and things were starting to feel normal in my world—the panic attacks stopped, and I was sleeping through the night. Dylan wasn't around as much as I'd worried she'd be, and Jason had been busy with the business, so when Reed and I went to visit his dad a few times, it was just like old times. Rosie had practically moved in, taking on most of the caretaking that Jason had said he would do. I know this set Reed's mind at ease, because he constantly worried about his dad.

It was almost Reed's birthday, and I had decided to surprise him with a camping trip, much like the one he'd given me when we first started dating. I wanted to feel connected to him, connected to us, and I thought bringing us back to the place where I'd first given myself to him completely would do that.

I hadn't let Reed touch me since the day I found out I had miscarried. I wasn't flinching at his touch like I had for days, but I still found excuses to stop our kissing from progressing any further. I could tell Reed noticed, but he'd never been pushy with me about being physical. I was usually the aggressor, and I knew that to get back to where we were with our sex life, I'd need to be the one to lead us there.

The weekend before his birthday gave me plenty of planning time. Reed's game was in Colorado, so I wouldn't get to see him until the team got back into town. I was spending my Saturday with Sienna for the first time in months. Always up for planning surprises, she was excited when I asked her to join me for a little shopping spree. I needed to get some picnic gear, just enough to make things romantic. I'd borrowed the camping equipment from Buck the weekend before and stashed it in my gigantic trunk.

Sienna and I were cruising the various aisles of Target and almost had everything on my list when we stopped in front of the baby supplies. I froze. I hadn't thought about it in weeks, but with that small flash of pinks and blues, it all came rushing back to me, and I went catatonic.

"Nolan, are you okay?" I felt Sienna's arm reaching around me, snapping me back.

"Oh, uh...yeah. I'm okay," I looked back at the soft quilt hanging from a display and the various piles of baby toys and onesies. Everything around me was so small, so tiny, so precious. I couldn't seem to come to grips with how quickly something could be here and then be gone. It all happened in an instant.

"Do you think I'll ever have kids?" I asked, swallowing hard and looking up into Sienna's eyes. It was the first time I'd said this out loud. I knew I wasn't ready now, and I felt so guilty that I was relieved when I'd lost the baby. Our baby. Reed's baby. But I was also terrified that I'd never get another chance. That this was it for me.

Sienna just squeezed me harder and pulled me into a full hug. "Nolan, of course you will have kids. What happened is something that happens all of the time, to a lot of women," she was stepping back now, holding my hand a little and looking at me curiously. "Have you talked to anyone? I mean, you know I think you still need to talk to Reed, but you might also want to talk things out with someone else, someone who can help you put what happened behind you."

I just bit my lip a bit and nodded. I knew she was right, but I also knew I wouldn't talk to anyone. If I had my way, I'd erase what happened from Sienna and Sarah's memories, too. And even better, I'd erase it from my own.

I dropped Sienna off at her apartment after lunch and was heading back to my parking lot when I heard my phone beep. Still paranoid about reaching for my phone while I was on the road, I pulled over into a Starbucks and dug through my purse. It was a text from Gavin.

Hey, the dingle twins managed to line up our last three tests today. If you can make it, we should be able to knock everything out and put together the final findings and report – and be done with those jackasses forever! Let me know if you're in – we'll meet at the library at 2. –G

The thought of finishing my nightmare psychology project was inviting. I knew it would be a long day, but Reed was going to be gone until late Sunday, so I thought I might as well make the best use out of my time and get the dingle twins out of my way.

I'm in. I'm at Starbucks, want anything?

I waited for a few seconds to see if Gavin had an order. He wrote back quickly.

Chai. Thx.

I grabbed a strong coffee for me, and a chai, and made my way to the library. I probably should have offered to get something for the dingles, too, but I was pretty sure Gavin wasn't with them yet. He and I both tried to limit our time alone with those two.

I could hear them as soon as I walked into the study room. It was a weekend, so thankfully we were the only group in that part of the library; otherwise, I'm sure those two would get us kicked out. Their real names were Steven and Cory, but I just couldn't get myself to even think of them as anything other than our nickname for them.

"Hey, what? No love for me, Sugar?" Cory said, reaching his arm around me like we were buds. I just smirked at him, annoyed, and he quickly took his arm from my shoulder. "Sorry, no touching. Got it."

I handed Gavin his chai and then tossed my backpack to the floor and took a spot at the end of the table. Gavin dove right into work mode, and I was grateful. He assigned Steven and Cory specific jobs—ones even they could handle—and we set up the three rooms for testing. Our subjects arrived within the hour, and we were done with all testing by 4 p.m.

When it came to compiling results, I was the master. I had our main spreadsheet organized within minutes, and Gavin was fetching copies from the printer for us to evaluate as a group.

"I don't know, these people look like a bunch of dummies," Cory said, leaning back and plopping his feet up on the table. His attitude must have annoyed Gavin, because he flung his feet back to the floor without even lifting his gaze to look at Cory.

"There are two dummies here, and they aren't on this spread-sheet," Gavin said, chewing on his pen cap and refusing to make eye contact with them. His nonchalant insult made me snort-laugh a little.

"Hey, man. That's not nice," Cory said, tossing his pen at Gavin who only looked up at him briefly and then went right back to work.

"So Nolan, what's your deal?" Cory was moving on to me now that he'd worn out his welcome with Gavin.

"Sorry, not sure what you mean," I said, taking Gavin's lead and not looking up to engage him.

I felt him shift in his seat and lean forward to put his elbows on his knees. Steven was joining him now, too. "I mean, you're like totally committed to your boyfriend and shit, right?" He was smirking at me, and I didn't like it.

"Yes, I'm like *totally committed to my boyfriend, and shit,*" I said, still not engaging, but becoming more and more pissed off.

"Hey, I didn't mean anything by it. Settle down, settle down," he was chuckling.

"What a cocky asshole," I thought.

"I was just thinking…you probably haven't partied much. Or done anything really *college experienced*, or nothing."

"I'm pretty happy. Besides, I don't have a lot of time to party… when I'm carrying two losers on my academic shoulders," I said, tapping my pen on their unfinished report pages.

Despite Cory's inability to launch a sentence, he was right. I wouldn't give him the satisfaction now, but his words did have some truth to them. I noticed Gavin studying me, too, and I could feel the intensity of it without even looking. I just forged on with my work, and the room stayed silent for several minutes. Gavin finally broke it.

"We should give you a college experience," he said. I snapped my eyes up to meet his, not sure where this was going but pretty sure I didn't want to experience anything with these three. Gavin must have sensed my fear, because he started chuckling and backtracking a bit.

"No, no. That's not what I meant. God no," he laughed. "I mean, we've been working our asses off on this project…*or at least some of us have.* Anyhow, we should celebrate when we're done tonight. Let's hit a club or something. I've got a buddy who's playing on Mill. I bet you'd like his stuff. We could just kick back, dance, shoot some pool, down some beers. Whataya say?"

It was clear the dingles were game, but I knew that the only person Gavin was really asking was *me*. Most of me was repelling the idea of going out tonight. But then there was also that small part of me—the part that craved to live just a little—that was fighting to say yes. It was a harmless night out. And Reed would be gone. Before I could talk myself back out of it, I just smiled and nodded.

"Okay, why not," I said, throwing my pen down and standing to head to the restroom.

When I walked into the ladies room, I headed right to the sink and mirror, splashing a little water on my face and looking at myself, my hair knotted atop my head and a pencil holding it in place. I pulled the pencil down and let my hair fall to my shoulders, shaking it out in sexy waves. I hadn't thought about how I looked in months. And even though it wasn't for Reed, it was nice to think about being pretty for someone.

―――

We didn't get everything printed, bound and labeled until 8 p.m. By this time, I was usually heading over to Sienna's or Sarah's to crash on their sofa and watch whatever stupid movie or TV show I'd talked them into recording for me. I had gone to clubs, but they had all been in Tucson, and I was always with Reed. I was a little nervous about getting in without an ID, but Gavin told me not to worry. He knew a lot of the people at the place we were going and was pretty sure I could pass by unnoticed. I just hoped I could fit in with the clubbing crowd.

My wardrobe hadn't changed much over the last two years. I hadn't really thought about that until now, but looking at my sparse closet and shoe selection had me a bit embarrassed. The guys had all headed to their various rooms, and we all planned to meet downstairs before heading out. I decided to keep it simple and put my red heels on with a pair of jeans and a tight black tank top. I left my hair down and made up for the boring outfit with some heavy eye shadow and lipstick. I gave myself a once over, took a deep breath, stuffed my keys and phone in my small handbag and headed out the door.

I took the elevator down, nervous about walking in these shoes and running into Gavin on my way. I pulled my phone out briefly and thought about sending Reed a text but decided I would just talk to him in the morning. I knew he didn't really like Gavin, but I thought the fact that I was out with a group might assuage his concern a little.

"Daaaaaaamn, girl!" Steven said as I rounded the corner by the front desk and met up with him and Cory. "Your man know you're going out looking like that?"

I blushed a little at the attention. As much as I thought Steven and Cory were idiots, I also had to acknowledge their attractiveness. They were both in the same fraternity and spent far more hours in the gym and by the pool than in class. Brown hair, dark skin, tall and lean—they were made for recruitment posters and college calendars. They also got around the sororities quite a bit. I had yet to see them with the same girls twice and was pretty sure they shared their women often, too. As much as I wanted to experience a little taste of college freedom, I was confident I never wanted to be *that* wild.

"Gav, hurry up man, let's get goin'!" Cory shouted over my shoulder. I turned to see Gavin walking toward me, his eyes intent on my face. As he got closer, he shoved his hands in his pockets and looked down, almost embarrassed that I'd caught him staring.

"Sorry, had to find a clean shirt," he looked up again, chewing the inside of his cheek and winking at me. He held out his elbow for me to take, and I hesitated. Not wanting to offend him, I reached through his arm and let him walk me through the door and along the walkway outside. When the twins were far enough in front of us, he leaned in and whispered in my ear.

"You look...really nice," I heard his gulp.

I let go of his arm after that and wiped my sweaty palms on the sides of my jeans. I needed to be careful. I didn't want to give Gavin the wrong impression, and I didn't want to forget what mattered to me, either.

————

Gavin was right. We got into the club without any trouble. The crowds were still filtering in slowly, and the band hadn't started to play yet. To kill time, Gavin ordered a pitcher of beer and challenged me to a few rounds of pool. The twins were sitting along the bar working on a group of freshmen girls who looked star struck by them. I just rolled my eyes, embarrassed by my gender.

"Okay, how about we play some nine-ball? Do you want me to teach you how to play?" Gavin asked, assuming. I was going to play along with this, and it would be fun.

"Sounds fun. Okay," I said, grabbing a stick from the wall and standing at the head of the table while he racked the balls.

The dingle twins and their female fans had moved over to the stools by the poolroom and were watching now. It was funny to see the girls react to their new eye candy. While the dingles were good-looking boys, Gavin was downright sexy. He was wearing a tight black shirt that accentuated his toned chest and abs and the scrolling artwork on each of his arms. He paired it with his usual faded jeans and black Converse shoes. He also wasn't wearing his usual black-rimmed glasses, which made the blue of his eyes stand out even more than normal.

"Okay, I'll break and show you how it's done," he said, moving me to the side to watch. I bit my tongue a little to force down the giggle of superiority that was dying to escape me. I'd been playing pool since I was 4; my grandpa was what you'd call a *shark*, and he had taught me well. When I was little, he would set me up on a chair so I could reach the center of the table, and after 16 years of play on his professional table at home, I was pretty threatening with a cue.

Gavin broke well and explained the basics of the game to me while we circled the table. Nine-ball isn't hard. It's just a game of counting, really. You shoot the balls in numerical order. The trick is planning out your shots in advance so you're never left in a corner. I watched as Gavin took his next shot and knew he wasn't going to be much competition. To make things interesting, I decided to play up my novice skills for a little longer, missing my first several shots and sighing in frustration.

"You're doing great; it's okay, you'll get it. I've been playing for a while, so that's why I'm so good," he said, his eyes crinkling with his confident smile. I almost felt bad. *Almost.* I was still going in for the kill.

"I think I just need a goal. I'm good with goals," I said as I pulled the balls from our practice game out of the pockets, and rolled them in the center to rack them.

"Okay," Gavin said, scrunching his brow and not really following me.

"Sorry, I'm not making much sense. I'm just a competitive person by nature, so I'm thinking if there's something I can win, maybe I'll play harder," I squinted my eyes and looked around the room a bit, pretending, as I knew full well what I was about to propose. "Ah, how about this. If I can win *just one game*…but only *one*," I was playing up my desperation some, "you and the dingles here have to wear my red lipstick out on the dance floor."

"Haaaaaaaaa," Cory laughed, completely taken by my acting skills. "That's funny. You're so on. There's no way you're winning."

Gavin leaned into the bar and had a pensive look, not as convinced by my performance. He was chewing on his bottom lip for a few seconds, considering, and finally spoke up. "Okay, but what if I shut you out?" He wasn't as trusting as the dingles, *smart man.*

We stood there in a staring contest for a few seconds, considering each other's bluffs. I was starting to think that maybe Gavin had been holding back a little, too, when he chimed in with his idea.

"If I shut you out, you have to kiss each of us on the cheek, with the red lipstick, leaving your mark behind—so that way everyone here tonight will know you lost a bet," he said. He smiled with tight lips, laying down all his cards. He was definitely holding back. But I was still pretty sure I could surprise him. My grandpa had won thousands at the tables and had trophies named for him in Vegas.

I'd been taught by the best, and I was about to put all of my faith in those skills.

I reached out my hand to shake Gavin's, and the bet was sealed. "You're on," I said, sliding the balls into the rack with flair, just to show the boys a hint of my skills.

"Fuuuuuck," I heard Steven whisper to Cory. It made me giggle.

I leaned my weight to one side and posted my cue on the floor, grabbing my glass of beer with my free hand and taking a big chug just for effect. I was getting better at holding my liquor. "You wanna break first or do you just want me to run the table right now and win the bet," I smiled and winked, just as Gavin had done minutes before.

He just laughed at my boldness and waved me through. "By all means. Show me what you've got," he said, sliding into one of the stools by the dingle twins and their harem.

It had been a few months since I'd played, but I wasn't very rusty. I broke and sunk the one ball right away. Two, three, four and five went soon after. I strutted around the table with a cocky swagger just to show off my new confidence, and then polished off the rest of the balls in a matter of minutes. Just to be a bit of an asshole, I tilted my stick sideways when I was done and blew the chalk off the tip. Gavin just nodded, smiled and looked down before reaching out to shake my hand again.

"Well played," he said. "I knew you were holding back. I didn't think you'd be *that* good, but I knew you were playing me."

"Why'd you take the bet then?" I asked, feeling a little guilty for flaying him in front of everyone now.

He just turned to look at the stunned dingle twins and then looked back at me. "Wearing lipstick for the next 30 minutes out there on that floor is worth every ounce of embarrassment knowing these jack-offs have to, too," he laughed.

I smiled and took another drink of my beer. I was having an amazing time. I felt freedom I hadn't felt in weeks, and the weight of my secret was temporarily lifted. "Play again?" I asked.

"Damn straight," he said, racking the balls. I let him break this time, and as I had suspected, he was better than he'd let on. I was still the stronger player, but he was good. And we competed for the next 30 minutes until the band started playing and we all headed to the dance floor.

The boys were all good sports, proudly wearing their red lips until the shiny makeup wore from their faces. The dingle twins were able to wear theirs off quickly by making out with a few various women at the club. Gavin's took a little longer, and after 30 minutes, I felt guilty and handed him a napkin to wipe the remaining color away.

I wasn't sure how many beers I had drunk, but I was working on a nice buzz when the main band started playing and the floor became crowded with moving and gyrating bodies. The band was amazing, somewhere between hard rock and alternative pop. They played a few cover songs that I loved and a few songs of their own that surprised me.

I was in my own world, dancing with my arms over my head and my hips swaying, when a strange guy reached around my stomach and pulled me into him. I turned to face him and put my hands up against his chest to push him away, get some distance. But he quickly pulled me close again. I was starting to panic a little when I saw Gavin's tattooed arm reach in between us, and heard him say, "Sorry, man. She's taken."

I smiled with relief as I turned to dance with Gavin now. "You okay there?" he asked, his hand on my shoulder. I just nodded and raised my eyebrows a bit. "Sorry, some guys are assholes," he said a little loudly so that my groper would hear.

"Thanks," I relaxed a little. Gavin still had his hand on my shoulder, and we were both swaying back and forth some. I was aware of his touch, but decided to pocket it as innocent, and kept enjoying myself. We danced like that for another two or three songs, until the band decided to slow things down. I was about to head to the seats when Gavin grabbed my hand to stop me.

"One dance?" he asked, giving me puppy-dog eyes. "I did wear lipstick for you."

I laughed a little and gave in. "Okay, one dance. You were a good sport," I said.

Gavin held my wrists and moved my hands behind his head to lay them along his neck. He slid his hands slowly down the undersides of my arms, and then they came to rest along my hips, pulling me close. The song was slow and erotic, and the couples left on the floor were all very into it. Not sure where to look, I laid my cheek flat on Gavin's chest. My heart was kicking up some as my brain swirled from the buzz of the alcohol and the dangerously inviting smell of Gavin's cologne. I felt his chin at the top of my head and tilted my face up to look at him. He was biting his bottom lip and looking at me with unmistakably hungry eyes. I felt his hands slowly work their way along my rib cage and slide barely under the edge of my bra as he moved them to my back again and then low along my hips once more, his fingers flexing and digging into my skin with a touch that was full of want.

This was definitely one of life's defining moments. So I ran.

I pushed back from him and told him I had to go outside to get some air. I walked quickly to the table, grabbed my purse and headed out the back doors to the alleyway where I knew I could get a moment alone. But I hadn't counted on Gavin following me.

"Nolan, I'm sorry. I got a little carried away," he was right on my heels.

"No, don't. It's okay, we both were drinking, and it was just a weird night," I said, turning to face him and stopping so my back was against the opposite wall.

Gavin stood across from me with his hands in his pockets, almost like he was locking them up to keep him from doing something stupid. I couldn't seem to find any words to help the situation, so instead I just stood there staring at him, blinking. My heart was racing, and my palms were sweaty. And I was pretty sure I was going to be sick later from the alcohol. I shut my eyes for a few brief seconds, trying to reset my thoughts and get myself back to normal. I pushed my hands through my hair and opened my eyes again to see Gavin staring into me.

"Oh, hell," Gavin said, lunging for me and grabbing my face

between his hands, kissing me hard and stepping into my body so we were pressed against one another. Instead of stopping him, I kissed back. I grabbed his wrists at first, a false protest, almost so I could tell myself I'd tried to stop. But I didn't. Not really. I reached behind his head and pulled him closer, fisting his hair and clawing my fingers up under his shirt. We kissed like this for several seconds before reality hit me, and I pushed into his chest. Hard.

"Gavin, I can't," I said, panting as I stumbled a few steps away from him. "Oh my god. Oh my god."

I started crying, the tears fast. I was walking away backward. He stood there, just as shocked as I was. I wiped my mouth along my arm, trying to erase what had just happened. "I'm so sorry. That was wrong. I can't…Oh my god."

I just turned and ran. I had made it only a few blocks away from the scene of my horrible slip when I felt my stomach churn and I bent forward to vomit in the gutter. People were walking around me, avoiding me, somehow completely unfazed by my throwing up, which I did four more times before I made it back to my dorm.

I had pulled my shoes from my feet and was walking along the sidewalk barefoot. The front desk girl gave me a disapproving look as I buzzed into the door and walked by her. I must have smelled like a hooker. I felt like one. I caught my reflection in the elevator on the ride up, my make-up smeared and my hair tangled in all directions.

I headed straight for the bathroom when I got into my room, stripping my clothes into a pile and crawling on my hands and knees to the shower floor, where I hugged my legs in close to me and wept. I rocked back and forth, willing my nausea to subside. The hot water turned my skin bright pink, and my hands were turning into raisins by the time I shut the water off and pulled the towel from the bar to join me on the floor.

———

By the time I awoke, the sun was shining through the bottoms of my curtains. I had slept the entire night, naked on the dirty tiles of my bathroom floor. My world was spinning as I straightened myself, sitting on my knees, not quite ready to fully stand. I grabbed the bathroom door for support and got to my feet and made my way to my bed where I had thrown my purse last night.

Last night.

I wasn't so drunk that I didn't remember. I remembered everything. *What had I done?*

I reached into my purse and pulled out my phone to find a text from Reed. I swallowed hard, almost afraid to read it. As if somehow he already knew how I'd betrayed him.

Miss you baby. See you at 4. XXOO

I had four hours to get my shit together. And the secrets were just piling up.

Chapter Twelve

Reed

WHEN MY POPS told me that Jason would be staying at the house through the holidays, I thought long and hard about cancelling Thanksgiving and Christmas—just kidnapping Nolan and taking off for Hawaii for the month.

He said that Jason was looking for his own place down in Tucson. He was moving back to Arizona permanently, taking on a bigger role with the dealerships and the company. But he wouldn't be able to move into anything until January at the earliest. I hated that he was there. Coming home was my center, my time to let my mind stop spinning. Everything important was in that house and town…and when Jason was there, well, he just had a way of shitting on things.

The holidays were still more than a month away, though, so I'd face life with Jason when I had to. I was looking forward to my trip with Noles for my birthday. She said it was a surprise, but I was pretty sure she was taking me camping. She wasn't very good at keeping secrets, and I'd seen our camping gear in her trunk the few times we'd taken her car out.

More than getting away, I was anxious to be alone with her. Things had been off lately. I was pretty sure the crap with Dylan and my brother was part of the problem, but we were just plain out of sync, too. If I didn't know how much she loved me, I would have thought she was trying to gain the courage to dump my ass—the way she flinched when I touched her, and cut our kisses short, pulling her lips tight. I had talked to Trig and his girlfriend Amy about it a few times, and they told me it was probably just the long distance thing. Of course, Trig was always filling my head with shit about how long distance relationships never worked, so he wasn't very convincing at lifting my spirits.

I was looking forward to our usual Thursday afternoon more than normal. The Sunday after the Colorado game had been especially weird. I drove up to ASU to take Nolan out for dinner and had planned to spend the night, but she said she was tired. She was off in space through most of our dinner conversation, said she was just super stressed about her big psychology project. When I pressed her on it, she got defensive, told me I wasn't helping things with the draft pressure I'd thrown at her.

I was hoping I could ease a little of her stress today. After a few long calls with Dylan, we pretty much narrowed down my most likely options in the draft to San Diego or Seattle. And with Sean's help, I was able to pull together some pretty good research on transferring from ASU's special education program to San Diego State's. I was pretty sure most of Nolan's scholarships would transfer, too; not that it mattered. Whether she liked it or not, I was going to pay the rest of her tuition once I got signed.

Amy offered to help me with researching Washington and Oregon schools next. Anything I could do to show Nolan how easy this next move was going to be had to take away some of her fears.

When I pulled into her parking lot, it was a little later than my usual visit. I knew she was probably already up in her room, so I sent her a text and told her I was running late and would just meet her upstairs.

I stole a candy from the dish at her front desk, mostly because it was funny how the freshman girls that worked the afternoon shifts acted when I did. Today, I winked at them when I passed by, which sent them into whispers and giggles. "Funny, if my life had gone the way of Jason's, I'd have slept with every single one of them by now," I thought.

I skipped the elevators and took the stairs to save time. With 15 floors in her building, it took forever for the elevators to make their way back to the lobby floor. I heard a couple arguing when I was coming closer to Nolan's floor and thought about stepping out a level early to give them some privacy when I realized it was Nolan's voice I was hearing. I slowed a bit then, trying to get a handle on what she was saying…and who the dude was on the other side of the conversation.

"I'm not angry. But please, you need to drop this," I heard Nolan say in a half-whisper, her voice full of frustration.

"Nolan, I just don't think you're being fair to yourself, that's all I'm saying…" I wasn't sure on this one, so I stood still for another minute, just waiting him out.

"Gavin, you don't know anything about me," I heard her sigh now.

Gavin. Fucking asshole.

"I don't drink often, and I think we can both see why now. The other night was just a HUGE mistake at the end of a really shitty week. That's it."

My blood was boiling now, and I was pretty sure I was going to punch Gavin in the face in about seven seconds. But I wasn't fast enough and heard him speak one more time.

"Well, it wasn't a mistake on my part. I made the decision to do everything I did that night. And I'd make the same choice again, right here, right now."

His words trapped me—ground me to a fucking halt. I heard Nolan sigh once more, followed by the sound of the door opening and slamming shut. I watched Gavin's feet climb the stairs above me to his floor, and I stood there frozen in fury. *What did that asshole do to my girl?*

I hung out in the stairwell for about 15 minutes, just trying to sort through the conversation I'd heard. I didn't know what to do next. Part of me wanted to barrel into Gavin's room and hold him up against the wall until he broke, but the other part of me knew I only had half the story. And that part was making me sick.

Finally able to get my legs to work, and tired of the strange looks from freshmen passing in and out of the stairwell, I climbed the rest of the way to Nolan's floor. I took a deep breath when I swung the hall door open, unsure of what I was walking into. Her floor was clear, no one around. I drug my feet to her door at the end and stood in front of it for a few seconds, not sure what words would, *or should*, come out of my mouth when I saw her.

Leaning my forehead on the door, I rapped on it lightly a few times, almost like I was hoping she wouldn't hear it and wouldn't answer. I straightened up when I heard the bolt unclick for her to let me in. She flung the door open and turned back around to walk back to her closet, smiling at me briefly over her shoulder.

"Hey, was just changing. Thought maybe we could go out, grab a bite? Mind waiting just a few while I get ready?" She spoke calmly, as if the conversation I had heard minutes ago never happened. I had no idea how to play this, so I thought I'd just see what turned up.

"Sure, sounds good. Take your time," I said, walking over to sit on the edge of her bed. My suspicion had me looking at everything differently. I lifted the corner of her comforter from her bed, touching it to see if I felt anything different. I lifted her jacket to my nose, smelling it for…for someone else. I touched her pillows and then stood to slip open her top drawer, curious and now full of paranoia. I saw her figure pass from the open closet door to the bathroom, and I started some, like I'd been caught.

"Just one more sec, I promise," she giggled.

All I could think was, "What the hell was going on?" I felt like I'd landed in a *Twilight Zone*.

I was full on pacing now in the center of her room, my mind debating with itself over whether or not I should confront her about what I'd heard. I tossed my hat on her desk to dig my fingers into my hair, my stomach fluttering more now—not with butterflies, though. She was just stepping out of her closet door, dressed cute-as-hell in a black shirtdress and tall boots, almost making my worries dissolve, when we both turned to face her door. The light tapping was accompanied by a voice. *His fucking voice.*

"Nolan, it's me. Open up, please? I feel bad...I...I didn't want to make you upset," Gavin said, clearly upset himself, though not as upset as he was about to be when I was the one to open the door for him.

I turned to Nolan and got the confirmation I needed when she just stared at the door, eyes wide, face ghost-white and mouth slightly open. She turned to look at me, and in that brief instant I just held up my hand. "Don't," I said, a little short, then put my hand over my mouth and rubbed my chin a little to force myself not to say anything I'd regret. "I'll get this."

When I opened the door, Gavin just stood there—he was still and stared right back at me. He pushed his lips together in a tight, knowing smile and then nodded a few times, looking down at his feet. "Reed...how's it goin?" he said, reaching his hand out to shake mine. I stared at it for a few seconds and then just chuckled and walked into the room, turning my back on him.

"Well, I don't know, Gavin. You tell me. How's it going?" I said, the asshole version of myself coming out to play now. I leaned into Nolan's desk and took Gavin in as he walked into Nolan's room, his hands buried in his pockets. Nolan was sitting down now, at the edge of her bed, her arms folded tightly across her body, her eyes still wide...*and glossy?*

"Did you tell him?" Gavin said softly, nodding in Nolan's direction.

"Tell me what, Gavin?" I interrupted. I didn't like the way he was making Nolan feel, and more importantly, I didn't like him.

He just sighed heavily and looked down at his feet, and he flexed them a bit and stepped side-to-side, thinking. He tilted his face back up to make eye contact with me, sucking in a long breath before he spoke. "I kissed her," he said, shrugging his shoulders and smiling on one side of his mouth, as if it was all some fucking innocent game.

That's all it took.

Within a half second, my fist was making contact with Gavin's bony fucking face. I hadn't punched anyone in a long time, and it stung like hell. But the rush it sent through my blood was enough to ignite a whole new wave of rage. While Gavin was busy stumbling backward and holding his nose, I flew at him and pushed him hard into Nolan's wall. I grabbed fistfuls of his collar and jerked him violently into the wall a few times before getting in his face.

"You piece of shit, you keep your hands off my girl! You hear me?" I spoke through gritted teeth. I was getting ready to shove him once again, when I heard Nolan's voice break through the noise in my head.

"Reed, stop! Stop! Don't, you're hurting him!" she said as she grabbed my sleeve and yanked one of my arms from Gavin's. With her distraction, Gavin was able to shove me back and force me a little off balance. He didn't swing at me; he just forced some distance.

I was breathing heavily, and Gavin was wiping his nose along his long sleeves, a small stream of blood coming from it now. He leaned back against the opposite wall and turned to look at Nolan, who was standing between us now, her back to me. He was shaking his head, and the face he was making was too damned familiar. I don't know when the words formed in my head, or if they even did, but as soon as they left my mouth I knew they were going to ruin me.

"Did you...did you kiss him back?" I asked, my voice cracking a little now. Nolan just kept her back to me for a few seconds, and I saw what was happening reflected in the shame on Gavin's face. "Nolan?"

Her shoulders started shaking, and she brought her hands up to cover her mouth. She turned to face me so slowly it killed me. By the time we were eye-to-eye, her face was wet, and her eyes were red with guilt. I slid off balance a little, bracing myself on the edge of her desk, my fingers digging into the wood. I wouldn't let her gaze go. I just kept it. Taking in a deep breath, I asked her one more time. "Nolan, did you kiss him back?" I asked.

Even though I already knew, when she nodded *yes*, and closed her eyes, it was like someone had stabbed me in the heart. My entire life just whirled by me at once. My dad, my future, my grandmother's goddamn ring...everything was fucking ruined! Unable to take being in this room another second, I pushed from the desk and stormed out her door, throwing it closed behind me with such force that it bounded back open and the sound reverberated down the hall.

I got to the stairwell and flung that door open, too, and was sliding down the stairs several at a time; my feet couldn't get me from this fucking building fast enough. Then I heard her voice—her pathetic-sounding pleas. And it all just broke me again.

"Reed! Please, don't leave. You have to understand, you have to let me explain!" she was chasing me down the stairs, and I knew she was going to fall if she kept up that speed. I just stopped when I was one floor away from my freedom and turned to wait for her. When she saw me, she stopped at the top of the steps, again putting a hand over her mouth while she cried and shook.

"Nolan, when I said *never*...I fucking meant it," I said, solemnly while I shook my head and looked down at the steps between us. "What...what the hell happened?"

She looked up and took in a deep breath, wrapping her arms around her stomach again like she was forcing herself not to be sick. When she looked back down at me, she just shrugged. "I don't really know. It just sort of happened..." she was soft, full of shame.

I turned to look away from her for a bit, just to reset my thoughts, and put my hands on my head. "Nolan, how does something like that just sort of happen? Was it...a small kiss?" I was turning to look at her again with hope that it was something innocent, but when her body started convulsing again, I knew there was nothing innocent about what had happened between her and Gavin.

Shaking my head, I started backing away from her slowly. "Noles, I don't think I want to hear anymore. I...I just can't," I was cold now. I didn't want her following me, but I didn't want to be mean. And I knew if I heard anything else she had to say, I was going to be. I was at the main floor and was reaching to pull the door to leave when she caught up to me one last time, her hand on my shoulder just breaking me all over again.

"Reed, please!" she pleaded.

I turned to look at her, so damn close to me. Not thinking, I just reached up to grab both sides of her face and kissed her hard, willing myself to erase the pain. But the more I kissed her, the more her body shook, and the more I thought about her lips on Gavin's, and how she actually wanted them there. I pulled away quickly and pushed her back gently. I scrunched my brow a bit, thinking, and finally found the courage to ask.

"Are you...into him?" I was afraid of her response. And when she didn't give me one immediately, I stumbled off balance a bit again, hit in the face with an entirely new devastating fact.

"No, I'm not...I just...I don't know how it all got to this...oh god," she was covering her mouth again and squeezing her eyes shut.

I just reached for her wrists to take them in my hands and pull them to my lips so I could kiss them softly. "I have to go," I said, my heart broken as I turned away from her.

"What do you mean? Are you coming back? Are we...okay?" she was blubbering now.

I just shrugged my shoulders a bit at her words. "I don't know. I don't think so," I said as I let the door fall shut behind me.

Chapter Thirteen

Reed

I DON'T KNOW how I got home. I don't remember a thing about the drive. I know I thought about stopping at my pop's house, talking it out with him. But honestly the thought of telling my dad about what Nolan did just ripped through me almost as much as the act itself, so I kept driving.

Somehow, I had made it back to my dorm room. It was early still, the sun barely setting. Normally, I'd be bringing Noles home from dinner, distracting her from homework, wrapping strands of her hair around my fingers and blowing on her neck while she tried to read or concentrate. But instead, I was laying flat on my back, staring up at my dorm room ceiling, miserable and alone.

I held the box with my grandmother's ring in it for two hours, flipping it open and then shut. Finally sick of flipping back and forth between what I had wanted a day ago and what I was faced with now, I just set it there on my chest, open and taunting me. Part of me registered the sound of my door, but I didn't realize I wasn't alone anymore until Trig broke into my numb silence.

"Woah, damn...is that what I think it is?" he said, reaching for the box on my chest. Reacting, I flipped it closed and pocketed it before he got too close.

"It's nothing," I said, sitting up and rubbing my hand through my hair to try to hide the wallowing that clearly had been done over the last hour.

"Oooookay then. You hungry or something? Didn't you eat with Nolan? You know you turn into a bitch when you don't eat," Trig was trying to be funny, but I wasn't in the mood.

"I'm not hungry," I said, standing and sliding on a gray beanie and then a sweatshirt. I started pacing around the room on a hunt for my shoes.

"Dude, you a'right man?" Trig asked. I locked eyes with him for a minute, and then continued looking for my shoes.

"I can't find my fucking shoes. Do you know where they are?" I was short.

"Uh, no. I'm not your *fucking shoe keeper,*" Trig shot back, calling me out a little on my attitude. I just sighed and sat back on the edge of my bed, holding my forehead in my hands and rubbing my temples.

"Sorry. I didn't mean to be a dick. I've just had a shit day," I said, holding a little back, and unsure if I wanted to get into it with Trig.

"Aw, what happened man, lovebirds fighting?" he said with a chuckle. He was trying to lighten my mood, but he had no idea how dead right he was. I just rubbed my hands on my face and finally stopped, holding my head in my hands and shrugged. Trig got it right away. "Ah shit, man. I'm sorry. Wanna…talk about it?"

He was uncomfortable. So was I. And I wasn't ready to talk yet. I finally spotted the laces of one of my shoes under Trig's bed and stood up to grab them. "No talking. I wanna go to the bar. I'm buying, you in?"

"Fuck yeah," he said, grabbing his keys and jacket. "We've got late practice tomorrow. Let's go."

I was about four beers in at Cooler's before I felt like opening up about things to Trig. Even then, it took him asking again about the ring he'd seen for me to start talking.

"So seriously, man, was that an engagement ring I saw you flashing around? Is that what happened? Oh...wait! Did you ask, and she said no?" he was making up his own story now.

"No, jack off. That's not what happened," I said, taking a big drink and finishing the rest of my beer. I pushed the mug to the side, tapping the top of it to let the bartender know I wanted another. Rubbing my eyes a little and scrunching my brow, I finally started to fill Trig in. I told him about the conversation I'd heard, and how Gavin actually had the nerve to come back up to her room.

Trig was ready to drive back up to ASU to beat his ass with me, but I just bought him another beer and told him to sit his ass down. "Thing is, man...she kissed him back," I said, pushing my lips tight, gritting my teeth and staring at the edge of the bar in front of me. That was the part that was killing me most. "I wish I could fix this by just taking it out on that asshole, believe me. But I can't. Something's wrong. It's been wrong for a while, and fuck, man? She kissed him back..."

I shook my head more and started on my fifth beer. My stomach was rolling over with hunger, so Trig and I ordered some nachos and got comfortable for the night. We were going to be here for a while.

"Sorry man," he said, just shaking his head. "I never saw this coming. I mean, I know I give you shit about long distance relationships and all, but that's only because I never thought you'd really have to worry about it. Hell, my girl is here with me, and I almost fuck things up on a weekly basis!"

I laughed a little at him. Trig was a good friend, and I was lucky I'd found him. But I knew he wouldn't be able to help. I was pretty sure no one could, and definitely not tonight. No, tonight was about me drowning my thoughts, throwing a huge-ass pity party, and finding a way to quit being so damned angry with Nolan. A little stupid from drinking, but still in control of my actions, I pulled my phone from my pocket and sent my best friend Sean a text. He was used to these, and he was my bro. Had been since high school. He would know what I should do next.

Hey man. Nolan cheeeted on me – need 2talk2u. don't freakout. i didn't do anything stupid. Drunk tho. Really fucking drunk!!!!!!

I pocketed my phone and went back to my beer. I was sipping on it like a fucking baby, when two giggling blondes bumped into me, one of them grabbing onto my arm to catch her balance.

"Oh my god, I'm so sorry," she giggled more. She was flirting, and it was obvious.

"No problem," I said, turning my face back to my beer and trying to ignore Trig's elbow into my side, telling me I should fix my problems by making bigger ones.

"Hey, my friend and I are trying to find a way home. You guys have a car?" she was leaning over into me now, pushing her breasts against my arms, and making them impossible to ignore. And I was looking…seriously looking.

I turned to Trig for a few seconds, chewing on the inside of my cheek, my mind sorting through all of the possibilities.

If not this one, then there would be another, and then another.

Taking things into his own hands, Trig just smiled at me and held my stare while talking to the girls. "We walked, ladies, but we'd be happy to walk you home, make sure you get there safely," he said, holding out his arm to take one of them, and willing me to do the same—*daring* me.

I downed the rest of my beer, still staring at him, and then threw a wad of cash on the bar and turned around to smile at my distraction. "Sure, let's go ladies," I said, smiling at her from the side of my mouth and letting my heavy eyes focus only on her. She snuggled in closely when I did that. Her skin smelled like peaches, and her long waves of hair tickled my bicep.

I'm not going to lie, it had me thinking about what she looked like under that short-ass dress. Maybe I'd been missing out?

Trig and I walked the girls two blocks in the opposite direction of our dorm, and my head was swimming the entire time. I was either going to say goodnight, and head home to pass out—or fight through the dizziness, and make myself feel better by making a decision I'd probably regret in the morning, but would feel so damn good right now.

The girls talked and giggled the entire way to their place, but I couldn't tell you a damn word they said. When we got to the steps up to their apartment, Trig hung with me for a few seconds, walking them all the way up to the door. But when they invited us in, he just held up his phone and said, "I got things, but my boy will stick around." He winked at me and skipped down the steps.

Drunk, I followed them inside. The blond that had been walking with Trig just smiled at her friend and said she was going to take a shower, leaving us alone in their living room. Everything looked fuzzy, and I felt enormous in their frilly, girly apartment. I wasn't sure what I was doing here, but I wasn't ready to leave yet either. I pulled my hat from my head and shoved it in my back pocket, pulling my sweatshirt up and tossing it on her couch.

"You want anything to drink?" she said, kicking her high heels from her feet and sliding to her kitchen.

I just stared around at my new surroundings, still debating with myself and fighting my instincts. "Nah, I'm good. I should…" I was about to say *go* when she came back out to the living room, her dress now hanging around her hips and her black bra exposing everything I had been dying to get a better look at.

She walked right up to me and held on to my arm while she pulled her dress the rest of the way down. My mind wandered, "Shit. She was fucking hot!" Her black panties left very little to the imagination, and I was really fighting the urge to just throw her over my shoulder and carry her into her bedroom. Everything started happening in slow motion, and I was pretty sure I was making the dumbest face, my mouth wide open and panting like a dog. My eyes were so heavy, my mind was racing minutes ahead, imagining running my hands over her body and taking off the last bits of clothing she had on. It was all right there, waiting for me.

She stood to her tiptoes and pulled on the collar of my T-shirt to reach her lips up to my face. I let my eyes fall shut for a second, and then her teeth were tugging on my bottom lip. The shock of it knocked me off balance, and I took a step back, my eyes shooting open in an instant.

Fuck! What was I doing?

"I'm sorry, I…I have to go," I said, grabbing my sweatshirt and turning from her before I changed my mind. Feeling a little guilty, I stopped at her door before opening it. "I'm sorry. This isn't how I am…You're a really pretty girl."

I couldn't get myself to fully look at her face, but from the periphery, I knew she was embarrassed, and I felt bad. But somehow, I stopped myself from doing something really stupid.

———

By the time I finally woke up Friday, I only had a few hours to spare before Trig and I had to get ready for practice. He must have come to a lot earlier than I did, because he stuck a Post-It on my forehead telling me he took off to the main hall for food and would just catch me at practice.

The entire last 24 hours felt like a damned nightmare. If it weren't for my god-awful raging headache, and the fact that the stupid ring was sitting on my night table staring at me, I might have been able to convince myself I'd dreamt it all.

After guzzling from the gallon of water we kept cold in our mini fridge, I forced myself to dig my phone out from my pocket. And there it was, staring at me—an undoubtedly *minutes-long* voicemail from Nolan. That stupid flashing green light was giving me the middle finger, over and over again. I'd listen to it, but not now. "Maybe after practice," I thought. Instead, I slid open the text from Sean.

First of all, dude, you can't just drop something like that on me without more to go on. WTF? Second, I'm around all day. Just waiting on Becky to finish a midterm and hanging out around the apartment all morning. Call me when you're done lovin' on the toilet ; -)

I missed Sean. He was, in so many ways, the brother I wished I had. Everything about him was good. When I decided to grow up, I told myself I would try to be more like Sean. I always thought it was a damned miracle Noles picked me over him in high school. And an even bigger miracle that he didn't fucking hate me for it, too.

It was almost 2 p.m., and I was pretty sure he'd be gone, but I gave him a try anyhow. I was about to hang up and just shoot him a text when I heard him answer, breathless.

"Yo, what's up man?" he asked, still breathing hard.

"Hey, sorry. I was a little late getting started today. Did I...interrupt something?" I teased him. He and Becky were living together, and I'd caught him more than once trying to talk to me while Becky was *distracting* him.

"No, dumb ass. I was just lifting weights out on the balcony. Not all of us get personal trainers and shit to keep up our workouts," he gave it right back to me.

We bantered back and forth for a few minutes on nothing important, and then finally settled into the serious stuff. I brought Sean up to speed, and then sat there silent while he thought about things and got over the shock of it all. I knew it would hit Sean pretty hard, too—one, because he was truly a brother to me; and two, because he loved Nolan almost as much as I did.

"Okay, so let me just ask you this...what is it you really want?" he started.

I thought about it for a few seconds, not really sure how to answer that question.

"What do you mean? Like, do I wish I could go back to that hour before I drove to her campus, and didn't know she kissed that asshole? Yes. Or better yet, do I want to go back even more, before she kissed him at all, and just show up magically and stop it all? Yes. But that's stupid...and I feel like," I swallowed, knowing what I was about to say rung a little with truth. "I feel like maybe it would have just happened at some point anyway. Like I would have just been putting it off, the inevitable, know what I mean?"

Sean just sighed. I could almost see him nodding through the phone.

"I'm right, aren't I?" I said quietly.

"Reed, I don't know. But I think maybe this kiss is just the tip of your problems," he was laying it out straight. "But…and I mean this…I don't think you're ready to quit on what you two have. You love her. Like, really love her. You always have, and you know it. You need to talk."

I took in a deep breath and lay flat on my bed again, staring at that same stupid dot on my ceiling that I'd been looking at since yesterday. "Yeah, I know. You're right. You always are, dick head," I joked, trying to lighten the situation, and my miserable-ass mood. I was pretty sure I was heading to ASU after practice. Some things just weren't meant to be said over-the-phone.

Chapter Fourteen

Nolan

SOMEHOW, I kept managing to find new lows. I was working on maybe two hours of sleep over the last 48 hours, and it was starting to make me paranoid and full of anxiety—something which I already had a tough time managing with ample amounts of sleep and low stress.

When Reed shut the door on me yesterday, I crumbled. I sat there in the stairwell sobbing for an hour. And when I made it back up to my room, I just kept going. I ignored Sarah and Sienna for the entire day, just texting them that I was busy, putting them off. I wasn't ready for their dose of advice. And worse, I wasn't ready for Sarah to be pissed off at me. I knew she would be.

I'd done this. And I knew if I just let Reed in earlier, I could have avoided it all. But I'd made a mountain out of my problems and guilt, and rather than deal with it all, I got carried away in stupid fantasies. I liked Gavin, sure. He was smart and handsome, and had that musician thing that made girls get stupid. But he didn't have my heart.

I dialed Reed's number on an impulse last night, spilling my guts to him. I was thankful, at first, when I got his voicemail. Voicemail wasn't intimidating, at least not when you were throwing caution to the wind. I told him everything. I told him how sorry I was that I'd been so cold toward him, how freaked out I was because I was pregnant, but how guilty I felt now because I'd lost the baby. I started crying harder when I admitted that aloud, just saying the words cut through me like a knife and forced me to pause on the phone for a few seconds—choking on words and heartbreak. I told him about what really happened the day I fell from the treadmill, about the heartless doctor who gave me a stack of brochures and a condom, along with my miscarriage diagnosis—and about how my fucked up head and drinking turned into the worst decision of my life when I kissed Gavin that night. I downright begged for him to forgive me. I laid it all out on the field, nothing left.

And then I waited.

As each hour passed, the fact that Reed wasn't calling was hitting me harder and harder. I figured he was probably ignoring my call and message at first. I thought about texting him, trying to force him to see my name and face. But each time I grabbed my phone, I chickened out, thought it was better to let him work through what he had heard and seen.

I knew I wouldn't be able to avoid Sarah and Sienna forever, so I texted them and told them to meet me at the Starbucks for coffee. Sienna, always perceptive, knew something was up almost immediately, texting me back:

You okay?

I was done lying.

No. Not at all.

. . .

I managed to take a shower and pull on some sweats and my warm Uggs. It was starting to get chilly at night, and I wasn't up for driving, so I planned on walking. I was stuffing my keys and some cash in my pocket when my phone buzzed. I was anxious and excited at first, but then I saw it was Becky. Knowing I couldn't put this off forever either, I answered while I locked up.

"Hey Becks," I said, knowing what was coming.

"Hey…are you…okay?" She knew. That must mean Sean knew, which meant at least Reed was talking to someone—that made me feel hopeful.

"No, not really," I sighed. "Becky, I don't know how it got to this." Becky didn't know the full story, and I didn't think I'd be able to fill her in on everything, including the pregnancy, in the short walk to the coffee shop. I was pretty sure Sean would know about it soon anyhow, though, and by extension, Becky.

"Reed called Sean. I'm sure you know," she sighed. "Has he called you yet?"

"No…" I lingered. "I keep waiting. Actually, I got a little hopeful when you called."

"Oh…I'm sorry. I'm sure he'll call, Noles. Sean said he was pretty tore up, but he got through to him."

The tears were starting to come again, so I wiped my eyes with the corners of my sleeves. I was passing people on the sidewalk now, so I tried not to give too much away, but I wanted to know everything Becky knew…she was my only connection to Reed.

"What happened, Nolan? Was this guy, like, just hitting on you all the time or something? I mean, do you like him? Do you know him really well?" she was trying to give me the benefit of the doubt.

I just let out a big breath and shrugged, even though she couldn't see it. "I don't know. I mean, yes, he's really good looking… and he's smart. His name's Gavin, he's in a lot of my classes with me. We've worked on a lot of projects together, and he's always been flirty, but that's it."

"Did he just blindside you? I mean, how did the kiss happen?" she was trying to understand.

"Becks, I was pretty drunk. I remember it, but sort of like it was a dream. Or more like a nightmare. We were out celebrating, a bunch of us were. And you know me, I never go out…but it just sounded like so much fun. And I was so stressed…you know, from school," I was vague with that last part. "We were playing pool, and everything was fine. And then there was a band, and we were dancing and then Gavin got close and we were dancing really closely, and he touched me a little, not like *that*, but still…it was pretty clear what he was suggesting. And then I bolted."

"Well, that doesn't sound so bad. Did he kiss you while you were dancing? I'm sure if you explained this to Reed he'd see…" Becky started to suggest, but I cut her off.

"No, no. It wasn't while we were dancing," I said, the tears threatening again. I hung my head in shame and bit my lip a little. "He followed me outside, and after a really intense stare-off, we kissed each other. Becks, I didn't stop him. Not for a *looooong* time, at least."

Starbucks was only another block away. We both hung on the phone in silence for a few seconds, and I was starting to worry that I'd lost Becky, too. Then she finally spoke.

"Nolan, it's not as bad as it sounds. I think maybe Reed's mind is making it worse than it is. You just need to explain it to him. It was a kiss. You didn't sleep with him, and I'm guessing you never plan on kissing him again," she joked a little.

I just laughed in return. "No, I really don't. I don't even like him that way, Becks. I just want to rewind the whole damn thing," I said, starting to feel a little optimistic.

I hung up with Becky as I walked into Starbucks, where Sarah and Sienna were waiting for me. I went through the entire story again with them, and, after taking my lecture from Sarah, left feeling even more encouraged. They were both proud of me for finally coming clean with everything to Reed, even if it was on his voicemail.

I checked my phone every 15 seconds it seemed during my walk home, feeling phantom vibrations and believing each one was a call or text from Reed. It wasn't, but I knew he had only gotten off from practice an hour or so ago. I was actually in a place where I was looking forward to my night of laundry and some much overdue lit reading—thinking my mind would actually let me focus for the next hour or two—when I saw Gavin leaning against my door, looking down at his phone while I approached. Seeing him just zapped me of all energy.

"Gavin, what are you doing here," I said, probably a little harsher than I needed to, but I didn't want to send any mixed signals.

He looked up and moved over while I pulled out my keys. He shoved his phone back in his pocket, shrugging a little, "I'm not stalking you...I promise," he said wryly, smirking at me a little.

"I know, I'm sorry. It's just...I think we, you and I, probably need a little space. I'm trying to work through some things..." I wasn't making much sense, and his presence just had me flustered.

"I get it," he said, not making me go on any more than I had to. "I just wanted to make sure we were okay...apologize. Do you have a few minutes? Just to talk," he raised his shoulders a bit when he spoke, trying to prove his innocent intentions.

I just laid my forehead on my door as I pushed my key in the lock and turned it. Letting out a deep sigh, I twisted my face to look at him, his puppy dog eyes begging me. "Sure, but only for a few minutes. I have a lot to do, and I haven't really been able to focus lately," I admitted.

Gavin followed me into my room and pushed the door closed behind him, but not completely, I think not wanting me to feel threatened. I appreciated that. He was twisting his hands together in front of him, a little uncomfortably while he paced around, deciding where he should sit. He finally sat at my desk chair, leaning forward and putting his elbows on his knees. I pulled my things from my pocket and went to work grabbing my laundry and cleaning supplies.

"Look, Nolan. I'm not going to lie. I like you. I like you more than I should. And I know it's a problem, it creates problems...but I think there's a part of you that likes me, too. Maybe...just a little," he was making things worse, mostly because I did like him...but not like he liked me. And I didn't want to lose that thing we had, what-

ever it was, before I went and kissed him and made it all compli-
cated. But I also knew I didn't want to lose Reed. And that was
more important than anything.

I stopped stuffing towels and T-shirts in my laundry bin and sat
on my bed, across from him. I blew the hairs out of my face, and
then rubbed it with my hands, thinking, searching for the right
words to say. There weren't any, so I just started talking.

"I do like you, Gavin...but..." I held up my hand to stop his
smile from growing. "I'm *in love* with Reed. What I feel for you is a
close *friendship*, and I know it's not what you want to hear, but it's all
I have to give to you. I never should have let it get as far as it did
that night. And I'm so sorry that it gave you the wrong idea. But I
can't be with you. I can't give up what I have, because it means the
world to me—and it's killing me right now, knowing how badly I
hurt Reed."

I stood up to walk over to Gavin a little, his head was hanging
down, and his brow was bunched. I knew he didn't expect me to
leap into his arms, but I also think he thought he could chip away at
me a little today, make me doubt my heart. "I'm sorry, Gavin," I
said right in front of him.

Tilting his head up a little, he just bit the tip of his tongue and
nodded, chuckling quietly, mostly embarrassed, I could tell. I
wanted to make it better. "I really am flattered, though. You have to
know, most of the girls in this building would smack me right now at
turning you down. You're kind of the resident *hottie* you know," I
smiled, joking, but also being honest. Most of the freshmen in our
dorm were in love with Gavin, always showing up at his door to ask
for help with ridiculous things, just so they could talk to him.

Unable to stand the tension in the room any longer, I turned
back to my laundry pile to look like I was ready to leave. Getting my
hint, Gavin stood, a little less confident looking than when I let him
in a few moments earlier. "Well, I guess, thanks for being honest,"
he half smiled. "Brutally honest..."

"I'm sorry. I really didn't mean to be *brutal*," I said, following
him to my door.

"I'm kidding. You weren't. I just really hoped for a different response," he said, opening the door a little and backing out. "I just haven't met anyone quite like you…not since Maya. You're really smart and beautiful…"

He stopped at his words and lingered on my face for a few seconds. I was feeling the heat from his stare, and it was making me uncomfortable, and forcing me to look down. I held on to the side of the door to keep myself grounded, ready to close it if I needed to. I flinched a bit when he reached up to sweep a few strands of hair from my face, but then shut my eyes when he tucked them behind my ear. When I opened them again, he was looking at me, *really* looking at me. And I knew by that look, that we couldn't be friends. For him, that would never be enough.

"Thanks, that was really nice of you to say," I said, smiling and genuine, because it was. But I had nothing to give back. Unsure of what to do, I just reached up to hug him a little. "Thank you for understanding," I whispered.

Gavin hugged back, a full hug with everything that came with it. I felt every single fingertip slide behind me and squeeze. And as we pulled apart, I felt his lips graze the side of my cheek, and then he hovered by my ear for just a brief second. "I had to try," he said, grinning as he backed fully away, and then turned to go upstairs.

I closed the door as soon as he was gone and leaned back on it, pushing the hairs from my now flushed face. What the hell? I'm not the girl that has boys fighting for her. This was awful. I pulled my lit book from my shelf and plopped on my bed, opening up to the beatnik section. Laundry could wait; I just wasn't feeling it any more.

Chapter Fifteen

Reed

IT WAS like the worst fucking nightmare, and it just wouldn't end.

I left practice and headed straight for Nolan's campus. I didn't have my phone or my wallet, and I was pretty sure I was going to have to stop back at my dad's house to get cash for gas. I just had to *get* there. The more I thought about her and what happened, the more I wanted to give her the chance to explain it away. I was so pissed at myself for almost getting carried away with some one-night-stand the night before, how could I blame Nolan for the same damn thing?

But that all flew right out the window the minute I got to her floor and saw that asshole with his hands all over her. He was leaving her room, and I watched him kiss her face and whisper something in her ear. The way she reacted to it, flushed and heated, was enough to send me over the fucking edge.

He backed away as she closed the door, and when he turned around, and stuffed his hands in his pockets with the huge-ass smile on his face, I just wanted to vomit. He knew I was there; he didn't even look up when he got to the stairwell door. "What are you doing here, Reed? She doesn't want to see you," he said, not even man enough to make eye contact with me.

"Who are you to tell me what she wants," I bit back, bracing myself for a fight.

Gavin walked back into the stairwell, just smirking, and I followed him in. He stopped after only a few steps and turned back to look down at me, leaning on the handrail in a way that just oozed of condescension. "I'm the guy that's here, that's who. Who are you? The guy that shows up every few days, and keeps her locked up in a fucking box so she can't really live?" He was attacking me with his words, and I could feel my pulse kick up in defense.

"She's my girlfriend, bro. You need to back the fuck off," I said, stepping up one level to meet his gaze and challenge him. But he stepped down to meet me, our chests inches apart while we stared each other down.

"I'm not going anywhere. I'm the one that was here for her last night, when you just left, and she wants me here," he had a hint of something on his face, not quite a smirk, but it was superior, and it was making me question things.

"What...do you mean...you were the one that was here for her last night," I said, my teeth pushing into my bottom lip, as I stared at him and my heart thumped through my entire body.

He just chuckled a little and looked down, shaking his head a bit, like I was some fucking joke, an embarrassment to myself. I was being a fool.

"I don't need to tell you what I mean...*bro*...you know exactly what I mean," he finished then slowly started backing up the steps, keeping his eyes on mine, while I stood there as the earth crumbled beneath me. My body was shaking, and I was struggling to get a full breath. I wanted to charge after him and slam his body into the wall, but his words, his confession, had me paralyzed. I watched him turn slowly as he reached the landing to the next floor. Then, just before he reached his door to open it, he leaned over the rail and gave me one final knockout punch.

"Time to move on, man. She has." His words followed by the smack of his door shutting.

I just stood there, wide-eyed, in the stairwell for the next several minutes. This was the second time in two days I was living this nightmare. It was like *Groundhog Day*, and I was Bill Murray. I looked back at the door to Nolan's floor and thought about busting into her room and questioning her, but I didn't really want to hear any more excuses. I kept replaying her face when she confessed that she had kissed him back, and the thought of her admitting to *much more* just killed me. Had she been unhappy for a while? Did she want to break up weeks ago? Months ago?

My feet somehow had carried me back to my Jeep, and I sorted through my thoughts all the way to my dad's house. Truth was, Nolan had been unhappy, almost from the beginning of our semester. It always felt like she was pulling away, but she still seemed so happy to see me. And she made the effort, too. Drove to Tucson to see me, came to my games. But I wasn't around…and when I wasn't, and Nolan was alone, I really didn't know what was happening. The thoughts were making me sick.

I was close to empty when I pulled into the driveway. My dad and Rosie were sitting at the breakfast bar eating pasta when I came in. The house smelled like a home, a smell I could get used to. That's how Nolan's house always smelled. Since Rosie had been staying to care for my dad, meals were becoming a common occurrence. Not just the usual frozen ones either, but slow-cooked, all-day-prepared meals.

"Reed, what are you doing here, son?" Pops said, sliding out a stool with one of his crutches to make room for me. "Come on, plenty to eat. Rose made a real good dinner tonight."

A little deflated, I slumped over to my dad and took a seat while Rosie got up and fixed me a plate. She put the pasta in front of me and kissed my head while she squeezed my shoulders a little. "Always good to see you, mijo," she said, sitting back down to finish her dinner.

"You staying the night, Kid? Or what," my dad asked, not even looking up from his plate; he was so engrossed in his meal. I sort of worried that my dad was going to eat himself into another heart attack with all of the food he'd been eating while he was laid up with his leg. But, I also knew Rosie, and she found a way to make the most amazing things out of low-cholesterol ingredients. She wasn't above tricking my father into being healthy.

Swirling the spaghetti strands around my fork and spoon, I just nodded. "Yeah, I think so. That okay?" I asked.

"Sure is; Jason's out until tomorrow. It'll be nice to just be me and you again," he said, but then Rosie cleared her throat a little to remind him she was here. "Oh, and Rose of course." He looked up and smiled at her, and I thought for just a second that maybe I caught a hint of something else. But I let that go, and instead went back to thinking about my own broken relationship.

———

I thought about calling Nolan the morning after I spent the night at my dad's house. I thought about it again that night, and then again every night for the next two weeks. But every time I got my phone out and started to punch in her contact, I stopped and realized she wasn't calling me either. Then I thought about that prick Gavin, and the words he spoke. "She's moved on." *Maybe, she has?*

My birthday came and went. I made an excuse with Pops when he had a big dinner planned, told him Nolan had some internship thing at a special needs camp. He bought it, which was amazing, because I was shit at lying. I couldn't seem to get myself to make it real. We weren't talking—hadn't talked for almost three weeks. But for some reason, I felt like if my dad still thought everything was fine, then maybe we'd find our way back, and no one would ever need to know.

I suppose part of it was pride, too. I felt betrayed, yes, but I also felt oddly ashamed. It felt like everyone knew my girlfriend had left me for some tattooed nobody, like they just stared at me, and pitied me. I knew I was just being crazy, but my head was doing a lot of crazy things lately.

Somehow, though, I managed to keep the football side of my head on straight. My numbers were ridiculous, and stories were starting to swirl on ESPN and in the papers about what I might do next season. Dylan and I talked frequently, even more so now that she was seeing my brother. She told me all of the press was common for a quarterback my age, in a draft year like this, so I just kept my mind on that—focused on the prize. Where going to the NFL was a future dream before, it was an out-clause now, a way to start over, and become a third version of Reed Johnson—not the shithead teenager or naïve college guy I had been, but my own man—free to date any woman I wanted, whenever I wanted, and however long I wanted. *Maybe* I'd try that for a while.

Chapter Sixteen

Nolan

IT WAS ALMOST THANKSGIVING BREAK, and I hadn't heard from Reed in more than a month. I checked my voicemail like a paranoid drug dealer almost hourly. But there was never anything. I was a shell of myself, as if each night that passed, and I didn't hear from Reed was one more night that a piece of me died. I wasn't eating, and I had skipped a lot of my classes, too. I was actually carrying two Cs, which I knew was going to screw me as far as my scholarships were concerned, but I couldn't seem to get myself to care.

Sienna had taken it upon herself to make sure I was up and out of bed every morning, knocking on my door before my first class, and waiting me out until she had proof that I was showered and dressed. But I often just undressed as soon as she left, or just bailed in the middle of my morning lecture, blending in with the crowd of slackers that sat in the back rows. I completely missed two midterms and blew off another writing assignment as well, which was what was hurting my grades mostly.

While Sienna was on academic duty, it seemed Sarah had

agreed to be on social duty, coming over every Thursday and Friday night, and forcing me to dress up and leave the comfort of my dark and depressing dorm room to go out dancing. I always went, but I usually just sat at some table and drank while she danced with guys who hit on her at the bar.

Gavin still stopped by to check on me regularly, too, always reminding me that I *had options*. But the more he reminded me, the more I was repulsed by him. I didn't even think he was genuine any more, especially since I'd seen him at the bar one night with Sarah and watched how he danced with a few of the other girls. I was just a challenge to him, and he had ruined me in his quest.

I had told Reed everything, and he was completely shutting me out. I think what hurt the most was the constant stream of questions running through my mind that I just didn't know the answers to: Was Reed mad I didn't tell him about being pregnant? Was he upset about losing the baby? Was he relieved that he didn't have to be a father now? Was he dating someone else...or *lots* of someones?

To make matters worse, when I was able to fall asleep, I usually awoke a few hours later with my heart racing from a nightmare. They weren't always about Reed, but the ones that were made me cry. I had started to relive the accident, it seemed. Only, in my dreams, Reed never made it out of the Jeep. Sometimes it would explode, other times I would see him in the driver's seat with the steering wheel cutting through him, his face white, and his lips gasping for breath.

I shared my dreams with Sienna, and she had suggested I make an appointment to talk with one of the school counselors, but the thought of opening up about everything I'd been through to a stranger just terrified me. And there were people out there who had *real* problems, I thought, problems far bigger than mine. No, the counselors were for those people who were dealing with things like a death in the family, a psychological break or meltdown of some sort. Not girls who got knocked up, and then cheated on their boyfriend.

I hadn't heard from Sean or Becky in a while, so when they called me the weekend before the break, I was a little surprised.

"Hey, Noles," Sean was chipper. It was strange, especially since I had convinced myself that he hated me by this point.

"Hey…uhm, how are you?" I asked with hesitation. I had been hiding out in my dark room for so long, I no longer knew how to interact with people, and my conversation felt stilted and awkward.

"We're good, we're good," Sean laughed a little. "We're leaving a bit early to come home for break—on the road right now. Becks is driving…hey, don't kill us, okay? Eyes on the road, you can talk to her later…Sorry, she misses you and wants to talk."

Hearing Becky's laugh and Sean's voice was comforting. "That's so exciting. I can't get out of here until Tuesday; have to finish some work at the writing center. But maybe when I get into town, we can meet up for burgers or something at MicNic's?" I asked, my mind imagining everyone piling into Reed's Jeep, just like we used to—instantly making me sad as I realized the low probability of that happening.

"That'd be awesome…" he was waiting to say something more, I could tell. "So…are you going to the game Thursday?"

Reed's game—against us: UofA and ASU squared off every Thanksgiving break. I wanted to be there desperately, especially knowing that it might be Reed's last. But I wasn't sure I was welcome.

"Uh…I don't know Sean," I started, but he cut me off.

"Noles, you have to go. You know he wants you there. Besides, Buck will insist on it," he was acting as if nothing was wrong.

"Sean, you don't know that. We…Reed and I…we haven't talked. Not in a long time. I think he's moved on," I admitted it out loud, and it made me choke a little.

"Yeah, I've heard you both say that same shit. I'm not buying it. Look, it's clear you two have some issues to work out…" he paused, thinking of how to say his next sentence. I appreciated that he was dancing around my miscarriage. "But look, you have to start somewhere. I think Thanksgiving will be good for you."

I soaked in his words. I couldn't see how me sitting in a football stadium—where Reed might not even know I was there—would be good for us, but I was a little comforted knowing that I could go without his even knowing, just hiding, blending in, and taking in his last rival college game for my own satisfaction.

"Noles? Are you there," Sean asked.

"Oh, yeah…was just thinking. So…okay, yeah. I guess I'll go to the game. Maybe I can go with you guys?" I asked, hoping.

"Of course! We'll see you at Buck's for Thanksgiving anyway," he said, matter-of-factly.

"Uhm…what?" now I was confused.

"Yeah, so…Buck invited your parents, and since you and Reed both like to pretend nothing's wrong, everyone thinks you're together and lovey dovey, so we're all having turkey at the Johnsons. Happy Thanksgiving! See you there!" Sean hung up as soon as he was done.

Fuck! How was I going to get through this? I started to fast forward to the day, envisioning Reed staring daggers through me, and then me breaking down in tears in front of everyone, him telling my parents how I kissed someone else…or worse, that I had been *pregnant*!

I let my head buzz with possibilities, ways I could get out of going, all the way to the writing center for a special Saturday session. My tutoring seemed to be the only thing that still held joy for me, so I went religiously—often spending more time working on the poems and essays that the kids were writing than my own projects and homework.

There was one girl, Kira, who reminded me so much of myself, and I found that I spent a lot of my time working with her. Kira had been struggling to come up with a topic for the winter showcase. She suffered from Tourette's syndrome, her muscle spasms almost constant, and her stutter a continuous wall in her way. She was one of my older students, almost 18. She was a beautiful girl, but so trapped because of her disability. And for some reason—probably more than any of my other students—I wanted to help her find words that would chip away at her cage. I knew they wouldn't completely break her free, but I thought if we could just come up with something together, that she could recite in front of a crowd…

118

despite the pauses and stutters that would undoubtedly work against her, she might find a reason to keep trying.

But I wasn't much help to Kira today. We read through sonnets together, and she practiced saying lines, sometimes actually getting one or two out before her body and brain betrayed her. And I was proud. But when we sat down to work on her topic, I wasn't my usual glass-half-full self, spouting off options and ideas. Instead, I just sat there and tapped my pencil on my pad of paper, staring at the lines until they bled together.

When our hour was done, I just shrugged at Kira, who still smiled and hugged me despite my lack of enthusiasm for the day.

"Sorry, I don't think I was very creative today," I said.

She smiled to let me know it was okay. Kira didn't speak when she could find a way around it, and that's what made me sad the most. Because I'd read some of the things she'd written...and her words were beautiful.

———

Sarah called while I was walking back to my dorm. It was the afternoon now, so she was on Nolan duty.

"Hey, I'm outside. You should be proud of me," I was monotone and defensive out of habit. She was starting to harass me lately about my hair, and general look, calling me a vampire and recluse, which I suppose was not so far from the truth.

"Wow, she breathes! To what does the world owe this honor of your presence in the outdoors and sunlight," she sniped.

I laughed a bit, short and breathy. "Very funny. I had a special tutoring session," I said.

"Ah, gotcha. Thank god you have those, otherwise we might not ever get you out of that damn room of yours," Sarah said. She had quit being nice a few days ago. "Well, shower up when you get home. We're going out shopping today. Sienna's here, and we're making it a girls' day..." She had that tone, the superior one.

"Sar...I'm not feeling it. Can't we just check out Netflix and crash on the sofa or something?" I was going to lose my battle, I knew.

"Yeah, uh...no. We're going shopping. And then we're going to come back to my place, pretty your ass up, and go out to this new sushi place..." I tried to interject, but she just barreled right through my words. "Ah, ah...stop talking. And then...we are going to a club. And you are going to dance—with other guys, who are not Reed. Or Gavin. Or anything like either of them. And we are going to drink shots, off of guys. Well, Sienna says she's not, but we'll see... owwww! Don't hit me! Sorry, Sienna just punched my arm. Anyhow, get your ass over here before we have to come get you. You've got 15 minutes."

Deflated, I slumped my shoulders and walked the rest of the way to my dorm room. I didn't bother to change into anything spectacular after I showered, because I knew Sarah would just make me change again anyhow, so I pulled on my sweatpants and giant long-sleeved T-shirt that had somehow become my uniform lately and threw some make up and hair stuff in a bag. I was locking up and forcing myself to keep moving forward when I ran into Gavin at the stairs. He looked a little surprised to see me out during the day.

"Wow, haven't seen you out in a while," he was sort of mocking me now.

"Thanks for the reminder," I wasn't in the mood for him.

"Sorry...that was mean. I'm...just sorry," he looked down at his feet. "So, you've missed a few psych classes. We had a quiz this week."

I just looked at him, like he was transparent. I was on my way to failing. I felt so far behind that I just couldn't see how I'd ever be able to catch up. I'd gotten an email from two of my professors this week alerting me that I was in grade trouble. They encouraged me to see them. But I knew I wouldn't. I was pretty sure I could pull out at least a C, but I'd probably have to take both of the classes again. And even then, I was going to be on scholarship probation. My parents were going to be livid.

"Nolan, I can help you catch up. I can share my notes with you on what you've missed. We got an A on the testing project. You aren't *that* far behind," he leaned into me a little, trying to shock me into a response. Instead, I just recoiled a bit from his touch. This boy, who seemed so smart and handsome a month ago, just felt like the enemy to me now. I hated him.

"Thanks, but I'll be okay," I said, moving by him to continue down the stairs. Before I could get far, though, he had his hand on my shoulder and was stopping me.

"Noles, please don't go. I feel…I feel like you're mad at me. I promise, I heard what you said. I get it. I know that we're friends. I can't lie and say I won't stop wanting more. But I'll try to quit asking for it. Just don't shut me out, okay?" he was pleading with me in his eyes. And I didn't like that he'd called me Noles. That wasn't his name to say. Rather than make a scene, or draw this conversation out any longer, though, I just smiled instead.

"I'm not mad at you. I just have a lot of things I'm working through. I appreciate the space," I said, looking him square in the eyes to hope he truly did understand. But I still saw the hope in his face. No matter what, I wouldn't be running to him.

I thought I was going to be able to escape finally when I made one tiny tactical error. Gavin was about to turn and climb up the rest of the stairs, when he stopped and asked if I was heading out for the evening or spending the night with the girls. I shared too much in return.

"Sarah's dragging me out to the bar, some club with some hot new DJ. I think it's called 22?" The words rolled out of my mouth. When Gavin perked up with this new knowledge, I instantly regretted sharing it. I turned to leave him there, but not before he could say goodbye, for now.

"That sounds awesome. Maybe I'll see you there," he said, and thankfully, my face turned away from him, he couldn't see the pained look in my eyes, willing him to stay home.

————

As I expected, Sarah started dismantling my outfit, hair and face the moment I walked through her door. I think to cheer me up a little,

Sienna had brought me some of her handmade earrings, which Sarah quickly put through my ears and built a look and outfit around. They were colorful earth-toned beads and feathers, beautiful and normally a gift I would treasure. But they seemed too happy next to my face as I stared at them in the mirror. Sienna looked concerned when I caught her reflection, so I reached for her hand and squeezed it a bit to reassure her that I liked them, not wanting my friend to think I didn't appreciate her thought, because I did.

Shopping was tolerable, or at least as tolerable as it ever was for me. I gave complete control to Sarah. It was easier that way, and afforded me the opportunity to slip away to the empty place in my mind. She'd picked out a sheer black-and-white top and tight black pants for me along with a new pair of knee-high boots. The look was actually one I liked, a little sexy, sure, but sturdy and moveable.

Lunch was quiet, or at least, I was quiet during lunch. I listened to Sarah talk about the guy she met at the club last weekend, and how they had been texting, or rather *sexting* one another. She was excited to see him tonight, which I had discovered was the real reason we were going to the club. I wanted to bail, *in the worst way*, but Sienna was going, and Micah was out of town at his grandparents, so I couldn't leave her to wingman Sarah alone.

We got to the club a little early, which was good, because I was going to have to take in quite a few shots if Sarah wanted to get me on the dance floor tonight. Plus, I was constantly scanning the crowd, praying I wouldn't find Gavin. I hadn't been drunk since the night of the *incident*, and was a little wary about getting myself into more trouble. But the thought of numbing myself a bit tonight sounded appealing, too. I was tired of feeling sick—sick about losing a baby, sick about losing Reed and sick about losing my scholarships. And when the vibrating music hit my chest as we entered the club, I thought the faster I could wipe my memories clean, the better.

Sarah ordered shots for each of us as soon as we got to the bar. Sienna was more of a lightweight than I was, so she actually nursed hers a bit while Sarah and I tossed two of them back each, squeezing our eyes shut, and shaking our heads from the sharp bitterness that burned down our throats. I was feeling the effects almost instantly, which is what made me willing to head out to the dance floor with the girls.

Apparently, some big local DJ was at the club tonight, which made things a little more crowded than normal. To be honest, I liked the anonymity the crowds were giving me. We were packed in, body to body, and there was no room for strangers to notice me on the dance floor. I was starting to get comfortable, thinking there was no way Gavin would show up and hit on me, when I spotted his head several bodies away from me, swaying in the crowd. He had a few friends with him, some of them girls, and appeared to be distracted, so I moved to the opposite side of the floor and surrounded myself with more strangers.

I felt safe here. There was no way I would be tempted to let down my guard with someone else. It was just me—smashed between sweaty arms, legs, backs and torsos—all to the rhythm of the music. I didn't even need to know how to dance well, just push my arms in the air and move. Sienna seemed to like the lack of pressure, too, because she actually finished both of her shots and was now jumping to the music in the center of the floor with me. Somehow, Sarah managed to squeeze in with us, and gave me another shot, which I consumed quickly. Sienna refused hers, so I took that one, too, and let my eyes lose focus on the flashing colorful lights all around us.

We had been on the floor for more than an hour, and I had taken every shot Sarah pushed my way. That was her way of medicating, and tonight, I let her play doctor. My body was wet with perspiration, my thin shirt sticking to my chest and back, and my feet aching from the tall arch of my new boots, but I didn't care. I kept dancing, moving and staring at the lights. Sarah had found the guy she'd hooked up with last week and was in her own world, and Sienna had made her way back to the tables, wanting to slow things down. But I powered on.

As the night wore on, the music got sexier, more suggestive. I had completely left myself by this point, my body powered by the alcohol far more than by my brain. I felt strange hands brush the damp hair from my neck, and then watched them reach for me and run over my back, arms and breasts. And I just put my hands in the air and let them. I felt a freedom that I hadn't known ever and was comforted by the anonymous sea of drunken men and women. I was in the mix, ignoring life and my problems, and just letting the vodka, or whatever Sarah had fed me, power my limbs.

I don't know how long I swayed like this, dancing with my stranger, but my safe haven was rocked when I turned into the body that the arms belonged to, and found my face square into Gavin's chest. I was drunk, more so than I was the night I'd kissed him, but somehow my wits were with me. I pushed from him and threw his arms from my sides.

"Don't do that!" I said in an angry slur. I giggled a little at how it came out, giving Gavin the wrong impression, because he moved back toward me and wrapped me up again in his arms, moving his lips to my neck where he started to taste me. His touch felt disgusting, and I pushed him away again.

"I said don't do that!" I was more forceful now, and Gavin seemed to get it. His brow furrowed as he looked down, and then back up into my eyes, confused and upset. Leaning in, so I could hear him, he got close to my ear, his lips touching it a little, making me nervous.

"I don't get you. One minute you're kissing me, and don't deny it. You kissed me. Just as much as I kissed you," he said, pointing a finger at me. "The next, you're telling me you aren't attracted to me, don't see me as anything other then a friend. Then you let me dance with you...*like this!* for an hour before you flip out on me again. What's with you? Are you really *NOT* into me? Because I've gotta tell you, Nolan, you're body is giving me an entirely different story!"

My words were definitely unfiltered, the alcohol working its black magic as I pushed a hand heavily into Gavin's chest, biting my lip a little, and moving close to him, my teeth gritting. "I had a miscarriage, you asshole! And Reed hates me for it! And the whole thing fucking ruined me—and you just made it worse! So just leave. Me. The. Fuck. Alone!" I stormed away from him and headed to the other side of the club, not even looking back to check his reaction.

I holed up in the women's bathroom for more than a few minutes after my scene with Gavin, my emotions bouncing between tears and anger. I finally gathered myself enough to touch up my makeup and storm back onto the dance floor where I continued on my journey to forget everything…again.

I vaguely remembered Sarah telling me to go home with Sienna. And I even less recalled arguing with Sienna and refusing to leave until she left me there alone. However it happened, I found myself wandering out the back door after midnight, digging through my purse for my phone, and completely unsure of where I lived.

Panic started to hit a little, and every face that passed me was unfamiliar. I started calling out for Sienna, but my words were slurred. I giggled a little at how I sounded. But inevitably, I would start to panic and begin the cycle again. After bumping into a few strangers, and stumbling to my knees more than once, I sat with my legs in the gutter of the main road, and zipped my boots off, setting them down next to me. I pulled my phone from my tiny purse with a force that sent my credit card and driver's license flying into the road. Instantly, I was irrationally terrified that someone would find my license and realize I wasn't yet 21, so I crawled into the roadway on my knees and grabbed my cards. Cars honked and swerved around me, and I remember the lines left behind as the headlights passed my face.

I think a few people asked if they could help me, but I always smiled, or at least I thought I was smiling, and told them I was fine. Fine. I was so fucking far from fine. I was turning into a train wreck, and I was beyond anyone's reach. So I did what I always did when I was in trouble, what I'd done every other time I needed help over the last two years. I called Reed.

Chapter Seventeen

Reed

"DUDE, you just shot me, you asshole!" Trig yelled over the sound of gunfire blasting from our television. A bunch of the guys had come over to our place, and we'd been playing video games for a couple of hours now. I was starting to get tired of it, so I just started shooting all of my teammates to try to end the game faster.

It was nice to have the distraction, but I was tired. When I found out that Pops had invited Nolan and her parents over for Thanksgiving, I flipped my lid. I knew it was my fault for not telling him about the problems Nolan and I were having, but I didn't think I'd be forced to out our *up-in-flames* relationship at the dinner table in front of our family and friends, while we all said grace and thanks for everything wonderful in our lives.

I talked it over with Sean and had come up with a plan that he said he was pretty sure Nolan would actually go along with. I just had to talk to her about it. And that's where the big hang up was… we weren't really *talking*. And I wasn't sure I could look at her anymore. The more time passed, the more I thought about that smug asshole Gavin and the way he looked when I saw him. I couldn't believe Nolan would be into a guy like that, but I was starting to think that she had changed into an entirely different person, someone I didn't really know at all.

I heard my phone buzzing in my pocket, but just let it go to voicemail, and kept shooting random targets on the screen. When it buzzed a second time about two minutes later, I got annoyed. I ignored it then, too, but the third round of buzzing made me panic, and immediately think that something was wrong with my dad. I paused my game player and tossed my controller to one of the other guys. Pulling my phone from my pocket, I walked out to the hall so I could hear. When I saw the face and name staring back at me on the screen, my heart dropped to the pit of my stomach. Why was Nolan calling me? Why now, after all this time? At 1 a.m.? On a Saturday?

I almost missed the third call when something forced me to answer.

"Noles?" I was confused. I could hear traffic in the background, and people laughing. It sounded almost as if she had dialed me accidentally, a misfire from her purse. And the hurt I felt at that thought surprised me a little. I was about to hang up when I caught the unmistakable sound of her breathing.

"Reed?" she sounded upset, like she'd been crying. "Reed? I can't hear you. Are you there?"

"Noles, I'm here. I hear you. What's wrong?" I said, pulling keys from my pocket and flying down my hallway out of instinct. Then she started giggling. It was an off sounding laugh, though. Like she was...*drunk?* I put my hand on my forehead and pinched the bridge of my nose. Jesus, this was not happening.

"Nolan, are you drunk?" I waited while she finished a giggling fit, and then it turned into panicked breaths, and near crying again. Nolan, I'm hanging up."

That did something to her, because she started talking more clearly now. "No! Wait. No, no, no, no..." she was fighting to make sense. It was irritating me, and scaring me at the same time. I instantly regretted the times I'd put her through having to deal with me like this. "Reed? Don't go. I...I need help."

That was it; I was out the door now. I hated how weak I was, and half of my brain admonished the other half for giving into her, letting her run my actions still after breaking me in half. But I wasn't over her. I wasn't even remotely close to the start of getting over her. And she needed help, so I'd come.

"What's wrong, where are you?" I said forcefully, trying to get her to concentrate. She giggled a little again, and then stopped.

"I'm...at a bar," she burst into laughter again. I leaned my forehead on my steering wheel and banged it a little. This was not going well. And if I was going to drive 100 miles to come get her, I was going to need a whole lot more to go on.

"Yeah, I get that. But *what* bar?" I said, sarcasm winning out.

"I...I don't know, Reed. I'm scared. I don't know where I am," she was starting to cry harder now. *Fuck!* I was already pulling onto the main road for the highway.

"Nolan, you need to find out where you are. Can you tell me what you see?" I asked, grasping for anything.

"I see...people," she was giggling again.

Realizing I wasn't going to get anywhere this way, I tried to figure out where her friends were. "Where's Sarah? Nolan, I need to talk to Sarah. Is she with you?" I was crossing my fingers like hell that Sarah would be on the phone soon.

"Sarah left," she was giggling again.

"Okay, how about Sienna?" I asked, knowing it was less likely Sienna was with her. When I thought about who she could be out with if it wasn't her girlfriends, I wanted to scream.

"She's mad at me," she started giggling, but less than before. "I mean...she left. I didn't want to go home."

I knew there was no way Sienna would leave her somewhere alone, not when she was like this. "Okay, Noles. I need you to do something for me, okay?" It was like reasoning with a 4-year-old.

"Okay," she was almost listening.

"I'm going to call someone, find out where you are, but I need to call you back. Hold your phone in front of you, and I want you to watch it for when I call, okay?" I was trying to keep things simple.

"Okay, answer the phone. Got it," she was crying a little again. She was a mess.

I hung up with Nolan and called Sienna. I was counting each ring, hoping like hell it wouldn't go right to voicemail. When I heard her pick up, and heard the crowds and music in the background I felt relieved. I knew she wasn't far.

"Reed?" she was yelling a little into the phone. "Hang on, I can't hear shit in here. I'm going to the ladies' room."

I couldn't tell where they were, but I knew it was crowded, the techno music thumping in the background, and the constant stream of voices filling in the gaps.

"Okay, that's better. I can hear you. What's up?" she said, not even a hint of panic to her voice.

"Sienna, where's Nolan?" I asked urgently, just wanting an answer at this point.

"She's out on the dance floor somewhere. I don't know. I keep trying to make her come home, but she won't...why?" she clearly had no idea what had happened.

"She just called me," I sighed, pulling off at the next exit and pulling into a nearby gas station so I could talk.

"Wha?...Wait, where is she, Reed?" Sienna asked, now a little worried herself.

"I'm not sure. She just called me. She's all freaked out, said you two had a fight, and you left her at some club," I just killed the engine and tossed my hat on the dashboard, rubbing my face out of frustration. "What the hell, Sienna? She's fucking wasted. I can hardly understand her."

"Yeah, I know. She did shots—a lot of them. I've been trying to get her to go home for the last hour," Sienna said.

"Well, you have to find her. I think she might just be outside, somewhere close," I said, hearing the sounds of the music kick in again. Sienna was on the move.

"Hang on, I'm going out front. I'll find her Reed," she was just as frustrated as I was. When the music died off again in the background, I knew she was outside. I heard a few voices and the sounds of cars roaring by on the road. "Wait...I see her. She's sitting in the gutter...with her freakin' shoes off, ohhhhhh."

I heard Nolan's voice in the background, and laid my head on the steering wheel, exhausted by the whole thing. "What happened?" I asked, wanting answers but knowing Sienna really didn't have the time to give them to me. "Where's Gavin?" I asked, my mouth repulsing at saying his name.

"Gavin?! Why the hell would Gavin be here?" Sienna said, her voice a little muffled from laying the phone on her shoulder. "I got you. Come on girl...really, this time. It's time to go home, okay?"

I heard Nolan, "Mmmmm." She sounded sleepy. I knew this stage of a hard night out. She was near passed out. I couldn't even imagine what she looked like.

"Reed? Look, I gotta go. Thanks for calling me. I'm sorry you had to," she was a little short with me before she just hung up.

"What the fuck?" For the next 20 minutes, I sat there just thinking about what had just happened. I hadn't heard her voice in weeks, not that she sounded like herself at all tonight. But when I asked about Gavin, Sienna sounded like I was crazy. Maybe she didn't know that they had hooked up? Clearly they weren't dating or anything. My head was spinning, not sure what was right anymore, and I was just left missing everything that I'd finally started to come to terms with losing.

Chapter Eighteen

Nolan

I WOKE up on Sienna's sofa, my face crusty with dried saliva, and God knows what else. My throat was dry as hell, and I wanted to gulp glass after glass of water, except when I sat up my entire world shifted, forcing me back flat on my face into the cushions. I was still wearing my clothes from last night, and my boots were stuffed in the sofa cracks, almost as if I'd clung to them overnight like they were a teddy bear. I was pretty sure I never wanted to feel like this again.

The kitchen light flickered on, and I heard the faint sounds of coffee brewing and pans sliding from a cabinet. I pushed myself up on the sofa and cracked one eye barely open to see Sienna leaning on her hands across the counter staring at me. Not really ready to deal with the look on her face, I just grumbled and fell back into the couch.

"Well, good morning, sunshine," she said bitterly. "You ready to hear about the fantastic night you made me go through? Or do you want to throw up and whine about your splitting headache for a while?"

She was full-on banging pans on the stove now, flinging the

fridge door shut with extra muscle, and cracking eggs to fry so loudly you would think she was throwing water balloons onto the stove.

"Uuuuuuuuhhhhhg. Sienna, do you have to do *all* of that now?" I spoke, my face still buried into the pillow.

"Yes, Nolan. I do. It's 11:30 in the morning. I'm hungry, and I'm sick of watching you twitch and wail, and flop around my living room couch. I want to watch TV, so sit your ass up," she was bullying me. It was a side of her I'd never seen, and I both admired and hated it.

She was flipping cushions up to move me now, so I slid to the end of the couch to curl up in a ball, and keep my face buried in the covers and my hands. "Stopppp, I get it. I'm moving," I said, my voice defensive, like I had some right to be. I had no idea what events led up to me being here, but I knew that there were at least 7 or 8 ounces of vodka involved. My stomach felt like a tar pit, bubbling and full. I left my arm wrapped around my chin, my nose covered and protected from any smells. I hoped this would keep me from vomiting.

"Noles, I swear to God, if you throw up on any of my shit, our friendship is over," she said, flipping through the channels and not even looking at me.

"Geeeeeeze, what the hell crawled up your ass?" I rolled my eyes, or at least the one that was open.

At that, Sienna shut the TV off again and got up off the couch to return to the kitchen. I had pissed her off, and I knew I was acting like a major bitch, but I was so miserable that I couldn't seem to turn it off. "I'm sorry…" I half-heartedly grunted from my sofa corner.

She just scoffed. I listened to her bang around the kitchen some more, before I drifted back into a light sleep. I slipped in and out of it over the next two hours. When I heard the unmistakable sound of Sarah's voice added into the mix, I finally rose from the dead, my body a little more prepared to sit upright…and possibly take in some liquids.

"Jesus, Noles. You look like shit," Sarah said, tossing a clean T-shirt at me from the chair on the other side of the room. On instinct, I pulled my night-before top off and put on the one she'd thrown to me. When I saw the small traces of vomit on my new blouse, I realized how bad the situation probably had been.

I finally got up from the couch and slid into the kitchen to pour myself a giant cup of coffee and sift through Sienna's cabinets for aspirin. "You won't find it in there. Hang on, I'll get the bottle from my bathroom," Sienna said from behind me. I hadn't seen her and her words startled me a little. She came back seconds later with two pills, and I took them quickly, thinking the faster they were in my system, the faster the nail pushing into my skull would go away.

"Thanks," I said, sheepishly. I was embarrassed now, both because I remembered how I behaved to Sienna just hours ago, and because I couldn't remember much before that. "So…how bad?"

Sienna sat there on a stool, staring at me for a few seconds before she spoke. "Epic," she said.

Sarah chortled a little, causing Sienna to toss a wad of wet paper towels at her. "Fuck! What was that for?" Sarah said.

"That was for leaving me last night…in charge of…*this!*" Sienna said, waving her hand up and down the length of my body.

My mind raced, "Oh god, what had I done to make her this mad?"

"I'm sorry," I started right away, my instinct to repair things kicking in. I leaned my face into my hands and rubbed my eyes before settling back on Sienna. "What…did I do?"

She and Sarah just looked at one another for a little while, almost like they had some shared secret that they were terrified to tell me. The longer it took them to give me words, the more I worried and let my imagination fill in the blanks. Had I gone to Gavin's? Did I kiss him again? Did I kiss someone else?

"You called Reed," Sienna said, taking a slow drink from her coffee, her eyes watching me for my reaction, which was devastated. My stomach felt as if I'd just dropped from the highest point of a roller coaster, and suddenly, I knew I was going to be sick. I sprinted to Sienna's bathroom, and dry-heaved for about 10 minutes, my stomach clearly empty from whatever I had turned over the night before. My equilibrium finally giving me a break from the spinning apartment walls, I came back into the kitchen with Sarah and Sienna.

"What did I say," I whispered, staring at the floor, because I couldn't bear to see any more disapproval on Sienna's face.

"You weren't very coherent," she started. "You had slipped away from me, for just a few seconds. It was the end of the night, and you were confused. You thought we were fighting, because I wanted to go home and you wouldn't leave the damn bar."

She was getting worked up again, so I just put a hand on her arm and squeezed, forcing her to look at me. I gave her a crooked smile, one full of genuine regret. "I'm soooooo sorry," I said.

Finally sighing, she put her hand on mine and squeezed it back. "I know you are," she said, blowing out the air in her lungs a bit. "You were just…a lot to handle. That's all."

I smiled a little bigger now, but also showed my embarrassment. "Was Reed…angry?" I asked, still wanting to know what I'd done.

Sienna looked at Sarah again, exchanging glances just as they'd done before. "What? Oh my God, what did I say?" I was getting slightly more animated now.

"No, no," Sienna stopped me. "It's not what you said. It's what Reed said…and did, I guess?" Sienna looked at Sarah again for confirmation to keep going.

"What do you mean," I was desperate now.

"Well, first of all, when you called and sounded in distress, he dropped everything. He was literally miles into his trip down the highway by the time he got me on the phone. Noles, he was so worried about you," she said. I smiled faintly at this information, and my insides lit up with a hope I hadn't felt in weeks.

"He…came for me?" I asked, wondering suddenly if I'd seen Reed in my condition, too.

"No, when I found you—out front and in the gutter, by the way —he pulled over and stayed on the phone with me until he knew I had you handled," her words suddenly disappointing me.

I was about to leave it at that when I saw my two best friends exchange that look one more time. "Come on guys. What is it? I can take it. I mean, look. I can't get any lower than this."

Sienna came over to sit closer to me, almost like she was prepared to catch me if I fainted. It was making me nervous. "He seemed to think you were with Gavin," she said, her words completely unexpected.

I clenched my jaw and pulled my knees up into my body a little, holding in the anger. Gavin! He was going to ruin my life! I was about to unleash a tirade about the nightmare Gavin had been, when Sienna threw me off my road map.

"Don't worry. I didn't tell him he was at the club. I didn't think you'd want Reed to know. But, Noles? Is there something happening between you two?" she asked.

"Wha...me...and Gavin?" I asked, my forehead crinkle deep with confusion now.

"Yeah...I mean, he was awfully touchy feely last night," she said, and immediately my mind went to work taking inventory on everything that I did last night. I remembered dancing, and I remember letting people touch me in a way that this morning made me shudder and feel ashamed. But I didn't remember Gavin.

"Oooooooh, you totally don't remember at all, do you?" Sienna said, sliding over closer to me now, almost feeling bad. Her hard shell was breaking a bit.

I just rubbed my eyes with my hands, searching for more memories in my brain, but they weren't there. Sienna filled me in on what she saw. She said I also shoved him at one point, which I thought was good. Regardless, though, I knew I was going to have to have another conversation with him—and this one might be the most uncomfortable yet.

———

I managed to recuperate from my binge enough to actually attend a few classes Monday and Tuesday. I even made it to the writing center Wednesday morning to work with Kira. She had come up with an idea to turn her poem or essay into a song. She said she could usually get through more of her words if she put them to music, which fascinated me. I encouraged her to try it, and she agreed to let me write about it for one of my assignments.

I packed up most of my things for the long weekend after our session and made my way to my parents; the drive on my own through the desert giving me too much time to think. Sarah, Calley and Sienna had already headed to Coolidge, so I texted them when I was leaving so we could meet up at MicNic's for some much-needed catching up with Becky. And after an hour in the car, with nothing but my worries and guilt to keep me company, I was desperate for my girls.

Chapter Nineteen

Reed

TRIG and I pulled into the driveway of my pop's house late Wednesday night. Sean had texted me that the girls had gone out to MicNic Burger's for the night so he was going to come over to hang out for a bit. Our rivalry game against ASU was Saturday, so Trig and I had to head back to Tucson late Friday morning. I was glad he agreed to come home with me. I knew it was childish, but somehow it felt better having numbers on my side when it came to Nolan.

Sean was already at the house when we barreled through the front door, dragging our bags of clothes and loads of laundry. Rosie was there to greet us, and just took the bags out of my hands without me even asking. Bless that woman; she really knows how to spoil me.

Sean and Trig had met a few times before, so they fell into a comfortable conversation right away in the family room. I grabbed a few beers from the fridge and handed them each one before I headed upstairs to check in with pops. He was propped up in his bed with a breakfast tray on his lap and the remote in his hand when I walked in.

"Heyyyyyy, there he is," he said, muting ESPN and clearing a little space on the side of the bed so I could sit by him. I gave him a half hug, and then propped my feet up on the bed and stretched out, putting my hands behind my neck.

"Hey, Pops. How's the leg?" I said, sitting up and knocking a little on his cast.

"This cast crap is for the birds, Reed. It's so damned itchy," he said, whining as he tried to move his leg around to find a comfortable position. There clearly wasn't one, because he just sighed heavily and then leaned back into his pillows, defeated. I chuckled a bit at my stubborn independent cuss of a father.

I lay there next to him for a few minutes, just staring up at his ceiling. I kept trying to start my conversation, but I could never seem to frame the right words in my mind, so I just stopped and waited, hoping he would pick up on my anxiety and fill in the blanks for me.

"Well, shit or get off the pot, would ya?" he finally kicked in. *Subtle*, Buck Johnson was not.

Sighing, I sat up again, pulled Grandma's ring box from my pocket, and slid it on his lap tray, just shrugging a little at it, and curling the corner of my mouth up a little pathetically. Dad just stared at it for a few seconds, trying to figure out what it meant. Finally, he nodded a little and closed his eyes, shaking his head some. He reached up to grab the ring box, and flipped it open to look at it silently before closing it once again. Staring at the closed antique box for a few moments more, he finally looked up to make eye contact with me, and then held it out for me to take back.

"Pops, it's not going to happen," I said, my stomach sick with this reality. "Just…just give it to Jason or something, okay?"

I stood up and turned my back to him, not wanting him to see the pain in my eyes. Not wanting to show my weakness. But I was so weak. Nolan could bring me to my knees. In fact, she had. I snapped back when I heard my dad's familiar raspy laugh kick in. I turned to see him turning the box over and over in his hand, the corner of his mouth raised in a smirk.

"Reed, life is hard. I know you know this…or think you know

this…but let me remind you. Life. Is. Hard. It's ugly sometimes, and it throws shit at you, just like a 300-pound lineman charging you full tilt just looking to flatten your ass," he said, his eyes still focused on the small box in his hand.

"And sometimes," he looked up at me now, right in the eyes. "Sometimes, that lineman knocks the shit out of you. And it hurts. It hurts like fucking hell, the breath punched from your lungs, and the will to stand gone from your muscles. But you don't just sit there, roll your ass off the field and lick your wounds, right?"

I was staring at the box now, too, those damn visions of forever with Nolan flipping through my mind like an old-fashioned picture show. I saw our wedding, our kids…our life. God, I wanted it. But between those flashes of us in my head, I also saw her kissing Gavin, the look on his face when he left her room that night, the fucking swagger in his step, the kind that said he knew her intimately. Those thoughts made me flinch and look back down at my feet. Chewing my lip, I finally looked back up at Pops, and shook my head. "Dad, I will never love anyone like I love Nolan, and you know it. But…*fuck*. Dad, I can't talk about it, but it's just not going to happen. And that ring is killing me," I said, choking a little on my words and forcing down my emotions.

My dad just grabbed my hand and put the box back in it, wrapping my fingers around it tightly, and then patting them shut with his other hand. I reached up with my other hand and dashed away the tiny tear that was threating to escape, sniffling a little to get a hold of myself. I was losing it. I looked Pops in the eyes, pleading with him to understand, to let me off the hook, but he just held on tighter.

"Life is hard, Reed. But we get up," he said, sliding from the bed now to reach for his crutches and force himself to a stand. "I could give this ring to Jason, yeah, sure. But you and I both know that Jason—God love him—will never pick a girl worthy of wearing your grandmother's ring…and you and I both know there's only one girl who deserves it."

My dad carried himself on his crutches out the door, and down the hall, leaving me there alone in his room to stare at this damn box again. I wished he'd never given it to me. But he was right; there was no way I could give it back. It was mine to work out, or live with, and carry.

———

Jason and Dylan both pulled up to the house together early Thursday morning. Dylan looked like she was dressed for a charity gala, always so image conscious. Jason, on the other hand, looked like he had just finished a morning round at the golf club, his pompous sunglasses tucked neatly in the collar of his shirt as he walked into the kitchen.

"Morning, jerk-off," he said, tossing a wadded up receipt at me.

"I know what I'm *not* thankful for," I said, tossing it back at his face. He rounded the breakfast bar and put his arm around me for a squeeze.

"Oh, come on little brother. You know you love me," he said, kissing the top of my head with a Donald-Duck-ish sucking sound. I just elbowed him off me and wiped my forehead.

I was helping Rosie peel potatoes, the repetitive task soothing. I hadn't slept since my talk with my dad the night before, but instead, tossed and turned while I spun my grandmother's ring around in my fingers. I was fucking exhausted, which I thought would come in handy tonight and help me get a really good night's sleep before heading back down to Tucson for the game. Trig was still asleep in the spare bedroom upstairs, and I was so damned jealous of his happy-ass self.

Dylan walked over to the sink and rolled up the sleeves of her sparkling turtleneck to wash her hands. She smiled at me a bit, and I smiled back. I really didn't have a beef with Dylan. Yeah, she wasn't the nicest to Nolan in the past, but I think it was really more of her personality flaw rather than any actual malice or dislike for Nolan. And she was good at her job. She'd learned a lot from her father, and she was making some moves for me that I knew would set me up for life.

When she grabbed a potato and started to peel along side me, I chuckled a little. "What?" she said, stopping and putting her hand on her hip.

"Nothing," I said, shaking my head and continuing to laugh a little to my self. She was still staring at me, though. "It's just...you *sooooo* don't look like the kind of girl who would know how to peel a potato."

She just smirked at that and went back to work on her potato, peeling the entire thing in one cut, leaving a swirl of perfect curls on the counter before me. She turned around then and pulled a sharper, larger knife from the butcher block behind her. Turning the blade over in her hands a little to look at it, she finally rested it at the edge of the potato before lowering her gaze and then going to work, dicing it into the tiniest, perfect squares in a matter of seconds. The entire scene left me shocked—eyes wide, and my hands frozen in the suddenly inferior pile of potato peels in front of me.

"Ooooookay, so maybe you *do* look like the kind of girl who can peel a potato," I said, my smile wide.

Dylan blew the blade like it was a smoking gun, and then giggled a little herself, moving to the sink to rinse it off. We were just beginning to have a good time when Jason walked up and slid into one of the stools to put an end to it.

"What the fuck do you find so funny?" he said, rolling his eyes at me. I just stared at him, willing myself not to engage. Realizing how hard I was trying, Dylan actually came to the rescue, explaining her parlor trick to me.

"I went to culinary school for a while," she shrugged at me. I was surprised...and impressed. "I didn't really want to be a chef, but I just wanted to learn something completely different from the biz, ya know?"

Suddenly feeling possessive or something, Jason stood from his seat, and came over to stand behind her, and kiss her neck a little, popping a piece of raw potato in his mouth. "That's right, bro. My girl can cook, *and* she's fucking wild in bed," he winked as she elbowed him a little, embarrassed, but also clearly affected by his compliment.

No, I didn't mind Dylan. But Dylan *and* Jason? That was a little much to take.

———

I helped Rosie prep in the kitchen most of the day, avoiding Jason, who just sat on the sofa and watched football with Trig and my pops. Dylan had some business to finish and spent most of her day on a computer at the dining table until she moved to my dad's office, when Rosie started to dress the table for dinner.

Sean and Becky came over first, followed by Sarah, Calley and Sienna. Each time a car pulled down the driveway, I ran to the window like a damned golden retriever, waiting for his master to come home. And I was both relieved and sad each time it wasn't Nolan's car pulling in. It was only 5 p.m. and Sean had told Nolan to show up around 5:30, so I took the opportunity to rush upstairs and shower. I was suddenly nervous, like I was back in high school and gathering up the courage to kiss her for the first time—or ask her to dance.

I hadn't seen her face in weeks, months almost. I had heard her voice, yes, but it was weighted with alcohol when she called, and it didn't sound right. I noticed the small box on the center of my bed while I was getting dressed, and I grabbed it quickly, stuffing it in the drawer of my night table. I wanted to look good for Nolan, but I also wanted to look comfortable. I must have changed shirts a dozen times, trying to find the one that sent the perfect message; except I had no fucking clue what message I was trying to send. I was acting a lot like a girl. "This is ridiculous," I thought, finally settling on the long-sleeved black thermal and my dark jeans.

I was sliding down the stairs when I heard the familiar timber of her voice talking to Pops. Her words were clear, on the verge of happy. It was so opposite from the last time I'd heard her. I stopped a few steps from the corner just to listen.

"Nolan, my dear, you look lovely," Rosie said. I could see her reaching to hug Nolan, but still couldn't see her face. "OH! Honey, you didn't need to bring anything."

"I know…I…uhm. I just wanted to. I made it myself. It took me all day, I hope it's good," she sounded so damned unsure of herself all of a sudden. "It's a peach cobbler. I hope it's okay. I've never made one before."

"I'm sure it's delicious," Rosie said. "Here, let's put it in the fridge."

"No, it's okay. I know where it is, I'll take it," Nolan said, and then passed through the group gathered by the front door to head to my kitchen. I was frozen to the steps as I watched her walk away from me, completely unaware that I was watching her. Her brown hair had gotten longer. She'd curled it into waves, and wore a red sweater with tight black pants, and knee-high boots. She looked like a girl from some romantic movie—some main character that the boy sees once, and then spends the entire rest of the movie chasing, just so he could learn her name. "I was that lame-ass boy," I thought.

When I realized she was heading to the kitchen alone, I squeezed my eyes shut for a second, pushing my palms into them, a little confused at my thoughts. I had been so angry at her. But seeing her again? Well, that had me suddenly a lot less angry. I took a deep breath, and followed her into the kitchen. She was balancing the dessert in one palm and trying to open the refrigerator door with her other hand, not quite able to get it open.

"Need a hand?" I said, startling her. She jumped a bit, and the edge of the tray hit the corner of the refrigerator, knocking it sideways, and sending it in a slow-motion flip to the floor. She just stared at the pile of peaches and crust that spread the floor beneath her, her hand over her mouth like she'd witnessed some horrible accident. And then without warning, she started to cry, her hand hiding her face as she bent down to feel for pieces of her broken cobbler to clean it up.

My instincts kicked in, and I started to help. "Noles, damn. I'm so sorry. I got it, it's okay. It's fine. We have plenty of food," I said, trying to clean it up before she had to look at it any longer. She just looked up into my eyes then, hers so sad and puffy. She started to cry harder then, and I couldn't take it. I slid, kneeling, closer to her and just reached for her, pulling her into a hug in my lap.

"Hey…" I whispered. "It's okay. I got you. It's okay…shhhhh-hh." I just held her while her body quivered in my arms. I stroked her hair, and each time I tucked the strands behind her ear, she shook a little more, letting out everything inside. My girl was broken. She'd ripped my heart from my chest when she kissed another man, and then stepped on it when she let him spend the night with her. But seeing her cry like this…I couldn't handle it.

I was content to stay there the rest of the night. I wasn't hungry, and I was fine sitting in a pile of peaches, and flour and sugar. But my moment wasn't meant to last long as Jason rounded the corner just in time to break everything just a little more. "Whoa, what the hell?" he said as he saw spilt dessert on the floor. "Ooooooh, sorry… did I interrupt?" *He was such an ass.*

Nolan broke from my arms immediately upon the sound of his voice, rubbing her nose on her sleeve, and going back to work cleaning up the floor. "Sorry, I dropped the cobbler. I'll get it, Reed. You go," she said, willing me away.

"I can help," I said, reaching for her just a little. When she pulled away, it broke me all over again. She just looked up at me, her lips tight as she took in a deep breath.

"I'm good. Just go," she said before going back to work.

I stood at her words, and just stared at her busy hands. Rosie must have heard the commotion because she was in the kitchen now, too, and bending down with a towel to help. "Oh, Noles, your pretty dessert. It's okay, I'll get it sweetie. You go clean up. Why don't you use the spare bathroom," Rosie said, squeezing Nolan's hand to get her to stop. She finally looked up at Rosie and smiled, but her eyes still seemed so damn sad.

"Ooooooh, trouble in paradise there, little brother?" Jason teased, condescendingly, as he picked a crouton from the salad on the counter, and popped it in his mouth as he turned to walk away. I was instantly filled with rage and found myself grabbing a fistful of his buttoned shirt and twisting it to make him uncomfortable, my fist locked just under his chin. "Ah, I hit close to home, didn't I? You wanna take it out on me because your little high school romance didn't work out? Go ahead; hit me, you little shit. But you know I was right. And you can do better."

I stared him down, my face inches from his, my breathing ragged, and my heart pounding with more anger than I'd ever felt. I wanted to break his nose. But I also knew he lived to push my buttons, and I didn't want to ruin Thanksgiving. And then I looked past him and saw Nolan standing at the foot of the steps, not yet upstairs, just chewing on her fingernails and seeing...*everything.* Not taking my eyes off of her, I just thrust Jason's shirt collar back into his body and backed away, brushing off the front of my shirt and cracking my neck a little to one side. I finally looked back at Jason to see his arrogant smirk. I couldn't let him off completely. I looked back to where Nolan had been standing, and she was gone. I settled back on Jason, leaning in close one more time, taking pride in the fact that I almost doubled him in size now. "You're a dick," I said, holding his eyes for just a bit so he'd see I meant everything I said before turning to join the rest of my family in the living room.

———

Despite the hours Rosie spent in the kitchen working on every detail of our dinner, we managed to demolish it in a matter of minutes. The table was quiet for moments at a time while we all stuffed our faces with her delicious turkey, stuffing and gravy. Pops, Jason and I always ate like Neanderthals, shoveling food in our mouths sometimes with our bare hands, and picking up fallen crumbs from the table and pushing them into our mouths, too. My mother always hated it but Rosie seemed to take it as a compliment.

Tonight was the first time I'd had a real Thanksgiving meal in my own house, *ever*...and it was amazing! Even Nolan's mom praised Rosie on her cooking, which was saying something, since every meal I'd had at the Lennox home was the single best thing I'd ever eaten, each thing Nolan's mom made one-upping the last.

Nolan and I were sitting at the far end of the table next to one another, but like strangers. We were both putting on a performance it seemed. She would smile and nod at conversations, half leaning her head in my direction, but never fully settling in to make eye contact. I found myself challenging her, though, staring right at her for longer than I should. She was friendly, and almost flirtatious, but there was an underlying sadness to her that I couldn't deny. I just kept replaying her crying on the floor in my kitchen, so lost and helpless, and my stomach sank in fear that I had made her that way. I'd almost feel sorry, and then remind myself that she was the one who kissed another man...and maybe more, and then when I thought of Gavin, I balled my hands into fists on my knees and quit feeling so bad.

"So, Nolan...how's school going?" Jason was engaging her now, but he had that tone to his voice that he only made when he wanted to give me shit. Immediately, I was defensive.

"Oh...uh, it's fine," she just smiled and looked down to straighten the napkin on her lap. *Shit!* She was barely holding it together, I could tell.

"Huh..." he just said, taunting her.

"What do you mean...huh?" I said, not able to take it, but probably just throwing gas on the fire.

Jason slid his chair a bit then and sat up straight to meet my gaze. "Well, little brother..." I knew he was going to lay into me now, get me back for knocking him around in the kitchen a little, getting in his face. Jason didn't like to be shown up, even if nobody was watching. "I just mean it must be hard between the two of you, long distance and all. I just wondered if Nolan ever had to turn anyone down, break some poor ASU guy's heart?" He smirked, tempting me.

I felt my heart beating in my stomach, and the weight of everyone's stares bouncing between Nolan and me. They were all rapt with the conversation, smiling and waiting for our cute response. And I was so pissed at the part of me that wanted to let them all down—just to crush her a little, the part that wanted to say, "No, she never turns anyone down. Instead, she just kisses whatever asshole wants to get her into bed that night." But I didn't, I just looked at Nolan, every muscle in her face clenched, and leaned in to kiss her on the cheek softly. Then I looked her right in the eyes as I backed away and got my own little dig in, private and not for anyone but her. "Never," I said, holding her gaze, and instantly feeling regret for saying it as she fought to keep the water pooling in her eyes from falling.

Suddenly not hungry for dessert, I excused myself, and pushed back from the table to head upstairs and clear my head. I noticed Sienna's hand squeezing Nolan's under the table as I walked away, and immediately knew I'd made a mistake. "I'm such an asshole," I thought. But I had been so angry for so long, for once I just wanted to give into it. Turns out it wasn't worth it.

I hung out in my room for about 20 minutes, just lying flat on my back and staring up at my ceiling. I was startled when my dark room lit up from the hallway light as someone cracked it open. My heart jumped a little, thinking it might be Nolan, but then settled when I realized it was Sarah.

"Hey," I said, laying back down and folding my hands under my head. The bed flopped heavily as she lay down next to me.

"Hey," she said, mimicking me. We both sat there in comfortable silence for a while. I was growing to really like Sarah. She was real, always gave it to people straight, and I admired that. Of course, that meant sometimes I had to take what she was dishing.

"So…that was a prick move down there," she said, turning her head to prop it up on her hand and look at me.

Sighing, I put my hands on my face to try to rub away the memory of an hour ago. "Yeah, I'm sorry about that. My brother is a real asshole," I said, turning to her and wincing.

"Hmmmmm, yeah…he is," she said, then sat up, and looked down at me. "But I was talking about you."

The look she was giving me could have burned a hole through my eyes. I just stared right back into, owning it. She was right, and I knew throwing my vow to never cheat on Nolan in her face was the shittiest thing to say the moment the words came out. Not wanting to get into it with Sarah, and partly wanting to take my punishment, I just shrugged a bit, and lay flat on my back again, throwing my arm over my eyes. "Yeah, it was a prick move," I said.

We were quiet after that again until we heard the others start to stir downstairs. The sounds of chairs scuffing the floor and dishes clanking had us both sitting up. I was dreading going back down there to face everyone after the shit I'd said. And I was pretty sure after the stunt I'd pulled, Nolan's parents were starting to question us, too.

"Get your shit together, Reed. We're going out tonight," she said as she flung the door open, leaving me there without an opportunity to say no.

———

By the time I got downstairs, Nolan's parents had left, and I didn't see her either. I felt a weight lift off my shoulders, but it was instantly replaced with self-pity. I saw Sarah standing in the kitchen swinging her keys around one finger. "Sar, look…if nobody else wants to go, maybe we just call it a night," I started, but she just held up a hand in my face.

"Oh, everyone's going. Everyone," she said, turning me around to see Nolan standing at the doorway with Becky, Trig and Sean, her face at peace for the first time this evening.

We split into two cars, I took my Jeep with Trig, Becky and Sean, and Sarah drove Sienna and Nolan. We headed out to the Old Wheelhouse on the outskirts of town. It was an old-fashioned country bar, the kind where bands played honky-tonk, and the ranch hands came to spend their paychecks on beer. It also happened to have karaoke and pool, which is where I was sure Nolan would spend most of her night.

The girls got there before we did, and I as I pulled in to park, I watched them walk up to the front doors. Nolan was lagging behind —her hair slung over one shoulder. I wanted to reach out and touch it, kiss her neck. But instead, I just sat there in the Jeep, resting my chin on the steering wheel, and panting after her like a dog.

When we walked in, Sarah had found herself a spot on the dance floor already, working the crowd into some line dance and getting the attention of a few of the locals. I slid up to the bar next to Trig and Sean, and nudged Sean a little with my elbow. "Where are the girls?" I asked.

"They're in there watching Nolan sweep the floor with some guy at the tables," he chuckled. It was her favorite thing to do, hustle some poor sap into some stupid bet. She'd gotten us free drinks when we went out more than once. I loved watching her do it, but I never wanted to play against her. I was shit at pool. Trig seemed intrigued at our conversation and slid from his stool to go check out the match himself.

"Hmmm, maybe I'll take her on," Trig said, wiggling his eyebrows a little like he had a shot in hell. Sean and I just laughed. I nodded at the bartender, who slid over a beer before reaching out to shake my hand. I was a bonafide local celebrity in Coolidge, but the people here were more down-to-earth. It was comforting. Like home.

There weren't many options at the Wheelhouse—shots or beer. I started sipping mine when I felt Sarah slide into the stool on my other side.

"So, cowboy. You wanna dance? Or what?" she asked. I knew I didn't really have a choice, so I let her guide me by the hand out to the dance floor. It was some slow country song, so I just kept hold of her hand and put my other one on her back. This dance was going to be all about conversation.

"Look, Sarah. I'm sorry about earlier...," I started, but she cut me off.

"Just don't, Reed. I get that you're hurt, and pissed, and angry, and all kinds of other shit. But you need to cut our girl some slack," she had her bossy tone on now. She pursed her lips, almost like she was reigning herself in. That was *huge* for Sarah. "Reed...Nolan's on academic probation. She's been skipping *a lot* of her classes because of everything that's happened. Sienna and I have been taking turns trying to get her out of her room, but she never leaves it. She just holes up in there. The only thing she comes out for is to help her floor charges or to work her writing workshop."

I was a little stunned, and stopped our dance—not that it was much of one—to soak in her words for a moment. I knew there was something sad about Nolan, but I didn't think she'd ever be in academic trouble. Her scholarships were everything to her. Suddenly, I felt worse…about everything. Sarah and I weren't even really spinning anymore, but rather just swaying slowly in the middle of the dance floor, the only couple out there.

"Is she going to lose her scholarship?" I asked, curling one side of my lip and squinting my eyes to brace myself for more bad news.

Sarah just sighed at first. "I don't know. She won't talk about it," she said. "I think her grades are good enough to give her a shot to make up for it in the spring. But Reed? I'm not so sure she can pull it together—not without talking to someone."

I wasn't sure what she meant by that, and it killed me to think of Noles being so depressed and not having anyone to talk to about it, especially when I was supposed to be that one person, *her* person. I just looked down and pulled Sarah's hand into me so I could hug her now. I kissed the top of her head a little and thanked her for being a good friend. I felt her body weight fall under my embrace and, when she looked up at me, her eyes were glossy. I just smiled faintly, understanding her love for Nolan.

"Sar? Can you tell me one thing?" I said, leaning back to look at her again.

"What?" She was back to being tough, clearly her way of keeping her emotions in check. It made me laugh a little as I pulled her in for more dancing.

"Where's Gavin in all of this? I mean, I get it…you don't want to tell me about him…and what he and Nolan are…or do…or did…or whatever. But Sar, I gotta know. Did he just sleep with her, and ditch her once he got what he wanted?" I asked, my brow pinched, while my head tried to work everything out before she laid it on me.

Sarah just stiffened at my question, her feet stopping, and her face looking down at them. Her gaze flashed to mine in an instant then, her face confused and full of worry. "Reed…you know she *never* slept with Gavin, right?" She said, her words slapping me in the face and fighting against everything I had believed for weeks.

"Uh...what do you mean?" I said, backing away a little, my hands dropping to my sides.

"I mean...Nolan. Never. Slept. With. Gavin," she said it slowly and punctuated each word, drilling it into me, and angry at my accusation.

"Fuck!" I said backing away from Sarah faster now and heading for the front door. She followed me out.

I was pacing now in the dirt parking lot in front of my Jeep. I kicked a rock so hard it dinged off of one of my doors, and then pushed my hands through my hair and tilted my head up to look at the stars. "You're fucking kidding me!" I screamed loudly enough to turn a few heads of others that were just walking into the bar. Embarrassed, I put up a hand in an apologetic wave. Sarah was frozen, just watching me pace and work out everything in my racing mind. I stopped right in front of her and put my hands on either shoulder.

"Sarah. You're telling me that Nolan never slept with Gavin?" I wanted to hear her say it again.

"Reed. I can't believe you'd even ask that," her forehead was wrinkled like my words weren't even making sense. She shook her head slowly at me in disappointment, and I just started pacing again.

"I can't believe that fucker," I said under my breath. Sarah caught my arm to stop me then.

"What fucker?" she gritted through her teeth now.

"Gavin. I came to see her, not long after we fought. You know, when I found out that she'd kissed him? He was coming out of her room, and he said that he'd spent the night," I hung my head feeling foolish that I believed him.

"Fuck! That asshole played me to get me out of his way. And I just fucking waved him right in," I thought.

I was sick, and felt like I was going to throw up, though I'd only had a few sips of a beer. Suddenly, I needed to talk to Nolan more than anything in the entire world. I left Sarah standing in the parking lot and stormed back into the Wheelhouse and found Sean still sitting at the bar. He was working on his second beer now. I looked around a bit for Nolan but didn't see her, instead Trig was just playing pool with a few other guys. Urgency must have been oozing from my pores, because Sean caught on quickly.

"She's dancing with one of those dudes," he said, tilting his head to the dance floor. Some local in a cowboy hat was spinning her around the floor, and she was laughing. Where moments ago I was conflicted between loving the sight of her smile and resenting her for it, now I only appreciated it more than the air I was breathing. She looked happy—simply, deliriously and absolutely happy. I had missed those carefree eyes, and when I thought about the tears that fell from them on the day you're supposed to be thankful, I felt like the biggest asshole ever.

I leaned into the bar for the entire song, just watching her, soaking her in. She was suddenly flawless. I could look at her without seeing Gavin, and my gut sank thinking of how much suffering she had endured. I was lost in her when I started a little as someone pushed me off balance from the bar, falling to one knee just to catch myself.

"Hey, bro," Jason said, reaching his hand out to catch a hold of me. I grabbed it, and stared him down as I got back to my feet, and brushed off the dirt from my jeans.

"What are you doing here?" I asked, completely uninterested in his lame-ass attempt at bonding.

"Hmmm. Nice, little brother," he said, taking a drink from his beer bottle and setting it back down on the bar. I hated that he called me *little brother*. He'd always done it. Just another part of his faulty personality and constant need to make sure I knew I was less than he was. Truth was, though, I was ten times the athlete Jason was, and the attention I was getting was killing him.

"Dylan wanted to come check this place out. She likes karaoke," he made a sour face as he spoke. I think Jason liked the idea of being with someone *like* Dylan more than he actually liked *her*. Even more, though, I think he liked the fact that our mother praised him for picking such a *lovely girl*. My mom's need to marry one of us off to the Nichols family was, apparently, relentless.

I saw Dylan walk out of the hallway by the pool tables with

another blonde and in a flash my stomach turned. *Shit!* It was the girl I walked home that night with Trig! The one who stripped for me and I'd left half naked in her living room!

I wanted to sprint from the building immediately, but my muscles were rendered utterly useless after the rush of adrenaline passed through my legs upon realizing my newest nightmare was walking up to me, wrapped in a scantly dressed bow. Dylan was reaching up to kiss Jason on the neck, while straightening the strap on one of her shoes when she looked me in the eyes to introduce me to her friend. "Fuck!" I thought; I didn't know what to do.

The girl locked eyes with me right away, recognition washing over her. "Reed!" she squealed. Uhg, suddenly that near-mistake seems like a cliff-edge I had almost dove from. She reached up, and kissed my cheek as if we were familiar. Though, I suppose sadly, in some ways we were.

"Uh…yeah, hi," I smiled softly, trying to find a balance between retreat and polite. Sean was sliding away from me now, to go join Trig, escaping my personal hell and sensing that things were about to go very far south.

"Oh my God! You two know each other?" Dylan said, looking between me, and my mistake.

"Well…sort of. I…uh," I scratched at my head and turned sideways to find Nolan's eyes locked right on me while she danced with the cowboy. *Damn it!*

I smiled politely and turned back to Dylan again. "I'm sorry?" I said, my train of thought completely derailed.

"I said, you two know each other?" Dylan was clearly thrown by my reaction now.

"Oh, yeah. I walked her…" I paused realizing I didn't even know her name. In my head, I called her Peaches, because of the scent of her hair. "…home the other day."

Dylan must have been familiar with the story, because I caught a slight flinch in her face as she nodded and smiled a little. "Ohhhhh, I see," she smirked before looking back at Peaches.

Not knowing what to do, I did the only thing I could think of doing to get us away from Dylan and her judgmental gaze. "Hey, wanna dance?" I said, holding out an arm. Peaches slid right up to me and took my arm as we walked out on the same floor that Nolan was on, now nestled into some boot-wearing idiot for a romantic slow dance. If I survive the night without punching someone, it would be a miracle.

I started dancing with Peaches, and she looked up at me, her face both hopeful and indignant. "So," she said, biting her lip. A few weeks ago, I might have given in to a second chance with her, but armed with my new knowledge, that there was no Gavin—never was…? Well, Peaches didn't have a chance.

"So," I said, not really even looking at her.

"I'm Jenny, by the way. In case you were wondering," she said, a complete attitude coming to the surface now. I spun her around once in a twirl, mostly to get her out of my grasp and gain some space between us. Unfortunately, though, she giggled when I did this, drawing Nolan's attention. And the flash of hurt on her face was unmistakable.

"Nice to meet you…again, Jenny," I said, pulling her back in so her head was out of my line of vision. I watched Nolan walk back over to the pool tables with her cowboy and a few of his friends. At least no one would touch her while she was playing pool.

"You know, I'm not usually easy like that," Jenny said. I just nodded and smiled, still trying to keep an eye on Nolan, and my chest tightening as I watched her down three shots from a tray with her cowboy friends.

"I'm sorry…how do you know Dylan?" I said, fighting to put conversation out there that I didn't have to work at.

"Oh, she's my cousin," she said quickly.

Shit! This just keeps getting worse. I just swallowed in response to this new information. My muscles tensed, and I became even more careful than I had been with this dangerous girl.

"Oh, I had no idea," I shrugged tightly.

She must have sensed my distance and hesitation, because she sighed heavily and then rolled her eyes, spinning herself from my arms and back again. "It's okay, Reed. I knew who you were. And I was totally just hitting on you that night, the entire time. My roommate and I had it all planned," she said, just curling one side of her mouth into a guilty smile. "And you can relax. I didn't tell my cousin about how I stripped for you, and you bailed on me after I threw myself you. It's not really one of my finest moments."

Relief washed over me, and my feet felt like they had shed a little of the concrete that had been weighing them down since I saw her walk from the bathroom. "She just knows that you walked me home, and we sort of kissed but that you rejected me," she continued.

Okay, we did sort of kiss. I could live with this. And it wouldn't make its way to Jason for him to twist and use against me at some later date. I leaned back a bit and smiled at Jenny genuinely now, the breath that I'd been holding finally exhaling. "Yeah, so...I'm so sorry about all of that," I admitted. "I wasn't myself. I've been... dealing with something."

I was looking for Nolan again, and Jenny followed my gaze, and then looked back at me to see the pain in my eyes while Nolan laughed and brushed her hand along the shoulder of Mr. Cowboy. "Ah, yeah...I see that," she smiled with tight lips, soft and understanding. It seems I'd underestimated both Dylan and Jenny.

"You wanna tell me about it?" Jenny said, her head tilted a bit, and her shoulders rose like she was truly interested in hearing my relationship problems. I considered it for a moment, but then I saw Sarah's stare right behind her, and heard her cough loudly just to get our attention and force us to face her.

"Excuse me," she said, just cutting in and taking my hands.

I shrugged a little at Jenny, and just mouthed, "I'm sorry," as I gestured toward Sarah. Jenny just shook her head and rolled her eyes, walking back to my brother and Dylan at the bar.

"Thanks," I said to Sarah.

"Really? You're thanking me?" she said, a little confused.

"Yes. Yes, I am," I smiled. "That girl is a...well...she's not a bad girl. Let's just say, she was almost part of a *reallllly big fuck-up* though."

Not quite ready to trust me, Sarah just looked at me sideways, and continued our dance. "Ooooookay," she said, full of skepticism.

"You can fill me in on that another time. Tonight, though, well… we've got bigger problems."

She turned me around quickly so I could get a better look at Nolan—who was now sitting on her knees in the middle of one of the pool tables, flirting with taking her shirt off, while those pig-headed assholes stood around her hollering, and waiving dollar bills.

"Shit!" I said, quickly stepping away from Sarah and sprinting over to the poolroom. I pushed through the seven or eight guys who had gathered to watch Nolan's little strip tease, and put my knee up on the table to reach for Nolan's hand. She recoiled at my touch right away, though, whipping her hair back from her face and making eye contact with me enough to show the hate in her eyes.

"Fuck you, Reed. Don't touch me," she slurred.

Great. I wonder how many shots she'd downed when I wasn't looking.

"Okay, Princess. Time to go," I said, climbing completely onto the table now and lifting her high over my shoulder. She squirmed for a bit, kicking at the light that dangled above. "You wanna stop that now? I'm not letting you go, and you're only causing a scene. And you're about to bust a light bulb."

She huffed, and finally went limp over my shoulder, as I stepped down from the pool table and walked past Jason, Dylan and Jenny. I paused for a moment and looked Jason right in the face. "You breathe a word of this to anyone, and I swear to God, Jason…I will fucking kill you," I said, no hint of hesitation in my voice at all. I turned at that, and continued out the door, which Sarah, Becky and Sienna were now holding for me.

"Thanks," I said as they followed me to the Jeep. I dumped Nolan in the passenger seat and forced her to buckle up, slamming the door on her while she sat there and pouted. "I'm taking her to my house. Her parents don't need to see this. Can everyone fit in your car, Sarah?"

She just nodded and waved me on my way. I got in the driver's side and peeled out a little, the energy from what I'd just witnessed still coursing through me. Nolan was staring out the window, her chin balanced awkwardly on her hand. I just sighed heavily and kept on driving.

"Don't sigh at me," she said. She was picking a fight now. I recognized this; we'd done this before. But not since we were kids. I thought it was better not to engage, but something told me she wouldn't let that slide.

"Oh, more silent treatment, huh? Like when you didn't call me for six weeks, and I locked myself in a room, and cried," she spit the words out angrily, and I winced a little at them. She was so angry with me, and I couldn't say I blamed her, knowing what I know now. I kept my lips sealed, though, knowing any words exchanged between us tonight didn't count. Nolan just huffed again, and we drove the rest of the way in silence.

When I pulled in the driveway to my dad's house, Nolan had nodded off and was snoring softly in the passenger's seat. When I opened her door, I took her in for a moment. Her lips were crooked, half smirking, and I thought about kissing them for a second when she lurched forward and sprayed vomit down my leg.

"Damn it, Noles," I said lunging back. She looked up at me and wiped her chin a little and started shaking. She was crying again. God, I felt like such an asshole.

"I'm so sorry," she said, her hands making their way to her face so she could hide.

I shook my leg a little and reached over to unbuckle her. "It's okay; I'll shower," I said softly, not wanting to wake anyone and not wanting to scare her. She was so fragile, and it was killing me to see her that way. "Come on, I got you."

I lifted her in my arms, and her body went limp into me. I carried her up the stairs and into my bedroom. I'd sleep on the couch tonight. Nolan clearly needed to be near a bathroom. I knew I made the right decision when she rolled from my bed almost the instant I'd set her down and stumbled to my bathroom holding an arm across her mouth. She made it just in time for the entire evening's booze to escape her body. I'd never seen anyone throw up so much in my life.

I was just rubbing her back, pulling her hair into a ponytail when she finally seemed to be done and slid her body to sit right next to the toilet, her arm and cheek resting on the lip of the bowl. I stood and leaned back into the wall, away from her, and waited as her sleepy eyes fought to stay open. I was exhausted from the entire evening, but I couldn't take my eyes from her until I knew she was okay. And there was something in them, some sort of sadness that just wouldn't go away. It both captivated and crushed me all at once.

She worked her gaze up my body, almost as if she lacked the strength, and then finally came to stop right on my eyes. We stared into each other for several seconds when her lip started to quiver a little and the tears, the same ones I'd seen in the kitchen, started to slide down her cheek again.

"I'm so sorry, Reed," she said, and at her words I looked down, not able to look her in the eyes knowing that I'd been so cruel when she never actually slept with Gavin—and knowing that I almost made a worse mistake with Jenny, just to get back at her. She was sobbing now, sliding back to the floor, and reaching up for a towel to drape over her face and body, her hands clutching at it desperately. Her eyes still settled on me though—*those sad, amazing and beautiful eyes.*

"I'm so sorry, Reed," she started again, and I tried to hush her, moving forward and making the softest smile I could, my head shaking *no*, and begging her to stop her worrying. I just needed her to sleep this off so we could wake up in the morning and start fixing things.

"I'm so sorry I lost your baby," the words escaped her lips, playing out in slow motion while she slid the rest of the way to the floor and succumbed to the pull of sleep. All air left my lungs at the sound of her voice. My legs no longer able to hold me up, I slid slowly down the wall, fingers clawing at it to slow my descent, until I was finally sitting on the floor, too, just staring at her now closed eyes. Mine wide with shock, each nerve ending on my body firing with this new information, and my breath completely stopped. Had I heard her right? Did she say *baby*?

I fumbled through my pocket, and my phone fell to the floor next to me. I scurried more, trying to hold it in my shaking hands and, when I'd finally gotten it right, I scrolled until I found Sarah's number. I hit *dial,* and waited, still not having blinked since the words *lost* and *baby* left Nolan's lips.

"Reed? Are you home? Is she okay?" Sarah started, but I interrupted.

"When did she lose the baby?" I asked, no longer questioning what I heard, but just suddenly desperate to know. I heard Sarah sigh on the other end. "Sar, I need to know. Please…just tell me." I swallowed hard, and found my face wet with tears, my voice urgent and needing.

"I didn't think you knew," she said quietly. "There was no way you could have. It just didn't make sense."

"What do you mean?" I asked, my heart rate picking up a little with panic now as I realized everything my girl had been through —*alone.*

"Nolan said she called you, said she left you a message or something, but I couldn't imagine you not calling her after that," Sarah said, my body flattening on itself in an instant at her explanation.

"Shit!" I said, my hand now covering my mouth to hold myself together. "The message…fuck!"

I stood to walk into my room and shut the door to my bathroom slightly to keep Nolan asleep. "Sar, she did. I completely forgot. I was so pissed. I never listened!" I was manic now, my body shaking, and my guts twisting.

"Well, you better go listen," Sarah said, exasperated and clearly pissed at me.

I hung up without saying bye and dialed into my voicemail in seconds, only to hear Nolan's voice telling me everything:

Hi. It's me. I guess you know that, though. I…oh my God, Reed. I'm so sorry. I don't know how this happened. I don't want Gavin. I don't even like him. He was just there, and we were both in the wrong place at the wrong time.

(Sniffle)

I was so drunk. I haven't done that before. I was so upset—and he was flirting with me, and I let him make a pass, and I didn't stop him, and then it all hit me at once—and I ran home. Oh God!

(She was crying harder now.)

Reed? There's so much you don't know. I...I was pregnant.

(The tears were non-stop and her breath stuttered.)

I found out the night we made plans to talk about the draft. And then Dylan happened, and then you made plans to sign, and I was so afraid I would have to drop out of school, and raise a baby. I thought you wouldn't want me—or want us. And Tatum had tricked you with pregnancy in high school, and I remembered how you acted, how depressed you got. How it ruined EVERYTHING.

(There was a long pause while she cried harder, her nose running, and her breath hitching.)

I lost it. It was terrible. And oh my God, the blood. Reed, it was so awful. And it was all my fault...because I didn't want it. I didn't want to trap you. And I felt relief, at first. And then I just wanted to go back, back to when I was pregnant, so I could tell you this time. What if I can't get pregnant? What if that was your only chance to have a baby? And I was so selfish. I wished it away, Reed!

(She was crying hard again.)

Gavin found me at the gym when I passed out the day after my...my... miscarriage. I wasn't dehydrated, at least not from running. And I had just come back from your house, from seeing Dylan in your shirt. And Gavin took care of me. And I think part of me thought about that day when he kissed me. And yes, I kissed him back. But I wasn't thinking of him. I promise! Oh God, Reed. Please, please just call me. I can't lose you, too!

Those were her last words before my message cut off. I just sat there stunned, looking at my broken girl lying on the floor, covered in her own vomit. Her scholarships in jeopardy, her heart broken, and her faith in me completely rocked...all because I forgot to listen to a fucking message! *She'd thought she'd lost me, too.* I played it again, and let the tears fall down my face, blotting them with my fists, trying to *man up*, but also letting it all fall out of me at once.

When her words finished, I slid the phone to the corner of the room and crawled on hands and knees to her body. She was snoring lightly and didn't flinch when I brushed her long strands of hair behind her ear. I managed to peel her soaked sweater from her; she only wrinkled her nose a little at me, but her eyes remained closed. I picked her up and carried her to my bed where I pulled the boots from her feet and slid her pants from her legs. I went to my drawer to pull out my softest Coolidge football T-shirt, her favorite. I slid it over her head and carefully pulled her arms through the sleeves. She twisted sideways in my bed a little, pulling down on the shirt out of instinct. I pulled the blanket up her body, leaving her shoulders exposed so I could stroke them with my fingers for a while.

Finally satisfied that she was asleep, and staying that way, I kissed my angel's head and whispered in her ear. "I'm going to fix this; I promise." Then quietly, I made my way to the bathroom for a shower.

Chapter Twenty

Nolan

IT TOOK me a few minutes to figure out where I was. The smell was familiar, the shirt I was wearing…different, but familiar all the same. My head was throbbing, and my ears were being hit with a constant drumming. My stomach felt empty, but also like it had been through a boxing match. *I was destroying myself!*

I pushed myself to a sitting position and cracked my eyes open ever so slightly, confirming my suspicion. I was in Reed's bed. I looked around for any sign of him, but he wasn't there. I could tell he hadn't been. I must have been a mess—made quite a scene, I thought. I remembered most of it, up until he threw me in the Jeep and hauled my ass home.

I could hear the clanking of dishes downstairs and the faint sounds of some voices, though I wasn't sure who it was. I thought briefly about fashioning Reed's sheets together so I could repel out his window, but I didn't have my car here. I'd need to walk home. And I was in no condition to go for a stroll through the desert. Knowing I had to live up to my walk of shame, I worked to find my footing to stand.

It was late morning, maybe 11, so there was a chance most of the guests had left, and Reed and Trig were already on their way to campus. My feet were gripping at the carpet by the bed, and I was puzzling at my lack of pants when there was a light knock at the door.

"Hey…you awake?" Reed said as he stuck his head in slowly.

Embarrassed, I just pulled the covers over my lap and smiled softly.

"Yeah, uh…you sort of barfed all over your clothes," he said, chuckling a little and looking down at his feet.

"Oh God!" I thought.

He slid completely in the room, holding a small bag and a juice, closing the door behind him. "I got you a muffin," he said with a half smile, approaching me like I was an injured puppy. "Oh, and some juice. Thought you might be hungry? Or thirsty?"

I just stared at him, trying to make sense of his behavior. "Thanks," I said, my voice a little crackly from the rough night. I pulled the muffin from the bag, and picked small pieces off it and ate—not really hungry, but also unsure of what else to do in front of him; suddenly, everything about me felt raw and on display. I just looked back up and smiled. "It's good. Blueberry."

"Yeah. I know it's your favorite," he said, leaning against his opposite wall. We just stared at each other while I ate. Finally, he pushed off the wall and looked at his watch. "Hey, so, I have to get going with Trig. We have light practice today. But you're going to the game, right? You'll be there?"

He seemed intense all of a sudden, almost worried. Why was it so important to him that I was there now, after missing so many weeks? I shrugged a little and nodded. "Yeah, I'm going with Sarah," I said, my insides sick that there was no way out of this now. I'd have to go—worse yet, the deep-down part of me really wanted to be there.

"Good," he nodded once before coming over to stand right in front of me, my heart speeding up with every step he took. He put his hand on my shoulder and put his fingers under my chin to tilt my face up to look at him. He was holding his breath. He was...*nervous?* What the hell type of paradox had I fallen into? What the hell happened after I got in that Jeep last night? Then he leaned forward and placed his lips on my forehead. His soft touch made me shut my eyes to savor it. I also wanted to cry, something that seemingly happened at the drop of the dime lately. I just left my eyes shut, while he backed away, opening them to see him smiling at me again softly. "Okay, well...see you after the game."

After Reed left the room, I sat on the bed and picked at the blueberry muffin a little more before attempting some of my juice. My stomach felt raw, so I didn't force much down. I had lost a little weight over the last few weeks, and my clothes weren't fitting like they were supposed to. When I realized that I didn't have any clothes, I panicked a bit, and stood up to spin around the room to find a solution. My eyes zeroed in on the neat pile of my clothes from the night before folded on top of Reed's dresser. There was a tiny note on it that read *cleaned last night.*

My heart skipped for a moment, an unfamiliar feeling in contrast to the gut-wrenching ache I'd been nursing. Unsure how I'd gotten here, both physically and emotionally, I did what I always do in these situations—I called the girls. We made plans to meet up at Becky's, and Sarah agreed to come pick me up from Reed's, though I couldn't ignore the odd hesitation in her voice.

Once dressed and looking semi-decent, I cracked open Reed's door to make my way downstairs, holding my breath as the kitchen came more into view. My stomach sank when I saw Jason's back to me at the kitchen island. I hadn't had much interaction with him over the years, but the last 24 hours would hold me for a while. I took in a deep breath and forced myself the rest of the way down the steps taking comfort that Sarah would be at the door any minute.

I didn't make eye contact, only reached up to the cabinet to grab a coffee mug. But Jason wasn't going to let me go without conversation.

"Hey, good morning, sunshine. Quite a display you put on last night, with your near strip tease," he joked, holding his coffee just far enough away from his lips so he could spit out his biting comment.

I just turned and shrugged, a bit embarrassed. I wasn't going to engage. I'd learned one thing from Reed about his brother over the years—Jason liked to spar. And if you didn't put up a fight, he got bored quickly, and moved on. I turned back to the coffee and started pouring my cup.

"So…kinda awkward way for you to meet the rebound chick, no?" he said, his words hitting every nerve in my body. Not wanting to give him the satisfaction, I just let my muscles clench to take the impact of his fire, hoping it would soon pass, and I could just work out what he'd said with Sarah, Becky and Sienna.

"He did tell you about Jenny, right? Dylan's cousin?" He wasn't going to let this go. I turned to face him, the coffee cup to my mouth, masking the grimace on my face. I just shrugged again, and gave him a lopsided smile, but nodded *no*, honestly. No. I'd told him the truth, and given him the weapon he desperately wanted to destroy me with.

"Wowwwwwww," he let it drag out as he stood to wash his coffee mug, his back now to me. "Well, then, it must have really sucked to have found out last night. I mean, if he's going to make himself feel better, though, might as well be with a girl like that. I don't mean it in a crass way. What I meant was she's so opposite of you. That has to make it better, right? I mean, if it was someone more like you, you'd feel like you were just being replaced."

He just sat there leaning on the counter again, with a smug-ass grin on his face. I knew Jason was playing me. It's what he did. He had some bitter war with Reed ever since Reed started seeing success in high school, and it had gotten way out of hand. But there was also always some layer of truth to his shots; he wasn't a complete sociopath like Tatum. No, he collected bits and pieces along the way, and saved them up to use them against his enemies later, when they least expected it.

I heard Sarah pulling into the driveway, so I grabbed my purse and turned my back to Jason, and his satisfied fucking grin. Not wanting to let him completely get away with it, I sent one final shot over my shoulder. "Yeah, well you would know about being replaced, huh? Must have sucked when Reed filled your spotlight… and never gave it back."

I walked out the door at my words and didn't look back. I'd held it together in front of Jason, but once out of his view, I felt the life fleeing from my lungs. I was nearly hyperventilating when I got in the car with Sarah, who was rolling her eyes at me already, trying to punish me from my actions from the night before.

"Jesus, Noles. Just once I'd like us to get together without some fucking emotional scars, or wounds, that need tending to," she said, sighing as I shut the door, and we drove off. She felt bad instantly, though, as she always did, and slid her hand over to squeeze mine. "Sorry, just a little frustrated. I didn't mean it."

"I know," I said, biting at my lip and readying myself for everything new that I had to fill the girls in on.

We hung out at Becky's for the entire day, just lounging and watching old movies. I'd filled the girls in on how Reed was acting, as well as the accusations and gossip Jason spilled on me before I left. Becky and Sienna were both hanging on every word I said during the part about Jason, but Sarah seemed less concerned. When I was done, she just got up from the couch and slapped her hands on her thighs in front of her.

"Pffft, Jason's just an ass. He's just trying to get to you…and by getting to you, get to Reed," she said, turning to go fill her bowl with more chips.

"Yeah, but I did see Reed with that girl, and they were really close. She was flirty with him, like they knew each other. And it wouldn't be the craziest thing that he did something with someone else while we're apart…not that we officially broke up, but…shit, well? I guess we sort of did," I said, hanging my head down and just searching for something to fill that raw and empty feeling I had in my gut every time I thought of Reed.

"Noles," Sarah said, climbing over the back of the sofa to join our girls' circle again. "Listen. I got in his face a little about her last night, and he swore there was nothing there. He promised...and I'm pretty good at reading people. He wasn't lying."

She just started eating her chips again and picked up the remote to start the next movie. I slid into the sofa cushions next to her and pulled my knees up to hug them. "I hope you're right," I said, sighing a little.

"I am," she said, not even phased. Her confidence gave me a tiny lift, and I was going to ride that out for the rest of the night.

———

The ASU and UofA rival game was something special. And while I may have been a Sun Devil to the core, when Reed played, I was on his team—no colors, no sides. Just him. I rode up early with Sarah, Sienna, Sean and Becky; my parents were planning to come up later. Buck had gotten them seats next to his, with most of the other boosters. They were comfortable, and would be out of the sun. Sienna was leaving us to join the band, which sat near the visiting team's entrance for the game. Our seats were in the student section, so for tonight, I would wear red and blue, and show my support for the only man I'd ever loved.

Buck had a grill set up at the back of his truck parked near the stadium and was cooking for his alumni friends when we strolled up. He was starting to get around a little better now, his leg still in his cast, but he was able to stand propped up on his crutches. Rosie was with him today. I noticed how she cared for him, and it warmed my heart seeing Buck get the love and attention he deserved.

"There's my girl," Buck said, reaching out an arm to call me in for a hug.

"Hey, Buck. Good to see you standing," I said, hugging him back and reaching up to kiss him on the cheek. He smiled at my gesture, and it made me feel sad that there might be a day in the future where this man wouldn't be a part of my life. Reed left me confused this morning, and Jason left me feeling even more so. I didn't know where I stood, where *we* stood. But for the first time since I'd called him and poured my heart out with confessions on his voicemail, I wanted to talk—the real, soul-baring kind of talk. And my heart skipped a little that Reed might actually want to listen.

"Hate to tell you this, darlin', but your school's going to lose today," Buck winked at me, bringing me out of my daydream. Normally, I'd give it right back to him; our longstanding battle over who was superior among our Arizona schools, a tradition between us. But today I just had to agree with him, because deep down, I never wanted Reed to lose.

"I hope you're right," I said, smiling warmly. He understood, and just squeezed me harder.

We fixed our burgers and climbed into the back of Buck's truck to eat. We were happily stuffing our faces—the quiet sounds of chewing, and faint sounds of the band and crowd in the background, the only other distraction until the rumble of another engine pulled up next to us. I turned to see who it was and came face to face with the girl I dreamt about last night. She was blonde, her skin was perfect, and when she turned to face me, our eyes meeting, she looked at me with clear recognition. But she wasn't intimidated or ashamed. She was confident and acted as if she belonged here. Sarah's words echoed in my mind, "Nothing's there," and "he wasn't lying." I played her words over in my head like a mantra, but my own self-loathing had me wavering. Hell, truth was, I wasn't wavering, I was faltering, falling off a cliff. And when Jenny laughed and slung her hair over her shoulder—her bronzed shoulders, and blue eyes sparkling in the sun—I was suddenly transformed into my weaker, younger self, the girl who was never good enough.

"Hey, Pops," I heard Jason shout to his dad as he climbed out of the truck. I ate my food in silence, just watching as Dylan and Jenny, *the mystery girl*, climbed out. I felt Sarah slap at my leg, trying to force me to stop obsessing, and reminding me that she had already vetted this girl, and had deemed her meaningless to Reed. I wanted to buy into Sarah's sales pitch. But everything about Dylan and Jenny was manicured, and expensive, and perfect. She was gorgeous, even more so than I ever thought Tatum was. And she was everything I used to think Reed wanted...but I knew better now. *At least, I thought I did?*

I slid from the back of the truck to throw my plate in a nearby trash can, purposely walking the long way around to avoid Jason's attention. I paused afterward for a while, to watch through the windows of the truck as Dylan introduced Buck to Jenny. He smiled at her warmly, bringing her into a friendly hug quickly.

"She's Dylan's cousin," I reminded myself. "And the Nichols are like family. It's nothing. The hug means nothing."

I leaned against the truck for a while longer, just wanting a few minutes alone to settle my thoughts, when I was startled.

"So, I suppose you and I should meet," I heard an unfamiliar voice say from behind me. I jumped a little and turned around to see Jenny's perfect smile. Damn, she had a nice smile. It was warm and honest, the kind that could charm any man into giving her anything she wanted, and frankly, I was pretty sure I would give her anything, too. She just stretched out her hand, and I shook it, her grip firm but feminine, just like Dylan's.

"Hi...uh...hi, I'm Nolan," I said, suddenly wishing I'd stayed home. She just giggled a little at my awkwardness, and I hung my head a bit in shame.

"Yes, I know who you are. Dylan told me about you. You've known Reed for a long time, right?" she said, pulling a band from her wrist and twisting her hair into a bun on top of her head.

"Yeah, since high school," I said, my insides screaming that I was his girlfriend, that we were in love, that we were going to be together forever. But I kept that all in my head, because I wasn't so sure about any of it anymore.

"Well, it's really nice to meet you. I'm in the box, with Dylan, so maybe I'll see you after the game. We're going to stick around for Reed," she said with a wink as she walked away.

What the hell did any of that mean? Why was she here? Why was she sticking around for Reed? Was he expecting her?

Sarah's pep talk to me had suddenly lost all of its power, and I felt flat and discarded. I slumped back over to my friends and remained silent until we got to our stadium seats.

I looked for Dylan and Jenny throughout the game, checking all of the skyboxes, but it was too hard to spot them from our crowded seats near the field. I forgot where I was for a moment with ASU's fight song starting to play, but remembered quickly enough when the crowd around me began to *boo*. I stopped my clapping, and put my hands in my pockets, making a funny face at Sarah who had started to scream and cheer, until she realized we were in enemy territory, too.

When the Wildcats took the field, Reed was leading the charge. I had missed a few games since we hadn't been talking, and watching him run out next to Trig, his body pumped with energy, and his face serious, reminded me of how proud I was of this man. He'd always been a natural. I knew it the first time I saw him lead a team out on a field more than seven years ago, and his presence had only grown stronger. I found myself staring at him, willing him to notice me. But I knew that I was a dot in a sea of faces out here. And whereas a few months ago he knew right where to find me, right where I'd be sitting, today he didn't have a clue.

Reed marched out to the middle of the field with the other captains, and the Wildcats won the coin toss. Reed wouldn't be taking the field right away, instead opting to take the opening drive in the second half. I watched him join his team and lean over to talk with his coach before he set his helmet down and walked over to the tables to grab some water. He was all business on that field, his head focused on one goal only—winning. And that was how Reed was when he was dedicated to something. That's how he was with *us*. How could I have ever doubted this man? I didn't trust him not to leave me, I didn't trust him enough to tell him about the pregnancy, and then I was the one to betray his faith in me. And now all I had done was lose him completely. If he had fallen into Jenny's arms, well…there was nobody to blame but myself.

I was lost in my thoughts, my eyes not completely focusing, and instead making a blur out of the colors of Reed's jersey, when I noticed the rapid movement of his arm. He was waving…at me. He'd found me, picked me out of the crowd of 50,000 fans. And he was waving, for everyone to see. Shell-shocked and stunned, I stood motionless, until Sarah leaned into me a bit, in an attempt to get me to react. I just raised a hand and held it up, biting my lip a bit and smiling, hoping. I couldn't make out his features from this far, but I was pretty sure he was smiling too before he turned back to the game. He'd taken a pause just to find me, something he'd never done on this field.

"I told you," Sarah said, giving me one more elbow to the rib. I just kept the dumb look on my face for the rest of the night.

———

The one drag about college games was how long they took to play out. By the time the clock was ticking down, it was 11 p.m. As predicted, the Wildcats scored 63 points against ASU. It was a rebuilding year for us, yes, but Reed was also at his best this season. And he had an amazing team to back him up. He and Trig were pulled in the third quarter to save their energy for the bowl bid the Wildcats would definitely get. I found myself watching Reed's every move as he stood and walked the sidelines, hoping he'd turn to me just once more. He never did, but I also knew he liked to stay focused on that field. And the players usually caught hell from coach for taking their focus away from the field, even when they weren't in the game.

Sarah, Becky, Sean and I waited for the crowds to move out before we left the stadium, knowing we'd be standing outside the athletic department for a while waiting on Reed anyhow. Sienna joined us after changing. It felt like old times, the group of us waiting for Reed, so we could go out and celebrate. But I was quickly reminded that it was the present, not the past, when the others joined our group in the lobby.

Jason had his arms draped all over Dylan, possessing her, and eyeing the college guys who were checking her out. He wasn't jealous, but instead seemed to get off on the attention she was getting, just wanting to attach himself to her so everyone would know he was the man who was good enough. She was his prize, his trophy.

Jenny stood next to them, wrestling her hands a little, almost as if she was nervous. I watched her ask Dylan a question, and then Jason piped in giving her a response. She seemed uncomfortable, and I wanted to help her.

"God, why did I want to help this girl, who just hours ago put me in a jealous rage? What was wrong with me?" I wondered.

I was about to walk over to strike up a conversation with her, when Buck's booming laugh broke the quiet. He was hobbling on his crutches from the main locker room with Reed, who held the door open for him, rolling his eyes at his stubborn father. "I don't need you to get every door for me, you know," he said, loud enough so we all heard. He wanted us to know he wasn't helpless, but no one would ever think that. Not of Buck Johnson, anyhow.

"Yeah, I know…just let me do the little things though, okay Pops? Humor me," Reed said, his bag weighing over his shoulder. His hair was still wet, and his body damp from his shower. He was dressed nicely, like he was getting ready to go out for the night, wearing dark jeans and a fitted black shirt rolled at the sleeves to show off his engraved watch and strong, golden forearms.

He tilted his head my way for just a brief second or two, making eye contact with me once or twice. He was talking to Dylan now, almost as if he was getting directions. His face was smirking when he turned back at me again, like he wanted to share a secret with me. I was stuck on him, not able to move away, but the burning stare from Jason couldn't be ignored. His grin was less playful, more cunning and amused. Suddenly uncomfortable, I turned my attention back to my friends, and to Rosie who had pulled up with the truck so Buck wouldn't have to walk very far.

"So, what's the deal? Are we driving back home? You staying at my house?" Sarah asked, nudging me to attention.

"Oh, uh, I guess so," I said, half of me still yearning to hear Reed's conversation. We were starting to get up to walk away, my whole heart slamming into my stomach, overwhelmed with dejection, when I felt a hand on my back, and heard his voice.

"Hey, wait up," Reed said. I spun around to face him, stumbling into his chest a little so he had to right me back on my feet. "Whoa, there's no race," he joked.

I just smiled, eagerly, wanting his next words to be, "I forgive you," and "I love you," and "forever." Instead, he looked down, chewing the inside of his cheek a little, and pinching his brow as if he wasn't sure about what he wanted to say. "Hey, so...I was hoping maybe we could talk sometime...not tonight, I can't," he said, shrugging over his shoulder where Dylan, Jenny and Jason were waiting, my heart sinking all over again. "I've got a few things to run over with Dylan. And...God, I'd really love to put them off...but I can't. I tried. There's a lot in play over the next few weeks...but, I was thinking, maybe Friday? I know you have finals coming up. So, I wanted to talk before I lost you to your books, *super nerd?*"

Super nerd. Ha. He had no idea how far from that I'd been. I would be happy, at this point, to escape my psych class with a D. But now wasn't the time to lie out my pathetic fall from academic greatness to Reed. We didn't have the time for that. So instead, I just smiled and gestured to his waiting party. "Sure, Friday's fine. You should go. Your...people are waiting," I said, unsure of what to call them, *Jenny.* He just turned to give them the one-minute sign with his hand, causing Jenny to smile and wave. I winced at her happiness, still jealous.

"Okay," he said, kicking his hands forward into mine a little, my eyes zeroing in on his small touch. "I'll be there, at your dorm, at 7. Wear something nice." He smiled as he turned to jog back to the others.

He was coming to see me in person? I had expected a phone call. But he...was taking me out? My heart was flipping inside, full of possibility. But as I watched him walk away with Dylan, Jason, and Jenny, I caught myself a little, not wanting to fall too far. And when Jason turned to give me a small wink and a shrug, his head tilting to Jenny, I questioned everything all over again.

Chapter Twenty-One

Reed

WHEN I LEFT to join Dylan and Jason at the Hyatt restaurant for our business meeting, every single fiber of my body was fighting against me. But I knew I had to take this meeting. Dylan had arranged for an informal meeting with someone on the Chargers coaching staff. To make it all seem accidental and informal, we had to set it up to be like a real evening out...like a date. And when Dylan suggested that Jason and Jenny join us to just make it work, I didn't fight her on it much. *Dammit, I regretted that now.*

Seeing Nolan's face in the stands brought me home. I knew I'd owe Sarah hugely for sneaking me a text about where they were sitting before the game started. But damn if I wasn't relieved to have her on my side this time. People say shit about your life flashing before you in moments of fear and tragedy, but I had my life play before me the moment I locked eyes on Nolan. I remembered every moment I'd done the exact same thing, sought out her face in the crowd, just to know where she was. I'd been doing it since we were kids, really. Before I was hers, and she was mine. I didn't know what the pull was then, but I understood it now.

And I'll be damned if I was going to let it go without a serious fight.

I noticed the hurt on her face when she saw me leave with Jenny. I'd have to explain what really happened, where we went, and what she was doing there. I knew I would. But I had a lot of work to do before then. I had to make my girl *whole* again. And if there was anything that had broken on my watch, well, I was going to try my damnedest to fix it.

That's what I was doing at my mother's on Thursday, and why I had to put off my first step with rebuilding my life with Nolan until Friday. I had offered to take my mom out for dinner, hoping a public venue might soften her up a little, but she was excited to see me, and always hated to share our time together. She had a special dinner prepared, and we ate at her house with Sam. I liked Sam. I did. He was nice to my mom, and incredibly tolerant of her need to be in a spotlight. But he wasn't a fighter, like my dad. He was the kind to roll over and let her get her way. And I didn't need any extra players working against me tonight, so I waited to talk to my mother in private after dinner was done.

Sam had retired to his office to "Take care of some phone calls," he said, but I had grown to know that was when my stepfather snuck in his cigars and brandy. When he left, I joined mom out on her patio for coffee. I didn't really like coffee, but I'd drink it. I'd drink anything to make time for this conversation tonight. I was nervous, like a child asking their parent for something really huge, something that meant something to them, and required trust and faith. I think what scared me most was that my mom wouldn't have either in me, not about this. But I also knew that if I didn't try, I'd regret it for the rest of my life.

"Hey, Mom? I need to ask a favor of you," I started as we slid into the comfortable recliners that overlooked the sprawling pool and water features near her patio.

"Of course, Reed sweetheart. Anything, you know that, right?" she said, and I hoped like hell she meant it…because the alternative would be ugly.

I sat up and turned sideways to face her, my elbows resting on my knees, so I could stare into the steam coming from my cup, almost hoping it would reveal some crystal-ball message that would guide me through this. Taking a deep breath, I looked up at my mom, the woman who raised me, and had always told me she would do anything it took to make me happy. "I need you to help Nolan," I said, my stomach falling out of me, and my head getting light from the nerves that were now filling my body.

My mom's lips formed a straight line, not a smile…but not a frown. Her eyebrows were low, considering perhaps? She set her cup down on a table and sat up to face me, but kept her gaze down. Afraid? "Reed…what kind of trouble is Nolan in?" my mom asked, her body visibly shuddering.

"She's had some bad things happen this semester…sort of a really shitty run of luck," I started, my mom smacking my knee at my curse word. "Sorry, I just meant it for emphasis," I kept going, taking in another deep breath before getting to the meat of my request. "Anyhow, she's been distracted—like, *really* distracted, Mom. And her scholarships are in jeopardy. And you and I both know how much those mean to her, how important they are to her…"

I waited, watching my mom's face react to what I had said. She wasn't following where I was going, I could tell. I was going to have to come flat out and ask.

"Mom, I was wondering if there was any way you would consider reviewing her scholarship packet for your foundation award?" I pulled the packet from the bag I'd kept with me most of the night. I'd spent three nights working on it, pulling everything Nolan had saved on my computer over the last two years when she filed for scholarship after scholarship, and emailing Sarah to sneak me the pieces I was missing. My mom took the packet from my hands, her lips curled into a bit of a smile, stifling a laugh. Finally, she broke out in a giggle, and held her hand over her lips a little to feign hiding it.

"Whaaaat's funny?" I asked, my brow heavy with confusion now.

My mom laughed a little harder now, sliding the packet to the side of her and covering her face with her hands while she bent forward and then sat up, blotting the laughter tears from the corners of her eyes. "Oh, Reed honey…wow, you really had me going for a minute there," my mom said, fanning herself now, trying to recover from her strange giggling fit.

"I'm sorry?" I asked, not understanding.

"Well…when you started this conversation, I was so certain you were going to tell me she was pregnant. Honey, I almost stopped breathing at the thought of that. I mean, can you imagine? You having a baby…*with that girl?*" She was laughing again at her words. Her eyes were closed with laughter, in fact. A blessing, because never in my life had I been more ashamed, and angry, with the woman who raised me. I hated her words, and they were making me hate her. Of all things she could say, of all possible reactions, this one was not something I had prepared for, and it had me reeling.

I got to my feet suddenly and pulled out my keys to start walking for the door. I had to leave before I said something awful. But I was naive thinking my mother would make this easy.

"Reed, sweetie? Oh, come on honey…you can't blame me for laughing. I mean it's really quite a ridiculous thought. I was just so surprised." My mother was walking after me now, the *tip tap* of her heels on the patio stones grating on every last one of my nerves. I just turned and stared into her eyes, stone-faced, wanting her to see how I felt about the words she spoke.

"Reed…you know I can't give any special treatment for our scholarships, honey. My hands are tied," my mother said, just holding her hands up in a tying gesture, as if I didn't get it.

Pursing my lips, I just nodded and turned back to leave.

"Reed, sweetheart? Stay, finish your coffee with me," my mom was sounding more desperate now. I stopped at the doorway, my feet urging me to leave, but my heart telling my brain that now was the time to fight. I'd made a renewed vow that I would—against anyone and anything—*no matter what* when it came to Nolan. And deep down, I knew that I'd have to have this moment with my mother.

"I'm not staying for coffee…" I started, her face falling flat.

"And Mom? I'm not coming back to see you. Frankly, I can't stand the sight of your face right now."

My mother physically stumbled backward at my words, her hand flying to her heart like she'd been wounded. But I also knew she was playing me, making this about her. But this was about Nolan, and how absolutely cruel and hateful Millie Johnson-Snyder could be.

"Don't do that," I demanded, my voice growing louder and more confident. "Don't pretend you don't know what I'm talking about, or where any of this is coming from. You know exactly where this is coming from, Mom. You have never been kind to Nolan. You judge her, disrespect her, and discount her as your equal, as someone worthy of even being a woman in your fucked-up society world. And I'm sick of it. And I'm ashamed of you. I've tried to defend you because—goddammit Mom? What son wants to admit that his mother is so heartless, cold and prejudiced? But you are!"

"You've always said you would do anything…anything, Mom! Anything to make me happy—well, Nolan makes me happy! Fuck. Mom? She's my entire damned world! And if there is ever a day in the future, where I'm lucky enough to have a child with her—to make something so amazing…*with that girl*—well…you can bet your ass that my son or daughter won't ever set foot in a household full of so much hatefulness as this one!"

"So you know what? Just forget everything I asked for tonight. I don't need anything from you. I'll find a way to help the woman I love on my own. I'm sorry that I ever thought I could count on you," I spat out everything in a matter of seconds, my body shaking, and my eyes seeing actual red as I turned and stormed from my mother's house.

I had done the impossible. I had left my mother speechless. And it hurt my heart, but I also knew it was the right thing to do, and that I was right about everything. And I'd find a way to help Nolan without her. I peeled out of the driveway as I sped onto the main road, heading back to Tucson. I replayed my conversation over in my head the entire way back to my dorm, and every single time, I was satisfied, happy I'd finally said what needed to be said.

I'd had disagreements with my mother before, but never over anything truly important. This one was going to last, and I could just tell. I thought about talking it over with Pops, but I knew he agreed with me. There was no need to bring him into it. This was my disappointment to bear, and I was finally ready.

To clear my head, I spent the rest of Thursday night preparing. I'd brainstormed just about every single overly romantic gesture known to man, and I was half tempted to pull them all out for this one date. But I also knew I had to take things slow. I was pretty satisfied with what I finally settled on, and when I called Sarah to run it by her, she agreed. If you would have asked me in high school if Sarah and I would be as close as we'd become, I would have laughed, a gut-busting kind of laugh in disbelief. But now was a different story. We were close, and Sarah was no longer just Nolan's friend—she was mine, too.

Before I would be able to focus on the evening, I knew there was some shit I just had to get out of the way. I knew when Noles would be at her writing workshop. It was the only damn thing she still went to religiously, so I counted on her being gone for at least two hours. It gave me enough time to show up early and pay a little visit to Gavin.

I could hear his pussy-ass music playing on the other side of the door when I got to his room. I smirked a little to myself, thinking about how surprised he was about to be before I knocked softly on his door. I heard the music turn down and saw the shadows of his footsteps under the doorway before he opened. When he made eye contact with me, his face fell instantly. It may have been disappointment that I was not Nolan, but I also think there was a little fear in the mix, too. And I fucking LOVED that!

"Reed, uh…what's up, man?" he said, leaning into his door a little, trying to look relaxed. I could tell from the rapid movement in his eyes that he was anything but.

"Not much, Gav. Hey, you gotta sec? I think you and I need to talk," I said, just pushing my way into his room. His walls were an interesting mixture of posters, with deep quotes, poetry and music. I saw his guitar propped up in the corner, and my stomach turned just thinking about how he probably tried to use his talent to woo my girl. This prick needed to pay.

"Yeah, uh… come in, I guess," he said, shutting his door and shrugging at me. I was leaning on his desk now, my legs crossed, and my hands in my pockets. He pulled out one of his chairs and turned it around to sit backward. I chuckled a little at him when he did this.

"So, Gavin…remember that night I saw you coming out of Nolan's room?" I said, just diving right in. I'd played this scene over in my head enough times. I was ready.

Gavin just nodded a little, looking down and laughing to himself. "Yeah, I know that night," he looked up, smiling. "Look, what the fuck do you want, Reed? Let's not beat around the bush."

"Sounds good to me," I said. "I think you owe me an apology. And, frankly, I think you owe Nolan one, too…but you can just give me hers, because there's no fucking way I'm letting you anywhere near her." I had pulled my hands from my pockets at this point and crossed my arms at my chest to flex my forearms, just for effect.

Gavin just tapped on the back of the chair a bit, looking at his hands and nodding. Finally, he took a deep breath. "Reed, you don't own her. You don't get to make decisions for her or control her life. And if she wants to spend time with me, well…I'm sorry, but that's not my fault, and you don't get a say in it," he said. *Cocky motherfucker.*

I chuckled to myself again, looking down and shaking my head. "Yeah, you're right," I said, looking back at him, locking my gaze to his. "I don't own her. But neither do you. And when you spun that little tale the other night, you weren't thinking of Nolan. You were thinking of yourself, and how you could get me out of the way so you could make your play. Genius, really. I mean, damn, I can't believe I fell for it! But shit didn't really work out like you wanted. Did it, Gavin?"

We stared at each other for seconds after I spoke. He was thinking of his next move, what to say. But I knew he was out of the picture. Fuck, he was never in the damn picture in the first place.

He was a blip in my girl's emotional meltdown. And he'd taken advantage of her, and I wanted to knock his goddamn teeth out.

"I told Nolan I'd wait. She's just getting over you, but she and I make sense, and you know it," he said, his words flaming the fire in my chest, forcing me to my feet. He stood when I did this, moving around his chair so we were now standing face to face. My mouth went flat, a straight and angry line. I was going to put this asshole in his place.

"Here's what I see, Gavin. When Nolan needed a friend, she leaned on you. And then your warped fucking mind took that shit and ran with it. You took more from her than she wanted to give, more than she wanted you to have. You wormed your way in when she was at her lowest. And that's not *making sense together*, dude… that's fucked up mind games and selfishness," I said, putting a finger in his chest to knock him off balance.

He stared at me blankly, breathing slowly. I was satisfied, and I was ready to leave. I walked to his door and put my hand on the handle, turning to give him one last warning. "Gavin, it's time for you to end this shit. You don't get to be Nolan's friend now; you've lost the privilege, understood?" I asked, waiting for his nod. I didn't expect the asshole to put up a fight, nor did I expect the words he said next.

"You sure about that, asshole? I'm not the one who knocked her up, and left her alone to figure shit out on her own. I mean, who abandons his own baby? You're fucking weak, man," he said, barely getting the end of his sentence out before I had him pressed with his back flat against the wall, my nostrils flaring, and my eyes fighting against angry tears.

"You. Don't. Get. To. Talk. About. That!" I gritted through my teeth, inches from his face, my forearm pinning him still. "You got me? That's not yours to talk about. Ever. Not a word."

I could feel his breathing change; he wasn't as sure of himself as he'd been minutes before. I waited for him to nod in understanding before I let up on his shirt, shoving him once more into the wall. "You leave Nolan the fuck alone. Or I swear to God, I will rip your pretty fucking teeth from your mouth, and you can use them to strum your fucking guitar, understood?" I waited again, and again he nodded.

One more shove, and I let my hands fall back to my side. I left his room without turning around to see his face again. I was done with Gavin. My blood was pumping through my entire body, and I wanted to scream, but I reminded myself that my message was heard. And I was pretty sure Gavin understood me loud and clear.

———

It was seriously a good thing I had more than an hour to calm myself down after dealing with Gavin. I drove up to a nearby corner market to get a Gatorade and just reset my thinking. He had me so angry, and I didn't want any of that flowing over into the night I had planned. Tonight was important, and I had to be very careful. I pulled onto a neighborhood side road and propped my leg up on my seat, popping my headphones in one ear and thumbing through my phone to make sure I knew where everything was. I found myself obsessively checking the time, recalculating how long it would take me to get back to Nolan's campus. Finally, unable to stand it any longer, I pushed my keys back into the ignition and revved my engine.

I was 20 minutes early, but I could hear Nolan in her room getting ready. I paused at the door to listen in to her phone conversation a little. It was either Sarah or Sienna on the other line, I was sure.

"He said to wear something nice…but I don't have anything *nice!* And I don't know what to do with my hair. Oh my God! He's going to be here any minute…are you sure? Yeah, that's what I'm wearing. Do you think it's nice enough?"

There was a long pause in her conversation, and I bit my lip to keep myself from laughing outside her door. She was nervous, and it was the cutest thing in the whole damn world. I was starting to think she had hung up when I heard her start talking again.

"Okay, if you promise me that it looks good and everything's okay. You swear he's not going to give me awful news and just smash my heart to pieces? Because I can't take that...not again," she said. Her words broke my fucking heart. She was worried that this was some trick, or that I was taking her out to end our relationship, for closure. I leaned against the wall, listening to her finish getting ready for another few minutes, my mind heavy with the thought of Nolan staying awake at night worrying about us. I wanted to fix everything, but I knew it would also take time. We'd both lost trust in one another, and we were going to need to get it back for us to be whole again.

I took a deep breath, and finally rapped on her door, my forehead flat on it as I listened to her approach. I straightened my posture and readied the mixed bouquet of wildflowers I'd gotten for her at the store, when I heard the lock twisting.

"Hey," I said, just smiling softly and taking her in. Her hair was straight, and swept over one shoulder. She was wearing tight black pants and a dark blue sweater that hung off one shoulder. Her exposed skin drove me wild instantly, and I just wanted to take a bite out of it, but I had to take baby steps, so after giving her a once over, I forced myself to keep my gaze up high, at her eyes.

"Hi," she said softly, unsure of herself. I noticed the slight tremble when my hand touched hers as I handed her the flowers, and I took it as a good sign. "These are amazing. Thanks, I don't get a lot of living things in here. I mean...unless you count the mold I'm growing on my bread."

She giggled at her words, my heart leaping from my chest at the sound. I laughed at her joke, trying to set her at ease. "I wasn't sure if you had a vase or anything. I think they're okay in a cup or whatever," I said, looking around her room. It looked the same, everything still in its place. But somehow, it seemed darker, lifeless. It made me sad. Nolan found an empty cup near her sink and filled it with water, setting the flowers on her night table. It made me feel good to know that she'd wake up to such a vivid reminder of me, and of tonight. Now all I had to do was not fuck things up. "Easier said than done," I thought.

I held out my arm and guided her from her room out to the Jeep. We were both quiet, and with each minute that passed without conversation, the more nervous I became, my palms actually sweating.

"So…do I get to know where we're going?" she asked, flittering her lashes at me just like she used to do in high school. *God, I was done.* I took a deep breath, and turned to her with a full smile.

"Sort of. I'll fill you in as we go. Like, right now? We're going bowling," I said, buckling up and starting the engine. Nolan's face lit up a little. She liked bowling, but we'd only ever been once. Tonight was going to be about doing all of those stupid little things we never did, or didn't do enough. And bowling made my girl smile, which was the first thing on my list.

The drive to the bowling alley was dead quiet. I tried to fill the air with my constant flipping through the various radio stations, and when I caught Nolan tapping her leg to the rhythm of one of the oldie stations, I stopped. I loved that she liked the old songs. She had an old soul. That's what Pops always said. And something about hearing some doo-wop band sing, while I looked at Nolan's smile in the moonlight, seemed right.

I thought about reaching for her hand when we walked into the bowling alley, but she had grabbed her jacket and purse, and was hugging them close to her chest, I think partly to shield herself from me. She wasn't herself anymore, and she was so damned uncomfortable around me. It was killing me. I hadn't kissed her in weeks, and all I wanted was to taste her lips, crush my mouth to hers and make her drop her purse to the ground, reaching for neck and hair. God, the way she used to tug at my hair and wrap her legs around my waist like I was some sort of tree, and she was the spider monkey…I had to quit thinking about it, because tonight was about taking it slow. And right now, I was seconds from throwing that theory out the window.

We picked up our shoes and headed to our lane. I found a ball right away, but Nolan was always picky. She wanted the perfect weight, the perfect thumbhole, and the perfect color. She finally settled on an ugly lime-colored ball and set it on our return.

"Really? All that time, and you come back with the slime ball?" I teased her. Her smile was refreshing, and I watched her shoulders relax while she swapped out her boots for her retro black-and-white bowling shoes.

"Hey, fancy-ass quarterback. You might be able to throw a pigskin, but I bet me and slime ball can school you out here," she sassed at me as she lifted her ball and propped it on her hip like a six-shooter. Slow was going to be really fucking hard tonight.

I considered her wager for a bit, and it gave me an idea. "Okay, let's have some fun with this," I said, lifting my ball now and mimicking her pose. "If you win, you get to pick what we do next. But if I win, we go skinny dipping."

This marked the first time ever—in the history of my knowing Nolan Lennox—that I saw her jaw actually drop. I also knew she didn't like to back down from a bet. I raised the bar with this one, and probably threw my whole plan to shit, but I didn't care. She was chewing on her bottom lip and wiggling it side-to-side when she finally nodded once. "Okay, you're on," she said, a flash of passion in her eyes. I hadn't seen this side of Nolan in months, and if I had to throw 10 strikes in a row to keep it alive, I was going to summon everything I had.

I set Nolan up to go first, because I wanted to know exactly what I needed to keep up with each round. She was good at bowling, so I knew it wouldn't be easy. But, it wasn't a game of pool, so I had a chance. And the fact that she knew I did, excited me even more.

She scored a nine her first frame, and I matched her pin-for-pin. She followed that up with two strikes and a couple of spares, and I was starting to fall a little behind. I had to do something to get my edge back, so I headed to the snack bar while she was throwing her sixth frame and grabbed a pitcher of beer and some nachos.

When I came back, she had her arms folded and was staring at me like I was in trouble. I just shrugged a bit and gestured *what?* "So, I'm guessing I'm not getting a real dinner tonight then, Johnson," she said, reaching for a glass and pouring a beer.

I held out my glass, and she poured me one next. "Noles, are you telling me nachos aren't a *real* dinner?" I said, grabbing one that was dripping with peppers and cheese, and tilting my head back while I ate it, smiling at her while I wiped my mouth on my sleeve.

She reached for a pepper then, and just ate it straight, looking right in my eyes while she did. "It'll do," she said with a wink, and then took a small sip of her beer. I was glad to see her go slowly. I'd had my fill of Nolan and drinking when she threw up on my best jeans the other night.

She still seemed in control on the lanes. I was hoping to get inside her head a little, make her miss a shot here and there, but she was too cool for that. I was down seven pins by the time the last frame came up, and I knew I'd need her to miss at least one toss to have a chance. She was standing at the ball return waving her hand in front of the air when she turned to me, a cocky grin on her face. "Looks like I'm picking what we do next, Wildcat," she teased, turning around to reach for her ball as it slid up the belt.

Her back was to me and she wasn't paying attention. I capitalized on this moment. It was my only chance, and it was the slightest opening to do something I'd been dying to do since I'd picked her up that night. I rushed up behind her as she lifted her ball, and leaned forward so my mouth barely grazed her ear. "You…are beautiful," I whispered, lingering there just long enough for her to feel my breath and anticipate my touch that wouldn't come, and her body reacted. I backed away slowly, satisfied by the tiny bumps raised on her neck and arms by my breath. More than wanting to rattle her enough to win our bowling match, I wanted to see if Nolan still felt me. And I knew instantly then that she did.

She refused to turn around, but she walked up to the wood floor slowly, holding her ball delicately in one hand. She tossed it down the lane, and knocked over only a pin or two. She turned slowly to walk back to the return and locked her eyes on mine. They were serious now, not angry and not nervous, but considering perhaps? She kept staring at me until her ball returned and rolled into her hand. She lifted it, and walked backward to the lane before she dropped it, not even looking, down in the gutter, and pushed it to the pins.

She just fucking threw in the towel. On purpose!

She walked back to me, her eyes hooded ever so slightly, and her breath held. I picked up my ball, and held her gaze until I turned and lined myself up, and threw three strikes in a row. When the last pin fell, I turned at the end of the lane to look at her. She was standing next to the ball return, staring right back at me, hungry.

"Screw it," I thought, as I walked up to her and pushed my fingers through her hair, and covered her mouth with mine. I reached around to her lower back and lifted her into me, her feet gliding up from the floor slightly as she reached around and pulled herself up with her hands gripping my shoulders.

I kissed her for a full minute, and I kissed her hard. And she kissed back. The lanes were filled with nothing but old smokers and drunks, and no one cared about the scene we were making, but I knew I had to cool it off. If I was planning to make her go through with her bet—which I had no intention of letting her out of—I was going to need to slow this down.

I slid my hands to her face and pulled my lips away softly, looking into her eyes the entire time. She looked like she wanted to weep from the loss of my touch, so I just reached for the small hairs that had slid into her face and smoothed them behind her ear. I tilted the corner of my mouth into a grin then hoping that would ease her worry. "So…where's the nearest pool," I asked, reaching down for her hand and kissing the top of it.

———

I think maybe there was a part of Nolan that thought I was kidding or wouldn't go through with the bet. So when she told me the closest pool was probably at one of the nearby hotels, and I pulled right into the Tempe Double Tree Resort, I think she was reconsidering throwing that bowling match.

"You coming?" I asked as I hopped out of the Jeep and walked down the main corridor for the hotel. I heard Nolan shut the door timidly behind me, but I knew she was there. The pool was in the back at this hotel, which was good, because it gave us a certain amount of privacy. I didn't even turn around to see her reaction when I kicked off my shoes, yanked down my jeans, and tossed my sweater on a nearby chair. I ran at the pool and dove in head first, figuring getting the shock of the freezing water out of my system quickly was probably the best move. I began to rethink that when the first touch of the water left me breathless.

"Whooooooaaaa ohh ohhh ohhh," I screamed as I popped back up from the water. Nolan started giggling then, and shrinking herself out of embarrassment.

"Shhhhhhh, you're so going to get us in trouble. You can't be loud," she said, kicking her shoes off now. She managed to strip herself down to her bra and panties without pausing and realizing how crazy this was. She stopped, though, when she realized I was watching her every move. I'd missed her body, and I'd wanted to take a bite out of her bare shoulder all night. Seeing her porcelain skin delicately wrapped in tiny black lace about had me undone. Realizing she was nervous, I kicked off my boxers and tossed the soaking material up on the deck, grinning at her from ear-to-ear.

"Bet's a bet, sweetheart...pay up," I said, proud of myself. I kicked backward to the other side of the pool and propped myself on the edge with my elbows, watching and waiting.

Nolan looked around again and chewed on her fingernails while she stepped forward and dipped her toe in the pool. "Ohhhhh no way, that's fucking freezing!" she whispered loudly. Sometimes it was cute when she swore. She hardly ever did, and for some reason it made it special when she would—made her seem real, and in-the-moment.

"Nah, you get used to it fast," I said, my teeth chattering just a bit. "Come on in, the water's fine."

Nolan wrapped her arms around her body, hugging herself a bit, and then finally slid both straps of her bra down her arms before reaching around and unhooking the rest. She held the material in place for a few more seconds before she finally tossed it in the pile with the rest of her clothes. Instantly, I realized what a bad, and wonderful, idea this was at the same time. She was stunning, and perfect, and everything I ever wanted physically. And she was so fucking vulnerable.

She moved forward to the steps and walked into the pool quickly, dunking her head and then coming up, gasping for air.

"Shit! That's realllllllly cold," she chattered. "You asshole!" She splashed water at me then, and I laughed, reaching for her hands to stop them from flailing waves at me. When I finally grabbed hold of her arm, she relented instantaneously, and just stopped and stared into me, grazing her bottom lip with her teeth. She reached down to pull her panties off and tossed them behind her with the rest of our clothes on the deck.

"Okay, you win. Now what?" she said, her face challenging me. I just held her hand in mine and stood there in the near freezing water, my teeth no longer chattering because of the heat firing through both of our bodies. I moved a little closer and held her eyes with mine.

"Now I'm going to kiss you...again," I said, moving even closer, and reaching down to hold her up in the water at her hips. Her breath hitched at my touch as I leaned my forehead into hers, our breath combining with the frostiness of the pool water to make fog. I slid my hands up her sides, under her arms, careful not to take anything too far. I was fighting against every instinct I had, but I was determined to leave her wanting more tonight. When my hands made their way to her jaw and her face, my thumbs stroking each cheek, she closed her eyes completely, and she leaned her face sideways into my palm. Leaning forward, I kissed her softly. It was *our* kiss, slow, and patient, and tender. She didn't need to know how sexy I thought she was; she needed to know I still loved her. And this kiss was the only way I knew how.

I spun her around slowly while I brushed my lips on hers over and over, taking small nips at her bottom lip and tasting her softly with my tongue. It was probably only minutes, but it felt like I had been kissing her for hours. When her body finally started to shake from the chills in the night air, I stopped, pulling her close, her body pressed tightly to mine. *God it felt amazing.*

"I think we need to get you dressed. And I think we need to turn on my heater," I smiled, pressing my forehead to hers again.

"I th...th....think, that's a g...goo...good idea," she said, her body starting the quiver uncontrollably now.

I chuckled a little as I climbed out of the pool and pulled on my jeans. I handed my sweater to her to cover up with as soon as she climbed out of the pool water. We quietly gathered up our clothes and sprinted back to my Jeep where we redressed and cranked the heat, giggling like the 16-year-olds we used to be. When we finally got control of our laughter, I reached over and pulled Nolan's chin up toward me, and kissed her once more, softly, before leaning back into my seat, buckling the belt, and pulling out of the hotel lot.

It was maybe 11 p.m. when I walked her back up to her room and kissed her on the cheek to say goodnight. I could tell she wanted me to stay, and every piece of me wanted to. But that was too fast. Hell, I jumped over five or six spaces on the game board already tonight.

We had practice in the morning, and things were going to be pretty busy for me until the semester finished. We were getting ready for the bowl announcements, though we were pretty sure we had the Rose Bowl all sewn up. I told Nolan that we would pick up where things left off as soon as the semester was done, and that this was just the first of many dates like this, at least, I hoped. She grew quiet as the night ended, I think still unsure of where we stood. I knew we had to get our trust back in one another, and I knew she still worried about Jenny, and how I felt about her. But I planned on earning every piece of her back, and rebuilding her to be whole again, starting with her heart.

Chapter Twenty-Two

Nolan

I CALLED Sarah as soon as Reed dropped me off, spilling every word about our date, just like I was back in high school and had just received my first kiss. I couldn't believe I'd stripped naked in a public pool just to challenge him in some bet, but *Oh my God* it was the best bet I'd ever blown.

Reed's touch had the power to erase so many things. For one night, I didn't think about Gavin, or grades, or scholarships, or tuition. But when I tried to sleep that night, I did wonder about what Reed was thinking. He still hadn't brought up the miscarriage, but neither did I.

When I didn't hear from him at all the next day, I slipped back into my old habits, my room dark, and my fire instantly diminished. By the time Sarah and Sienna came to pick me up for our girls' night dinner, I had convinced myself that he was playing me, while seeing Jenny. I was hesitant to tell them my thoughts at first but, since I really didn't have anyone else to lean on, I found myself blubbering over burgers and fries at the sports bar we all went to.

"Nolan, you do realize that you're crazy, right?" Sienna said, leaning forward and forcing me to look her in the eyes. "Reed is about to get a bowl bid, he had practice all day, he's working with Dylan, and scouts and business people and, lord knows Buck's probably involved."

I smiled a little at Sienna's words forcing myself to consider everything with a fresh perspective. She was right, and I was automatically assuming the worst. It was something I needed to stop doing, and I was about to declare it publicly, when a glimmer flashed by my eyes briefly, but long enough for me to register what it was.

"Holy shit, Sienna. Is that what I think it is?" I said, pointing to her hand. She blushed a little, and then brought her hand to the table to reveal a giant diamond engagement ring. Sarah and I just stared at it with mouths open before reaching over and hugging her, screaming so the entire restaurant turned to our table.

"You bitch, you held out on us," Sarah said, slugging her on the shoulder a little. Sienna just rubbed it, and elbowed her back.

"No, I just couldn't seem to find the right time. He just asked me last night," she was beaming. I took her hand in mine and studied the ring even more while she told us the story about how Micah had led her on a treasure hunt around their apartment for what she thought was a special dessert. She said he had called her parents and got down on one knee and everything. My heart was soaring for my friend and racing with hope at the same time that maybe, someday, I would be the one my girlfriends were screaming over.

———

My worries from earlier in the day were laid to rest later that night when I got a string of texts from Reed.

I'm so sorry I was so busy today. Didn't have any time to call. But I missed you. No swimming without me ; -)
XXOO

He had signed every message the same, and I was a giddy teenager all over again. We texted or talked every night until the end of the semester, and we made plans for our second, second-chance date when I got home. I still couldn't seem to get myself to ask Reed about his date with Jenny that night after the game, or if it even was one. I seemed to be caught in this strange place between wanting to just trust him, and also being bitterly jealous.

I was heading to Sarah's with most of my clothes and shoes packed in a giant rolling suitcase, when I ran into Gavin in the elevator. He seemed to flinch a little at seeing me, and I wasn't so sure how to react to him either. We hadn't talked much since I quit going to psych, dropping the class under emergency with the promise of taking it again next semester—*hopefully with much better results.*

Uncomfortable, but also not wanting to be rude, I smiled at him faintly and motioned to his bag of belongings. "Heading home?" I asked, going for the obvious question. This was clearly polite conversation.

"Oh, uh...yeah. I'm driving out. It's good to have a car at home, ya know?" he said, nodding a bit at my bag. "You heading out with the girls?"

"Yeah, I'm driving in with Sarah. Calley took their car, and I like having someone to ride with," I said, letting the rest of the elevator ride go silent. We were both staring at the floor now, working hard not to make eye contact with one another. I don't know what made me speak up as the doors were opening and we were both wheeling our bags out, but something made me, like I needed closure. "So, see you in January?"

Gavin just nodded slowly at first, stopping in the lobby and looking down at his feet. "Yeah, uh...probably not, Noles. I'm moving into Cortez Hall. It's just a better spot for me, closer to the psych building and all," he said, sucking in his bottom lip a bit uncomfortably.

"Oh," I said softly, a little confused by this information, but also a little grateful that I might not have to see him again. "Well, maybe I'll see you on campus, or in another class sometime."

"Yeah…that'd be nice. I mean, I'd like that," he said, backing up with his bag and pulling his beanie on his head. "Take care of yourself, okay?"

I just nodded in return and let him walk out well before me so I wouldn't have to see him anymore. Our final exchange was strange, but there really was no way around that. I'd made it that way the moment I kissed him. But the thought that I might get a chance to earn back all that I'd lost, gave me hope, and there just wasn't room for Gavin in any of that.

———

Sarah and I were driving back to Coolidge on Sunday evening because of some dance recital she had managed to squeeze into for the weekend. Sarah's dance had really evolved. She was constantly being requested for senior choreography projects and being put in showcases at the arts college. I loved to watch her. The things her body could do were truly amazing. It was odd to think of her tough and rough personality when watching her bend and twist in ways so beautiful they almost brought tears to my eyes.

Sarah was packing the rest of her things late Sunday afternoon while I texted back and forth with Reed. He was at some fancy hotel in Tucson with a television crew waiting for the Selection Sunday announcement for the Rose Bowl. Our conversations were playful, and our texts were flirtatious, but never anything more since our skinny-dipping make-out session. I still hadn't asked about Jenny, but Reed also never brought her up.

I was so anxious for our next date, and for being home with Reed. I knew he'd have to leave right after Christmas for the Rose Bowl, and we probably wouldn't get to spend New Year's together, but there was something warm and full of possibility about the holiday season. Coolidge always had a holiday festival in the streets of the downtown, where every historic building was wrapped in lights, and families came out to share desserts, cocoa and popcorn. It was one of the best things about being in a small town.

The news cut in for a live shot where Reed was sitting with Trig and a few other players along with their coach. I texted him—teasing him a little, just to make him sweat.

Uh, so I just saw you on TV. You might want to check your hair.

The camera was still on him, and I saw him look in his lap to read my text. He immediately brushed his hand through his hair and bumped Trig's shoulder to ask him if he looked okay. I laughed out loud.

You are such a girl. I was just kidding : - P

I saw a smirk spread across his face next, and he looked directly into the camera, right at me, before he snuck his phone into his lap again and shot back a quick message. The station went to a commercial break just then.

That was not nice…but funny as hell.

My small prank had my mind spinning a bit, and it gave me an idea. I texted him back right away.

Hey, so…wanna make a wager?

I waited, and he wrote back in seconds.

Hmmmmm, I'm curious. What are the terms?

I grinned and slid down into the sofa so I could hide a little from Sarah, who was busy tidying things up in her kitchen.

When they interview you after the announcement, if you can work the word 'coconut' into your response, I will spend tonight in your room.

He responded instantly.

Tonight? In my room? All for coconut?

I wrote back:

Yes.

Reed was fast again.

Deal. You better have your PJs packed, Princess.

I giggled silently to myself. Truth was I was winning in two ways. I'd give anything for more time to reconnect with Reed, and seeing him work an absurd word into a national TV interview was priceless. Sarah had finished her packing and cleaning and was sitting on the corner of her sofa next to me. I looked up and told her we could leave as soon as Reed's school was announced; there was no way I was missing this.

The Rose Bowl committee made their announcement right after

the commercial break, and the camera turned to a room full of cheering UofA students, and then settled in on Reed, Trig and his coach.

"We're here with Reed Johnson, whose name is being thrown around in a lot of Heisman conversations lately...Reed? How excited are you to face Ohio State in the Rose Bowl?"

Reed was wearing his modest grin, his dimples deep, and his eyes squinted a bit from the attention. He was so amazingly talented, but he always hated being singled out as the reason his team was doing so well, even though he was precisely the reason they were. "Thanks for that, Wendy. Well...it's pretty awesome being in the Rose Bowl for a second year in a row. Ohio State is a great team, but I feel pretty good about our chances," Reed said, leaning sideways in his chair to get more comfortable.

"And what about the Heisman hype? Does that distract you at all?" the reporter questioned him again, pushing him for more. But as always, Reed was so cool in the face of big-time pressure. He just smiled again and chuckled to himself.

"I mean, I'd be *coconuts* not to be a little excited about the idea of winning a Heisman," he said it. He looked right into the camera after his answer, right at me, and winked a bit with a smile, before he continued on. He was adorable, and I was as in love as I'd ever been. "But it doesn't take away from the game. The game is my first priority. I worry about one game at a time. It's worked out pretty well for me so far."

"Well, alright then. Congratulations to you, and the Wildcats, Reed. We look forward to seeing this great match up," the reporter said as the camera angle swung wide. I was dizzy with giddiness one instant, and then suddenly lost it all the moment I saw Jenny standing in the background, her eyes bright and focused on Reed, while she clapped and cheered—all for him.

"Why was she there? And what was she to Reed?" I asked myself.

"Steve, I'm sending it over to you to give us a little insight into what Ohio State thinks about this match up, as well as quarterback Ian Herring. Steve?" the reporter signed off and the coverage shifted. I picked up the remote and turned the TV off only to find Sarah smirking at me, standing with her arms crossed.

"What?" I said, shrugging and trying to brush her attention off.

"You know what? You two are so syrupy sweet. It would be *disgusting* if I didn't love you so much," she said, punching me lightly in the arm. I had to smile at her words.

"Yeah," I paused and sighed a little. "It feels like we're almost back…I just feel like there are these big clouds out there floating over us, though, know what I mean? I still feel weird about Jenny. Is he dating us both? Was she just a one-night stand? And he still hasn't brought up my miscarriage, Sar. I mean, that's weird, right?"

Sarah turned away from me, refusing to make eye contact, and immediately my suspicion rose. "What? What do you know?" I questioned her, crawling over the back of her sofa to run into her, and force her to look me in the eye. She pushed her lips into a hard line and then exhaled heavily.

"Noles, Reed didn't know. Not at first. This whole time, when you thought he was ignoring you, ignoring what happened. He didn't know," her words were so foreign, they seemed impossible. I just shook my head, not understanding. She slumped her shoulders and grabbed mine to look me in the eye. "He never listened to the message. Not until I told him to."

My eyes went wide, my mind playing back memories of the last three months, trying to fit this new information together with everything I had done, everything Reed had thought, and where we were now. "When? When did you tell him?" I stuttered, my body shaking a bit with adrenaline and renewed understanding.

"The night we all went out…after Thanksgiving. He called me and said you mentioned it in your drunken stupor. You were a nightmare, by the way," she paused to point out before continuing on. "Nolan, he was crying and upset. He was devastated."

My heart broke a little thinking of Reed's reaction. "Was he angry?" I asked, suddenly feeling sick and leaning into Sarah's counter to hold my weight up.

"No. That's what I'm trying to tell you. Nolan, he was so upset over you and everything you were going through," she said, stopping herself short when I snapped my eyes to hers.

"What do you mean what I've been going through?" I asked, praying she hadn't told Reed every detail of my crumbling life.

"Yeah, Nolan. Reed and I, we've been talking. A lot. You're going to get pissed and find this out eventually, so you might as well know now. I'm worried about you. Sienna's worried about you. You're flunking out, losing your scholarships. You're a mess! And I told Reed. He knows everything," she said, her shoulders sagging again with the weight of it all.

I held my hand over my mouth just listening to her words, embarrassed and ashamed. I knew it was all true, but I still didn't like hearing it. I was the together one. I didn't fall apart. And the thought that Reed was just being nice to me, showing me attention, because he felt bad for me also ran through my mind.

"Nolan, stop that. You're getting ahead of yourself, I can tell," Sarah said, forcing my eyes to hers. "Stop it. You and Reed are figuring things out. It's not pity."

"Sarah, how do you know? What if it's all just guilt?" I said, my stomach twisting and my heart sinking a little more.

"Because, I know. I'm never wrong. Like...ever. Now grab your shit; we're going home," she said, turning on me and not letting me get another word in. It was her style. Tough and to-the-point, and I knew I was better off following her directions. I also knew I'd continue to worry silently.

———

Sarah and I were just turning onto the main desert highway when my phone buzzed, bringing me out of my self-pity funk for just a moment. I reached into my console and pushed until I found the talk button and put the phone to my ear.

"Hello?" I asked, not sure who was calling.

"Hey, honey," my mom said, her voice sounding a little flat and depressed.

"Oh, hi. I didn't see the number. Sarah and I are on our way. I just have to drop her off then I'll be home," I said, excited to be going home.

"Honey, that's the thing…" my mom started, my mind taking over and going in a million directions over what her next round of news could be. I was slowing down on the highway now, and Sarah was staring at me, worried.

"Oh God, what is it?" I said, choking a bit with panic.

"No, no…honey, don't worry. Everyone is fine. Everyone is just fine," she continued, knowing that I was imagining the worst. "It's the house. We…we had a small fire this morning. It was the laundry room, actually. Something about the dryer vent."

I relaxed immediately, my home being damaged—nothing compared to what my mind was conjuring. "Oh, thank God. Well, do I have to sleep on the sofa or something?" I asked, knowing I shared a wall with the laundry room.

"Well…it's a little bigger than that, I'm afraid. The fire destroyed your entire room. Honey, I'm so sorry," my mom was crying a little, giving me the news. I was just so relieved that everyone was okay, and that it was only a fire, only stuff.

"It's okay, really mom. I have most of the things I need at school. I'm just glad you and Dad are okay," I said, trying to calm her. She let out a big breath and seemed to settle again when I spoke. "Well, what's the plan then? Are we going to a hotel for a bit? Do they just board it up?"

"Ohhh, nooooooo. Honey, it's bigger than that," my mom said, and I could almost visualize her eyebrows rising as she spoke. "We're going to need to live with grandma and grandpa for a while. Your dad and I have the truck packed, and the insurance adjusters are coming out next week to figure things out. Work will be slow over the holidays, but we should be back in by spring."

Suddenly, the gravity of everything hit me. But it wasn't my home and my things—it was Reed. I wouldn't be near him, and I didn't think I could live without that right now. "Do…do we have to?" my voice broke a little as I spoke.

"I know it's really awful timing, Nolan. But the house, it just isn't livable right now," my mom said. "Hold on…" I heard her muffle the phone and could hear my father and her talking in the background. At this pause, Sarah slapped at my leg to get my attention. I just grimaced at her and mouthed "Hang on."

"Okay, I'm not totally sure how I feel about this. But your dad said Buck offered to let us stay in his guest house," my mom started, and I broke in, not letting her finish.

"Yes. Yes, yes, yes. Let's do that," I was overly enthusiastic, causing my mom to laugh nervously.

"Yeah, I figured that's what you'd say. Funny, your father was just as excited," my mom said, her tone noting a bit of sarcasm.

"That's just a long time for a grown man to live with his in-laws," I heard my father say in the background.

"Yeah, yeah. Okay, well, it seems like plans are changing. Why don't you come to the house just like you planned, and then we'll figure it out from there before we head to Buck's," my mom said, giving in, and giving me the greatest Christmas gift ever in the process.

"Okay, I'll see you in an hour," I said, hanging up, and then explaining everything to Sarah.

Chapter Twenty-Three

Reed

NOLAN'S HOME was in pieces, and when my dad told me about it, I wanted to run to her and be with her when she found out. I knew the loss would hit her hard when it sank in, but I had to admit, the thought of her being in my house, within reach, for the entire winter break had me filled with the excitement of a kid waiting for Santa to come.

My dad had left as soon as the TV interviews were done, and when he called a few minutes later to let me know the Lennoxes would be staying with us, I jumped in the Jeep and wasn't far behind. Practices were light for the next few days, but would get more and more serious the closer we got to the bowl game. It was always weird being on campus when everyone was gone, like a ghost town. We were given a couple of days off over Christmas to spend time with our families, and then it would be pretty strict, and the focus on football got serious. I'd still get to head home a few times to see Nolan, though, and that's all that mattered. I thought maybe she could stay in my room when I was gone, and the thought of her being there, sleeping in my bed, made me crazy, and I drove a whole hell of a lot faster.

My dad and I headed over to the Lennoxes late Sunday afternoon. I knew Nolan would be home soon, and I wanted to see how bad everything was before she got there, so I could try to ease her shock.

Her room was completely gutted, nothing left. Her clothes were charred shreds of their former selves, and her books and papers and charms that hung on her walls were blackened with soot and smoke stains. Nolan's mom said she seemed to deal with the news over the phone, but I knew when she saw what was left, how everything was destroyed, it would break her heart.

I reached down, and recognized a scrap of one of her T-shirts. It was a MicNic's shirt, probably her oldest. I remembered it from high school, she'd put holes in it she wore it so much. When I looked up to take inventory of all of her bare hangers, and realized all she'd lost, an idea struck me. I called Sienna to bring her in on my scheme, and we made plans to scour Coolidge's Goodwill stores over the weekend. I was going to do my best to replace what she'd lost—at least when I could.

Before long, Nolan was pulling into the driveway. Pops and I had loaded up his truck with the rest of her family's things, so hopefully she wouldn't have to be in her house long. My heart leapt at seeing her, and I noticed a smile on her face, too. It was a good start, and I'd just have to work my ass off to keep it there.

"Hey," I said, walking over to her car door and pulling it open while she stepped out.

"Hey," she said shyly. "So, I guess my room exploded." She had her sense of humor, another good sign.

"Yeah, it's pretty bad. I'm not sure you should see it," I said, reaching for her hand and locking my fingers with hers. She stared down at them, her breath stopping as she bit her bottom lip, and then tilted her chin back up to look at me.

"I'll be fine," she said, convincingly.

I led her around the back of her house, her parents and my dad following. Her dad was explaining what the fire inspectors had told him about the dryer causing the fire. Nolan just surveyed everything, taking it in. She poked her head through the exposed wall and floor, looking at the remains of her room. She reached up to blot her eyes, the scene affecting her more than she thought it would. I was worried about this. I just squeezed her hand tighter and pulled her in for a hug. She snuggled her face into my chest and turned to look up at me.

"I'm fine, I promise. It's just...a little hard to see, if that makes sense. I know it's just stuff," she said, her face a little more dejected now.

"Yeah, it's just stuff. The important things are all okay," I said, squeezing her again and kissing the top of her head. She grabbed onto the front of my shirt with her fists, resting her forehead under my chin for a moment while she kicked her feet and stared at the ground.

"Well, I guess it's a good thing you said *coconut,*" she laughed.

"Yeah, good thing," I laughed, too. "Tell me, how ridiculous was that interview?" I led her back to her car so we could all caravan to my dad's house, our hands still glued to one another. She got into her car and left the door open so we could talk.

"Coconuts? You are coconuts? That's the best you could come up with?" She teased me, poking at my stomach a little. I just shrugged and raised my hands. I'd won, and that's all that mattered.

———

When we got home, Rosie had already set up the guesthouse behind the garage for the Lennoxes. There were two bedrooms, but I hoped like hell Nolan wouldn't be staying in one of them. Even though she was 20, I still felt like we were kids when her dad was around. I didn't want to disrespect him, but I also wanted to have Nolan with me at night. Despite my wishes, she slept with her family for the first few nights. I wasn't around much, splitting my time between Pop's house and campus for practices, so I didn't push my luck until I came home for our full practice break on the 23rd.

"So, you're not planning on welching on that bet, are you?" I asked Nolan, kicking her feet from the barstool in our kitchen while she read the paper and picked at one of Rosie's famous omelets. She put her fork down and shoved my shoulder playfully and I pretended to be hurt. "Hey, watch the arm, killer."

She smiled big, her eyes crinkling, while she stuffed a full bite into her mouth. "I don't welch on bets, Wildcat," she said with her hot attitude. *So goddamned cute.* "I'll pay up. Tonight."

She didn't look at me when I walked around her, instead continuing with her breakfast and pretending like none of this affected her. I took advantage of it and leaned in, grazing my lips on her neck, and then whispered in her ear. "Good. You might want to nap. Because we're not sleeping," I said, biting at her a bit and then backing away when she turned to look at me, her eyes full of embarrassment and surprise as she looked around to make sure no one else heard. I just winked and walked outside to join my dad on the patio and left her there, breathless.

————

Night couldn't come soon enough. Nolan had spent the day with the girls, and I spent the entire afternoon getting everything ready with Sean. We had a lot to catch up on. When I told him that Nolan had lost a baby, it hit him pretty hard. Suddenly so many things were making sense. He was so enthusiastic about helping me set up all of Nolan's surprises. My dad liked to have everyone open presents on Christmas Eve, and Nolan would be at her grandparents' house for Christmas while I would be at my mom's with Jason—something that I was seriously considering skipping for the first time in my life. Tonight was our only chance to have a holiday just for us. And I wanted it to be perfect.

The sun was setting by the time Sarah's car pulled in the driveway, and Nolan hopped out. I had been waiting in the living room for more than an hour, everything ready for her to arrive. I texted Sarah, and told her not to let Nolan eat dinner so she'd be hungry by the time she got home. She clicked the front door open and stopped in her tracks when she saw the table dressed for two, candles and all.

"Wow, Reed. Did you do this all yourself?" she was surprised.

"I had some help," I shrugged. She knew Rosie did most of the heavy lifting. "It's Rosie's lasagna. I hope you're hungry."

She smiled and kicked her shoes off, sliding over to the table. "I'm starving!" she said, pulling out her chair before I could. I was a little disappointed so I grabbed her napkin before she could take that gesture from me as well, only I knocked over the water glass when I reached for it, dumping a full glass on her lap. "Oh man!" she shrieked, standing right away and reaching for the napkin to try to dry her legs. "That's cold stuff!"

Damn. I was ruining it already. I reached for the other napkin and tried to help her dry her now soaking jeans. "Stupid. I'm so sorry," I said. She just started giggling, instantly making me feel better.

"It's okay," she tossed her now soaking napkin on the table. "I think, though…I'm gonna need some pants."

"Right," I said, looking at the giant dark spots on her lap. I pointed to her and signaled that I'd be right back and ran upstairs to grab a pair of my sweatpants. I came back down and gave them to her, and she ducked into the powder room to change. I cleaned the rest of the water from the table before she came back out, my sweats draping on her body but looking *so good*. I just wanted to lift her in my arms right then, but I was determined to get the evening back on course. I went to reach for her chair again, but she just held up a hand, laughing a bit.

"I appreciate it, Reed. I really do. But I got it," she said. I slumped and just let her pull out her own chair and serve herself. *I was a nervous wreck!*

We ate Rosie's dinner, and each indulged in a piece of cheese-cake before I led Nolan over to the sofa. *It's a Wonderful Life* was on tonight, her favorite Christmas movie. I pulled a blanket from the back of the sofa and held it up, encouraging her to snuggle into my side. She hesitated, and then moved into me, her body warm. I could feel her heart beating in her ribs, and she was cautious at first before finally relaxing against me.

We watched the start of the movie in silence, all the way up to the point where the main character, George, runs to the bridge, desperate, and feeling like a failure.

God, could I relate—a couple of years ago I felt exactly the same. But I had this amazing girl, *this girl right next to me,* who pulled me out of my funk.

I could sense that Nolan wanted to talk. She would lean forward every so often and open her mouth before settling back down and deciding against it. When she did it for a third time, I had to laugh. "Good grief, woman. What's wrong? Do you have to pee?" I poked her sides, teasing her. She giggled and slid to the side away from me.

"No," she smiled, and then her mouth dipped just a bit. "I wanted to ask you about something...it's sort of been bothering me." Her lips were tight, and she was picking at her fingers, looking down. I reached for her hand and grabbed her, pulling her into me and laying her across my lap.

"Ask me anything," I said, kissing her lips quickly and startling her.

"Okay," she took a deep breath. "Are you...seeing Jenny?"

I started laughing instantly, causing her brow to scrunch. She sat up and pushed back from me some, her feelings clearly hurt. "I'm sorry. I'm not laughing at you, I swear," I said, pulling her back in. "I'm laughing at the thought of me with Jenny. Oh God, that would be awful. Mini Dylan!"

Nolan smiled at this. I did have to come clean, though. No more secrets. Ever. I brushed her hair back from her face and looked at her for a minute, considering my words carefully. "Okay, how much do you want to know? I mean, there is *nothing* bad. I promise. But the story of how I know Jenny, well...it might make you uncomfortable. I don't want to do that, not tonight, unless you want me to."

She seemed to consider this for a while, chewing on the inside of her mouth, thinking, and looking down at her twisting hands before meeting my gaze. "I'm good with it all. I want to know everything," she nodded and I nodded back.

"Okay. Well," I started, pausing to think back to the first night I met Jenny. I decided it was best to tell Nolan everything, so I started with the trip to the bar with Trig. When I told her about Jenny stripping in her apartment, her face turned sick. I held my hand up and finished that part quickly. I wanted her to know that I left Jenny standing there, that all I thought about was *her* that night. Then I told her about Gavin, and the words we'd had that night in her hallway, which made her angry.

"Son of a bitch!" she shot up from the sofa and stood now. "I trusted that guy! Oh my God, I was so nice to him the other day in the elevator. I was downright polite!"

She started to pace, and I just stood up so she'd run into me, and grabbed her, pulling her into a hug. "It's okay," I said. "And trust me, I don't think he'll be bothering you." I just looked at her and held her gaze, until I saw realization hit her. She didn't ask for any details, but I knew she got the point.

"So you're not seeing Jenny?" she asked one more time.

"No, absolutely not. I'm only seeing one girl. Haven't really seen anyone else since I laid eyes on her," I said, pulling out every ounce of Johnson charm now. It seemed to work, because she looked down and smiled faintly, kicking her feet and shrinking with embarrassment from the attention. She looked up then, and scrunched her brow a little.

"Alright, I believe you. There's just one thing," she started.

"Anything," I reminded her.

"Why were you going out with her, and Dylan and Jason the other night? And I saw her in the background at your interview, too," she said, her voice unsure again. I'd forgotten about that in the midst of everything else I had been planning. I had meant to explain my date to her, and instantly felt bad that I'd let her fret and worry needlessly for the last few weeks.

"I'm so sorry, I meant to tell you about that. It was a business meeting Dylan set up. She invited Jason and Jenny to make it less formal, so we wouldn't raise any eyebrows. God, I didn't want to go. But I had to," I said, looking her right in the eyes. "And she got a ride with Dylan, so she was just at the interview waiting around." I paused for her to take it all in, wanting to make sure there was nothing else standing between her heart and mine before I moved on with the rest of my plan. Finally satisfied, I moved on to phase two.

"So, do you want your presents?" I asked, heading to the kitchen where I had them stashed in a cabinet. Nolan put her hands over her face and turned red in an instant. "Uh, or not…" I stopped in my tracks.

"No, no," she said, shaking her head and frowning a bit. "I totally want them. I'm sorry. It's just that I didn't bring anything for you. I sort of haven't been able to do much lately, I've been…busy."

I watched her face carefully. I wasn't sure how much she knew I knew, and I didn't want tonight to turn into a self-help session, or an intervention. To put her at ease, I just smiled and bent down behind the kitchen counter to pull out her gifts. "Yeah, that's pretty crappy of you to not get me anything," I teased as I walked toward her, her face hardening with a toughness at my insult. "I guess you'll just have to spend two nights with me now," I winked, letting her know I was kidding. "Seriously, Noles, you don't need to get me anything. This was just something I wanted to do."

I slid the first box in front of her. It was one of my dad's old boot boxes, the largest box with a lid we had in the house. I didn't wrap it very well, opting to just tie a ribbon around it. She pulled the strings and looked at me with a smirk, clearly trying not to judge my very masculine wrapping job. "Hey, I was in a hurry," I shrugged.

She smiled, and then looked down, pushing the lid to the side. I held my breath as she reached in and pulled out the first gray T-shirt. It was my Coolidge football shirt. She held it up to her face and breathed it in, and watching her close her eyes and just take in my scent, so damned adoring and in love, had me lost. "It was always your favorite," I said softly. She just nodded and looked up, her eyes tearing. "There's more," I urged her on.

She pulled out a MicNic shirt next, just like the one she'd had for years. "Where'd you find this?" she held it up against her body, rubbing the softness of it and clutching it close.

"Ah, that one was hard. I had Sienna's help. We went to three different thrift stores, and that one was actually in the last one, all the way up in Florence," I said, acknowledging that I'd driven to the next town, 50 miles away, just to find a shirt.

As she took each shirt out of the box, she held it up and admired it for minutes, laying each one over the next against her, hugging them close. There were old movie shirts, concert T-shirts, Arizona tourist trap shirts—they weren't all exact replicas, but they were damn close. Nolan was never about the expensive designer labels. Hell, the girl owned maybe two dresses, and a skirt, still as an adult. But these stupid T-shirts? They were wrapped up in her identity. And I knew when she lost them that she'd feel stripped. And I just couldn't stand it.

"You like them?" I asked, reaching for the last one she'd pulled from the box and feeling it with my fingers, tracing the soft letters from some arcade that had shut down years ago.

She nodded without words, not ready to look me in the eyes. She wore her emotions, and I knew she was touched. But I didn't want this to be about her appreciation for me. I wanted it to be about her feeling happy, relieved and less lost. So, I sat there quietly —and waited while she put each one back in the box, and then slid it to the corner of the sofa. She scooted over to me and reached around my neck, giving me a full-bodied hug, her head resting hard against my shoulder. I heard her small sniffles and just caressed her head. "I'm glad you like them," I whispered in her ear, stroking her hair until she was ready to release me.

When she finally did, I slapped my hands in my lap and then asked if she was ready for the next one.

"You got me something else?" she said, her face turning guilty.

"Ah. No feeling bad, I told you, I don't need anything," I said, sliding over the second box. Nolan recognized it instantly, her eyes popping back up to mine.

"Oh my God!" she gasped, covering her mouth and grinning ear-to-ear. "You kept this? All this time?"

"You bet your ass I kept it. When a hot girl shows up at my door, and hands me a box of important things like this, I store it safely— even if she's pissed as hell when she does it," I said, recalling the time we'd broken up in high school. Nolan had showed up at my dad's house with her box of mementoes, thrusting them at me angrily. I'd put the box in my attic when she did and had forgotten about it until the fire. I knew it wouldn't replace a lot of the memories Nolan had saved in her room, but it was a good start. And they were all memories of *us*, and that's what I wanted her to hold onto most.

I slid her close to me again, and we both pulled out the various pictures and love notes I'd given her. She had dried the rose I gave her the summer before our junior year, its pedals flat and crisp now. She giggled when I tried to sniff it, and scrunched my nose at its stink. "It's for keep-saking, not smelling, idiot," she joked, giggling a little quietly.

I sat back after a while and just watched her as she went through the various items she'd saved in that box. I could tell when she was reaching back for fond memories, her body language telling me she was happy and remembering all of the good that was *us*. I couldn't take my eyes off her. Nolan had always been beautiful, uniquely beautiful. She didn't need makeup, or hairstyles, or skimpy clothing. She was a *what-you-see-is-what-you-get* American-blooded girl. Her long, brown, wavy hair caressed her shoulders, and framed her big eyes—eyes that couldn't bluff against her feelings if her life depended on it. Yes, she'd always been a beautiful girl. But as a woman? She was fucking stunning. And while the curves and softness of her naked body and the sexiness of her lips drove me wild, it was the entire package that had me starving for air. She was it for me. And I had to have her, for always.

She was walking into the kitchen to put the boxes back on the counter, when I noticed she'd paused in front of one of Rosie's sprigs of mistletoe that hung from one of the wooden archways. I raced to my feet and was next to her in seconds, my chest flat to her back while I slowly slid my hands up the sides of her arms, over her shoulders and into her hair, lifting it to reveal her long, slender neck. I breathed against it softly at first, smelling the strawberry scent of her hair and slightly tasting her skin before biting at her earlobe. I felt her body quiver, and she started to turn to face me, her eyes cautious, but full of want. I pointed up above her as she faced me.

"Mistletoe," I grinned, tilting one side of my mouth up, sinisterly. "You can't mess with mistletoe. I have to kiss you, it's the rule."

Nolan's face slid into a smile then too, her teeth grazing her bottom lip while her eyes shifted between mine and my mouth, her breathing getting more and more ragged with every second. My palms were resting on her hips, but they were hungry to touch her, feel her. I slid them to her back, and up the bottom of her shirt until I was gripping her bare skin, feeling the heat of it along my fingertips as I worked my way up and down, still holding her gaze.

She stepped into me more, our chests touching, and her nose tickling the center of my body, right where my heart lives. She tilted her head to look straight up at me, biting her lip harder now, her eyelids heavy. I felt her hands grip the bottom of my shirt and begin to pull it up, so I helped her pull it over my head and discard it on the floor. Her hands continued to roam, gripping my stomach, and then grazing up my chest and to my chin and neck and then back down. Our eyes were locked, and the tension was fucking undeniable. I wanted her. And she was giving me permission. But I was fighting with myself, afraid it was too soon, that our trust hadn't been mended enough.

I was lost in my head when I felt the coolness of her lips against my chest as she began kissing her way up to my neck, my breathing failing me now. I had a solid grip on the back of the sweatpants she was wearing, like a leash keeping my hands in check. I didn't have much restraint left in me, though. And when Nolan reached down to pull her own shirt up and over her head, pressing her bare skin against mine fiercely, reaching into my hair and pulling my mouth to hers hard, I lost control over everything.

Our tongues tangled as I reached behind her and lifted her to me, her legs wrapping around me and holding me to her tightly. "We can't stay here," I said into her ear as I kissed my way up and down her neck.

"Okay," she whispered, kissing me again and holding on tighter as I turned to the stairs, and carried her all the way to my room. I kicked the door closed behind me and walked us over to my bed, my lips never once leaving hers. I leaned forward, laying her down, and held myself above her. I stopped kissing her just long enough to look into her wanting eyes—just long enough to make sure this was okay, and okay tonight. When she slid up the bed and pulled me with her, I had the confirmation I needed.

I felt Nolan reaching for my jeans, and I stood to pull them off, returning to her in seconds, almost as if my body would suffocate without her touch. I peeled her bra down her shoulders before removing that, too. I kissed her breasts, taking my time, not wanting this night to end. I rolled her on top of me then, and she sat up, straddling me, her hands digging into my chest for balance, and her hair draping over our faces. I reached up to tuck it behind her ears, and she licked at her lips softly to moisten them. *Fuck. I was done.*

Gripping her head more, I pulled her back to me and sucked in her bottom lip. She was reaching to remove her pants, and I leaned over to my nightstand to pull out a condom. When I looked back, she was completely naked and ready, so beautiful and so full of fire. I knew I should stop, slow things down. But I just couldn't do it. I nodded to her, making sure this was what she wanted. And then she took the condom from me and finished putting it on me herself.

Within seconds, we were connected, our bodies completely in sync, and Nolan's eyes staring deep into mine. I reached up to grab her face between my hands and kissed her tenderly, slowly, and passionately as we made love to one another, the faint sounds of Christmas music drifting up to my room from downstairs. Time felt irrelevant, and our messy, recent past seemed so, too. All that mattered was now, and moving forward. Feeling her, smelling her, being able to touch her, and hear her, share my secrets with her— that's all I wanted in life.

"I love you," I breathed into her, "so fucking much."

I felt her body shake a bit, and noticed the small tears gathering at the corners of her eyes. I reached up to stop them with my thumbs, wiping each away and stroking her face tenderly. "Don't cry, Princess. We're okay. Everything's okay. I have you, and I'm not letting go," I said, kissing her harder now, like I was laying claim to her and binding us together forever physically.

"I love you, too. You're my everything," she said, her voice cracking as she spoke. I pulled her close to me, and we moved together—here in the same room I'd first confessed my feelings to her. We were kids then, our problems such adolescent bullshit. We'd grown so much. And we'd taken major fucking steps backward. But here we were, back to *us*. And there was no way I was ever letting go. Our bodies were wet with sweat, and our hearts were racing, as we both climbed together until I felt her body shudder, and I followed her, holding her tightly, and refusing to let go until I felt her body still with exhaustion.

I left my bed for a quick shower and turned out every light in the house, setting my alarm to wake us up at sunrise, hoping like hell we'd beat the rest of the house. But I wasn't letting Nolan leave my bed tonight. Her dad could beat my ass in the morning, and I'd deserve it. But I didn't care. She wasn't leaving these arms. I pulled my blanket up over us as I lay next to her and held her close, the beat of her heart the only sound I could hear.

My lullaby.

———

Nolan was stubborn about waking up in the morning. I knew my pops wouldn't care, but I was pretty sure hers would, so I started trying to wake her around 5 in the morning, well before the sun came up.

"Mmmmmmm," she brushed at her hair, flinching at my breath as I blew lightly at her face. "More sleeeeep."

She rolled over and pulled the blanket tightly over her head. So damned adorable. I pulled the corner of the blanket up and snuck underneath next to her, lifting it slightly and nestling my nose right against hers. "What do they call those? Eskimo kisses?" I said, nudging her cheek then with my nose.

She scrunched her face, still keeping her eyes tightly shut. "Ewwwww, your breath stinks," she said, raising her hand up to pinch her nose shut. I pulled it away and breathed at her again, just to tease her. "Gross!"

She peeked one eye open at me then. "Popeye," I teased her.

She smacked my bicep and pulled the blankets up around her nose. "Okay, okay. I get it. I'll brush my teeth. But *youuuuu* have got to get up."

I yanked the blanket from the bed, leaving her there half exposed and uncomfortable while I went into the bathroom. "That was a jerk move," she grumbled.

"Yeah, well, desperate times call for desperate measures, Princess," I said, tapping on my wrist to signal what time it was. This seemed to get her moving quickly as her eyebrows shot up a bit, and she jumped from the bed, pulling up her pants and running her fingers through her hair.

"Shit, do you think anyone's awake?" she asked.

"No, I'm pretty sure we beat the house up," I mumbled through my toothpaste-filled mouth. Nolan cracked the door open then and listened while I finished getting ready.

"Shhhhhh," she whispered over her shoulder. "I think we're good."

I followed Noles down the hallway and to the stairs, poking at her sides and forcing her to stifle giggles. We made it into the kitchen just in time to see Jason sliding through the front door, coffee in hand. I slid a mug over to Nolan, and she pretended to have just finished drinking when I picked it up from her, and asked her if she wanted a refill with a wink. "Yes, please," she said, grinning at me behind Jason's back.

The house started to fill up with people, and Nolan slipped out unnoticed to head to the guesthouse to shower and change, just as her parents came in to join us. Rosie started cooking breakfast, and by the time she was done, Nolan was back.

Christmas Eve was always a tradition at my dad's house. Most of his buddies from college, and their families came to the house along with some of his closest business partners. Pops always had a big Christmas Eve gathering; I think partly to make up for the fact that I always had to spend the actual holiday with Mom. Rosie seemed to be in her element, serving up sausage and biscuits to the dozens of people now filing into the house. She'd been helping my dad on Christmas Eve for years. And the time hit me in the face when her son Edmund showed up with a family of his own.

"Mijo, come here," Rosie said, squeezing my arm and turning me to follow her. "You remember Edmund? You were probably five years old when he used to babysit you. He's on leave for the holidays. George couldn't make it, but it's nice to have one of my boys here."

I shook Edmund's hand, and shook my head in disbelief. Here was this mature, grown man who I remembered looking like a teenager. Rosie was hugging Edmund's wife hello when a little girl with long pigtails came running up and leapt into Edmund's arms, burying her face into her father's chest. She reminded me so much of Nolan.

"Samantha, can you say hi?" Edmund said softly in his daughter's ear? The shy girl peered from under his arm, and smiled at me softly before ducking back into her father's arms.

"It's okay, maybe next time," I smiled at Edmund who just shrugged his shoulders.

"She's super shy. She'll warm up to you, though," he said, patting me on the back while he walked away to join his wife in the living room. As he did, Samantha popped her head above his shoulder and smiled bigger now, raising her tiny hand to scrunch her fingers at me for a covert wave. I raised my hand and gave her a small one back before putting my finger to my mouth to give her a *shhhhh*, like it would be our little secret.

Rosie's family was beautiful, and I found myself envious of her son. I walked out to the patio where I found Nolan talking with her parents, and for the first time in weeks, my grandmother's ring made its way back into my thoughts, it's weight comfortably back on my mind.

Christmas Eve was a full day of eating and drinking at the Johnson house. A few card games were in progress on the back patio and, somehow, old UofA football games made their way to the big screen TV, my dad and his college buddies camped in front of it reliving their glory days. Nolan's dad, Rich, seemed to like the stories, though, because he was settled in on the sofa next to my dad, honestly interested in every word. The scene made me laugh a little when I made my way to the front driveway to get a little air and look for my girl.

"Hey, you see Nolan?" I asked Jason who was leaning against the garage, smoking a cigar. He always smoked cigars on special holidays. I don't think he even really liked them, he just liked how important they made him look in his own mind.

"Nope," Jason said, uninterested.

"Okay then, thanks…asshole," I said the last part a bit under my breath.

"What was that?" Jason asked, walking up to me and stomping out his cigar on the ground. We hadn't been kind to one another in years, so why he was taking offense to it now baffled me.

"Look, man. I was just razzing you, no big," I said, backing up and turning around. Just then, I felt a fist slam into my back, knocking the wind out of me, and sending me forward on my feet.

"What the fuck?" I yelled, turning around and getting my balance, my feet under me now.

"What'd you say to Dylan about me? You tell her I'm a player? That I sleep around?" Jason was pissed, and unreasonable.

"Dude, what the fuck are you talking about?" I asked, holding my hands up now, ready to defend myself.

"Dylan took off this morning, said we needed some time apart, things were moving too fast," and as Jason spoke, I was starting to realize something. He actually liked Dylan, maybe even loved her. "So what did you do man? I know you said something. You hate me so much, can't stand my success."

"Jason, look…I have no idea what you're talking about," I said, backing off from him a little and shaking my head in an effort to get him to calm down.

"Ooooooh, wait a minute. I know," he had that tone suddenly. "You were jealous. You envy me because I have a real woman—and you're still with some fucking girl from high school. My girlfriend looks like a supermodel, while yours…" he let an evil laugh slip slowly from his throat. "Yours looks like a grocery clerk…just like her fucking mom."

I've wanted to hit Jason in the face for about a decade, but never in a million years would I have thought the feeling of my fist smashing into his nose would feel as satisfying as it did in that instant. If I had known, I would have done it years ago…and probably often. Within seconds, I had Jason on the ground, and was pounding at his jaw and chest and arms. He was scrappy, though, and had managed to wiggle out from under me and kick me a few times, too. We were both standing in a face-off finally, taking turns sending punches at each other's face, circling each other like boxers used to do in the ring, when my dad's voice broke through the bubble Jason and I seemed to be operating in.

"Boys! My office! Now! The both of you!" Pops yelled, his voice bellowing and the disappointment and anger punctuating each and every word. Jason and I turned from each other slowly, breathless, as we walked side-by-side toward the house. Our eyes remained angry and locked, but I realized that Nolan and her family had gathered outside now, too. And my heart sank a bit with worry that they had heard some of Jason's venom. He spit a little at the ground right before we walked in the house, and I felt satisfied knowing I made him bleed.

My dad was finally out of his cast, which meant he could pace back and forth in front of Jason and me like we were children. Being in his office on Christmas with a house full of family and friends was mortifying, but I didn't regret finally giving Jason the beating he'd deserved.

"What the hell was that?" Dad finally asked, leaning on his desk and crossing his arms. "Like zoo animals, you both are. You were raised better than that. You're brothers, start acting like it!"

Dad was angry, angrier than I'd seen him in my entire life. I was content to just nod my head, and apologize in order to get the old man's blood pressure back down to normal, but Jason couldn't let it rest. "Come on, Dad? Reed's out of control. He flew off the handle at me for no reason, sensitive pussy," Jason said, thinking he'd just be able to bluff his way through this, that I wouldn't call him on it. Well, I'd grown up since our last fight. I stood up from my chair and leaned over into him, my face close to his.

"You disrespected the girl I love, you asshole. You disrespected her family. You embarrass me, and I won't call you brother," I said through clenched teeth, slamming back into my seat and folding my arms again in an effort to control my anger.

Jason just rolled his eyes at my words and let out a big sigh. I watched as my father stared at him for a long time, finally drawing Jason's attention. "What?" Jason asked, rolling his shoulders as if he were innocent. "Oh come on, Pops. He's being sensitive, and stupid."

Dad cut him off then. "Just shut up, Jason," Dad said, his voice calmer now, but his words still carrying a bite. "I don't know where I failed you, but I'm sorry."

Jason was looking at the floor now, his eyes a little glassy, but his arms still crossed like mine, fighting everything. "Did you hear me?" Dad asked, forcing Jason to look at him. "I said I'm sorry. Son, I taught you everything I know about business. And man...you are one hell of a businessman. You're better than me."

Jason scoffed at my dad, looking down, embarrassed now.

"No, Jason. I'm serious. You are a better businessman than me," Pops said, holding his gaze level. "But Reed's a better *man*. And it's my fault. I didn't teach you enough about that. And I'm the one to blame. But I hope like hell you can come out the other end of this, because if you don't, you're going to live a sad life, full of anger and resentment. And you're going to be alone."

Our dad let his words hang there in the air, the heaviness a suffocating blanket on the three of us. Dad took turns looking each of us in the eyes, his face hard, and heartbroken. Jason and I sat still, our eyes locked straight ahead, not ready to acknowledge one another. When it almost became unbearable, Dad pushed off from the edge of the desk and reached for the door to leave us there alone. "You two take your time. Figure this shit out. When you're done, we'll have Christmas," he said, closing the door behind him.

Jason and I sat there in silence for minutes, careful not even to make a sound with our breathing. I was the first to break, turning my head slowly to look at him. And when I did, I saw the thin wet streaks left behind by the few tears he was unable to keep inside.

Something had gone wrong in my brother's life. I didn't know what it was—maybe he'd seen more of my parents' fights, maybe it was the end of his football career, and part of it was probably having my success constantly shoved in his face—whatever the trauma, it had left behind some heavy scars. But my Dad? Boy, he just went right in to cut them open. I hoped they'd heal better the second time.

Suddenly feeling guilty, I nudged my brother's arm with my own. "Sorry for the sucker punch," I said, also a little proud of how hard I'd fought him. He was still my big brother, after all. He chuckled a little and rubbed his jaw.

"You nailed me," he said, still not ready to look me in the eye. He looked down, and we were quiet for what felt like a full minute. "I deserved it."

Knowing the best thing I could do at this point was to leave my brother alone, I stood to my feet and patted his shoulder with my hand. "Yeah, you did. But I'm still sorry," I said, then I left him there with his thoughts.

———

Nolan helped me clean up the scratches and cuts on my face in the bathroom upstairs, never asking for details. I was pretty sure she'd heard more than I wanted her to, but she didn't seem fazed by any of it. By the time we made it downstairs, Jason had left my father's office and was now sitting outside on the back patio alone. A few of my father's friends joined him as the afternoon wore on, and by evening, he was talking and smiling again. But I had a feeling he was still chewing on my father's message, and I could tell it had affected him, saddened him. And it made me sad, too.

Dad got a fire going as the sun set, and everyone had finally gathered on the sofas, chairs, and floor in the living room. It was gift exchange time—Dad's tradition was always that everyone brings a gift fit for anyone in the room, and we all take turns picking and stealing, sort of like a *white elephant* gift party, but with things you'd actually want. Last year I ended up with a hundred bucks.

Before we started drawing numbers, Rosie walked around and

handed everyone a glass of champagne. I gave her a funny look when she handed a glass to Nolan and me, and she just smiled, and told me to wait to drink it. "Your father wants to make a toast," she said, moving on to serve the rest of the guests. Nolan and I just shrugged at each other and leaned back into the sofa to wait for everyone else.

Dad cleared his throat when everyone had been served, somehow able to make a noise loud enough to quiet the entire room. "I know, I know. Buck wants to talk more, you're all rolling your eyes," my dad joked, and everyone chuckled fondly. My dad could be long-winded when he wanted to be. "I promise, though, I'll keep this short. I have some important things to say on this day. A day that has always been about family to me," my dad turned to look at Jason, and then to me, raising his glass a little.

"You see? I'm a blessed man. I have had wonderful success in life, yes," he said, turning with his arms out, acknowledging the giant house we were all sitting in. "But I think we can all agree…it's family that makes everything worth anything on this earth. Family. Jason? Reed? I love you both more than the air I breathe. You two are my life and soul, and the most important things I've ever done. And you have always loved your old dad, no matter how much of a pain in the ass I might be. Whether I'm riding your ass about throwing the ball with more speed to get more distance…or nagging you about meeting with the lawyers to close the deal on our latest dealership—you just smile, and nod, and do these crazy things I ask because you love me, and you trust me. And I can't tell you how much that means to your old man," my dad was getting a little choked up, so he took a small sip of his drink, raising his glass a little and laughing. "Ha, that's good stuff. Almost done, I swear."

"Well, I'm asking you both to trust me…just one more time. You see, I've gone and done something a little crazy. But it's really all about family, so I'm hoping you'll be okay with it when I tell you," I looked at Jason as my father spoke, and we both made eye contact, shrugging, and wondering where the hell our dad was going with all of this. "Well…I guess that's enough beating around the bush. Rosie and I are getting married."

The room erupted in clapping, hoots and hollering, as everyone stood at once and collapsed on Rosie and my father, hugging them and congratulating them on their news. Nolan looked at me, her eyes wide with shock. "Did you know about this?" she asked.

"Not a clue!" I said, my own eyes unable to blink, but a smile stretching my face. My father started tapping on the side of his glass, getting everyone's attention again.

"Hold on, hold on everyone. We're not going anywhere. You can tackle us in a few minutes," Dad laughed, his full bellied laugh, the kind he did when he was truly happy. "Reed? Jason? I hope you two are okay with this. I wanted to talk to you about it first, but it just never seemed to be the right time…and well…Rosie, she's always been family. And over the last few years, what started as a beautiful friendship, became the deepest love of my life," my dad said, turning to Rosie and grabbing her hand with his, squeezing it and bringing it to his lips to kiss it. "When it's right. It's just right."

My dad had been married four times in his life, the three women after my mom each only sticking around for less than a year. But I knew this one was it—the one that would last. It felt right, just like my dad said. And as Nolan and I talked about it, while everyone took their turns congratulating my father and Rosie, we realized we'd been pretty blind to their romance.

By the end of the evening, my dad finally made his way over to us, and I smiled when Nolan embraced him, and then Rosie. She loved them as much as I did. "So? What do you think?" my dad asked, reaching for Rosie's hand and showing us the ring.

I just smiled at him, and shook his hand before he pulled me in for a full embrace. "You did good, Dad. Real good," I said, noticing Jason standing behind, for once a genuine smile on his face, too.

"Yeah, you did good, Dad," Jason said as my dad turned around to hug him, too.

Chapter Twenty-Four

Nolan

THE DRAMA of Christmas Eve had exhausted me, and I was actually looking forward to the low-key traditional Christmas we always spent with my grandparents. My parents and I left early Christmas morning to spend the day with them, arriving just in time for Gran's big breakfast. She made the most amazing French toast with bacon and eggs that always seemed like they came straight from a farm.

I slept a little in the car on our way. I had stayed up late with Reed, waiting for Christmas to arrive. We sat outside and watched the stars by the outdoor fireplace. We saw a shooting star, and both vowed to make wishes with our eyes closed. We kept them secret to seal them, make sure they'd come true. I knew it was a silly myth, but I was so happy in this moment, I was willing to grab onto any legend or mysticism with both hands just to wish it mine for keeps. I squeezed my eyes shut and whispered in my head for everything to work out for Reed and me, my wish mostly a direct assault on my enormous fear that as soon as Reed signed his name to a contract for an NFL team in the next few months that he'll be lost to me forever.

My dreams were scattered and brief, and they continued throughout the car ride to my grandparents. I seemed to be replaying Reed's fight with Jason, mostly hearing the harsh words his brother had said. Awake it was easy to rationalize everything. It wasn't me. I could be any girl, and Jason wouldn't be kind. He would threaten anything good in Reed's life because he was jealous. It made me curious about the pictures I'd seen of the two of them as smaller boys, Reed the little boy under Jason's wing. Year's ago Jason had a look in his eye that he'd fight to the death to protect his little brother. Somewhere along the way, though, that look had been replaced by envy.

My parents seemed to have been spared the verbal assaults of the fight, only witnessing the two Johnson boys pummeling each other in Buck's driveway. My mom worried about Reed during our drive, and I felt relief that she was on Reed's side without even questioning it.

As the morning wore on, I was able to relax more, almost letting go of all of my stress. My brother Mike joined us before too long, and we were finally able to exchange gifts. Our holiday was a lot different from the one at the Johnson house, just the six of us sitting on my grandparents' living room floor, and sliding mismatched wrapped boxes to one another filled with sweaters and homemade items. My grandmother had knitted me a scarf and a hat in ASU colors. Grandpa gave me his old pool stick, which of course led to a few rounds at the table. I was actually able to beat him from time-to-time, which I think made him proud.

My parents had given me a few ASU things, and each time I opened a box I felt a twinge of guilt about my dismal grades, and the fact that I could be in my last semester at ASU, flunking out and going down in fiery academic flames. My stress was once again picking up, when I felt a buzz on my phone and pulled it out to find a text from Reed.

Hey. So…my mom wants you to come over for dinner if you're able. Do you think your parents would mind if I drove you home later?

I stared at the text for a bit, and then put the phone back in my pocket so I could dissect the message in my head. Why would Millie want me to join them? I was embarrassed by my reaction, always assuming the worst, like it was some sort of trick. I had to remind myself constantly that Millie was an adult. True, she was cold and lacked empathy, but she wasn't calculating ways to attack me. I must have been making a strange face because my mom became suspicious and finally came to sit next to me on the sofa.

"What's wrong, sweetheart?" she asked, leaning into me a little and whispering her words to keep our conversation among us girls.

"Nothing's wrong," I started, pulling my phone out again and looking at the screen a bit while I sucked in my top lip. "It was Reed. He...wants to know if I can join him at his mom's for dinner. But...I don't know."

I just looked down, shrugging a bit. I was caught in such a weird place. Part of me wanted to run to Reed just to be with him more, while I had him. But there was this other part of me that was terrified of how Millie would probably make me feel, and I didn't know if I wanted to feel like that *on Christmas*.

"You know you can go if you want to, right? You won't hurt our feelings, sweetie, if that's what you're worried about," my mom said, reaching around my shoulder and pulling me in for a squeeze.

"Thanks, Mom," I said, thinking more. "I just hate to miss out here, though, you know?"

"Oh, you're not missing out. Your dad will doze off in the chair in another hour while your grandmother and I will clean the kitchen top to bottom and sit on the porch gossiping about her neighbors and the ladies I work with. Mike is going to speed out of here the second you leave to get back to his girlfriend, and you already made grandpa's day at the pool table."

I just smiled at her, still considering, and uneasy about going. "I'm really going to miss him," I said, admitting out loud for the first time ever my fears over Reed to my mom. She just looked at me puzzled, not sure what I was talking about. "Reed's...well, he's probably going to get drafted this year. He could go anywhere, really. And I'll be stuck here, in college." I threw in the college part not wanting to let on my fear that I'd, in fact, be stuck in the literal *here*, back at home, going to some junior college without hope of ever becoming anything.

My mom was quiet, her eyes falling now to show her understanding. She smiled softly and patted my hands. "Honey, that boy loves you. He loves you like nothing I've ever seen. If that's what you're worried about, well, let me just put a stop to that for you right here and now," she was giving me her best pep talk. And it might work if I didn't think that she was just doing her duty. I appreciated it nonetheless.

"Thanks," I just smiled back. I took a deep breath and resolved myself to make the most of the moment. I texted Reed that I'd love to join them, and then held my breath, waiting for him to write back. He finally did, saying that he'd pick me up in an hour, which meant I had an hour left to pretend I didn't have any worries in the world. I found my grandpa and challenged him to a few more rounds of nine ball, escaping my problems for a little while longer.

———

Reed hugged everyone in my family when he came to pick me up, even Mike. My family adored him—even my grandpa, who was truly a tough emotional nut to crack. Seeing how they all took Reed in made me feel proud of my family. We were simple and we didn't have fancy parties or give expensive gifts, but we loved with our whole hearts and without reservations or prejudice.

Millie's house was only 30 minutes or so away from my grandparents, so the ride was quick. I told Reed about the things my family had given me, and even put on my new knitted hat, which was a bit too tight, but I'd never let my grandmother know. When we pulled into the driveway, my breath caught, causing Reed to reach over and squeeze my hand. He knew how little I enjoyed being in Millie's company.

When he came around to help me from the Jeep, he stopped me in front of the door, holding both of my hands. "I think my mom is trying," he said, looking me in the eyes. It was strange for him to admit, even in this small way, to the way his mother treated me. And having him *understand* actually meant more to me than Millie being nice. I leaned forward and kissed him softly.

"Thank you," I said, my words more for him, than his mother.

He took my hand, and we walked up the drive through her enormous front door. I followed Reed through the foyer, to the large sitting room. I noticed Dylan and Jason sitting outside on the patio through the large wall of windows. I didn't think Dylan would be here, given what Jason had said during his fight with Reed yesterday, so I was surprised to see them holding hands and looking at each other across the table.

I just pointed at them and nudged Reed. "What's up with that?" I asked.

"Hmmmmm, well...Jason's trying, too," he said, his face forming a hard smile, and his brow heavy.

As we approached the patio door, I watched Dylan and Jason stand to talk with Sam and Millie, and the way Millie grabbed Dylan's hand and kissed her cheek like she was her own daughter had me swallowing hard on my own pride. That's all I wanted. It made me sick to admit it, but I'd give anything for Reed's mother to show me just half of the acceptance and affection she did Dylan.

I found myself suddenly wishing for super powers—invisibility, flight, time-freezing. Anything that would get me out of this place right here and now would be fine by me. I was smiling a little at my thoughts, when Millie's curt greeting jostled me to attention. "Nolan, dear. So good to see you," she said, leaning into me awkwardly to kiss at the air next to my cheeks. I froze at her move-ment and bunched my forehead, stepping back a little, almost embarrassed for her.

"Uh, yeah...thanks for having me over?" I still wasn't convinced my presence here was her idea.

"Of course. Nolan, you know Dylan, right?" she said, introducing us, her smile brighter as she touched Dylan's shoulder. It disgusted me.

"Yeah, we've met," I nodded, more uneasy than I was just seconds ago.

"Oh…" Millie said, looking around for something else to say. When she couldn't come up with anything, she just turned to Sam and started talking. That was it, my warm embrace by this part of Reed's family. *Yeah, she was trying.*

Dinner was stilted and awkward. Sam, thankfully, filled the silence with hunting stories. And despite my complete and utter disdain for the sport, *if you could even call it that,* I listened intently, hanging on every word. Reed kept hold of my hand under the table, even while we ate; I giggled the few times he dropped food from his fork with his left hand. For such a gifted athlete, he was shit with his left hand. Thank God, his right one healed after the accident.

We all headed to the sitting room for coffee after dinner, a tradition that seemed so bizarre to me. I didn't really like coffee, but I was just happy to not have been insulted over the last hour, so I sat there and gripped my cup, taking tiny sips of my drink that I loaded with cream and sugar just to choke it down.

Dylan and Reed were talking about Reed's upcoming press conference, and I was trying to put all of my focus on that when I felt Millie's polished nails tap at my shoulder, almost like a chicken's beak. I looked up at her, a bit bothered and I think she was surprised by my boldness. "I'm sorry, I didn't mean to interrupt," she said, pulling her hands back together and folding them in front of her. "I was just wondering, if I might borrow you, just for a moment," she asked, holding her hand out to point toward the door.

I looked at Reed, who was still involved with Dylan, and then looked back to Millie, whose face was growing full of impatience. Remembering Reed's words, that his mom was trying, I filled my lungs and calmed my nerves. I smiled up at her and stood to follow her from the room, looking back once more to catch Reed's attention. His eyes were wide, and I just shook my head for him not to worry, shrugging a little to acknowledge how strange this was.

We walked to Millie's office, and she closed the door behind me —instantly killing my spirits and diminishing my confidence to nothing. I felt like a grade-schooler who had been sent to the principal's office. Out of instinct, I sat in the large leather chair facing her desk and waited for her to administer my punishment. But instead of sitting across from me, Millie sat at the corner of her desk, leaning with one leg propped atop, an amazingly casual pose for her. She pulled her glasses from her face and folded them, sitting them next to her. She looked down quietly for a few seconds, almost like she was searching for the words to her speech. *Oh God, was I going to get a lecture?*

"Nolan, my son loves you. And I don't think you're good enough," she slapped me with this right out of the gate. No easing in. My emotions betrayed me as my eyes watered at her words, but I held my breath and willed the tears not to slide any further.

Millie sighed heavily, and I looked to see her looking down once again, pinching the bridge of her nose. "That came out cruel. I don't mean to be that way," she said, shaking her head. "It's just that Reed has always been my baby boy. He was all I had...for so long. And I had these plans for him. Who he'd marry, where they'd live? But that boy, he is stubborn. Well...you know this." She laughed a little, closing her eyes while she thought of Reed.

"Like I said, my son loves you," she said, reaching behind her to grab a large folder from her desk. "Reed came to see me a few weeks ago. He told me about your academic troubles."

I gulped. I actually gulped at her words, looking at my knees in shame and wishing once again for the damn super power.

"You see, my son wanted me to give you a scholarship," she chuckled a little to herself, more amusement at my expense. "I explained that we have rules, and the scholarships, Nolan? They just don't work that way."

Oh God, she was pitying me now! I wanted to curl up like a bug, and disintegrate into her carpet.

"But my son? Well, like I said. He loves you. And let's just say he gave me some things to think about," she said, touching my hand a little. I could feel her hand trembling, and was lost between wanting to shirk it from my skin and wanting to grab hold of it tightly. I was powerless, and I couldn't get myself to look her in the eyes.

"Nolan, I don't know you well. And I'm sorry. I know that is mostly my fault. But from what I do know, you aren't someone who is used to favors. You like to earn your way. And I can respect that," Millie spoke more comfortably, her formalities breaking down just the slightest bit, and my heart leaping at the word *respect*. "I sent your files to a friend of mine. Dean Howard is in charge of the Education College at ASU, and it seems she's quite familiar with you. She submitted your profile for the Summit Fellowship. Are you familiar with the program?"

I shook my head slowly. I'd heard of it, but really had no clue what it was.

"Hmmmm, well…basically your senior year is turned into an intensive study program under her direct supervision. You have to complete a major paper to be published in an academic journal and turn in several hours of hands-on experience. And in exchange for your tutoring in her class, your tuition is completely covered," her words were starting to echo as my head was racing through this possibility. I had spent the semester digging my own grave, and there was this chance now that I would actually be able to claw my way out.

Millie held the folder out for me to take, and when I did, I clung it to my chest, afraid to look inside.

"Nolan, I removed myself from the selection committee. It wasn't appropriate. I hope you understand," she said as she left the office and left me to sit there alone, curious about the direction my life would turn the second I flipped open the damn folder in my hand.

I set it flat in my lap, and with shaky fingers I turned the cover over to see the personal letter from Dean Howard, welcoming me to join her fellowship next fall. I gasped for air, my heart beating quickly, and my eyes stinging with relief. I read every word of the letter and every paper that followed, spending at least 20 minutes alone in Millie's office. The more I read through my files, and the details of the program, the more I realized what Millie had meant.

She had removed herself from the committee. I'd earned this honor all on my own. While I might not be good enough for her son, I had Millie Johnson-Snyder's respect. And with that in my hip pocket, I felt renewed optimism that someday I might just be able to win her favor completely.

Chapter Twenty-Five

Reed

"DUDE, get your head in the game," Trig laughed, slapping the back of my head with a towel after our morning workout the day of the bowl game. We did some light running, and I threw a few passes just to get a feel for the ball and the cooler air. Playing in California was amazing. Of all the BCS bowls, the Rose bowl was the bomb.

"My head's in the game. Don't you worry about me. You just make sure you catch the pretty little passes I'll be throwin' your ass, okay?" I gave it right back to him. He started laughing as he lay down on the bench across from me, stretching his arms out and taking up the entire bench. Trig was six-foot-four, and when he jumped, he seemed like he was 10-foot-plus, which made even my crappiest throws look pretty spectacular.

"Don't let coach hear you calling your passes *little*. He won't like that too much," Trig joked. "You know they're going to be gunnin' for your ass."

"Yep. I know," I said, laying back, too, and shutting my eyes, my head spinning with everything that was happening so fast. Win or lose, tomorrow morning I was declaring myself draft eligible. I had been ready for it all season, but now that it was here, this new step scared the shit out of me. If I failed, it was going to be on a mega stage for the world to see. I'd gotten used to being the big fish in the small pond; I wasn't so sure anymore that I was ready to swim with the sharks.

I heard my phone in my bag and sat up to dig it out. Trig started laughing at the ringtone Noles had put in for her number. "Man…is your phone playing P!nk?" he started poking fun.

"Yes. It is," I said back seriously, my face bluffing my embarrassment. I was going to play it proud.

"Well, alright then," he said, laying back down and popping his headphones in.

"Huh? That was easy," I laughed to myself.

I answered Nolan's call, excited to hear how close she and my dad were to the stadium. "Hey, Princess. Where you at?" I asked.

"We're getting off the freeway right now. Your dad's telling me some story about the Rose Bowl parade in 1994, something he did to one of the floats?" she was giggling a little, telling on my dad. I just rolled my eyes. I'd heard the story a million times. ASU was in the bowl that year, and my dad and a few of his alumni buddies managed to sabotage one of the ASU floats, spraying their flowers red and blue, UofA colors. I'd heard the story about a thousand times. Poor Nolan, this was only her first.

"I'm so sorry. You're too good to him. You can tell him to stop talking sometimes you know?" I said, also loving the fact that I knew Nolan would never say anything remotely mean or rude to my dad.

"Oh God, never. I love his stories," she said, her voice honest and true. My grin stretched ear-to-ear talking to her.

"Oh, hey! Tell Pops to pull in to the media lot when you guys get here. His name's on a list, so he gets VIP parking," I said.

"Got it," she said, muffling the phone a little as she relayed my words to my dad. "Okay, we're pulling in. See you in a few!"

She hung up quickly, which was good, because I was about to unleash some seriously mushy stuff, and I wasn't so sure Trig's music was playing loudly enough to block it all out. I headed down the main hall to the front of the team lounge, almost skipping like a schoolgirl. Here I was about to play in the biggest game yet of my football career, and my heart was completely, 100-percent focused on the girl about to walk through the doors in front of me. My dad swung them open first, but then he held one side open so Nolan could catch up and walk through.

Damn. She was perfect.

When we talked the night before, she told me that she was going to break her rules—go *full Wildcat* for me, but I didn't think she'd look like *that*! She had on a red version of my jersey that she'd tied in the back so it hugged her body, slumping a little over one shoulder. Her tight jeans slung low on her hips, showing off her smooth stomach and cute-as-hell bellybutton. She pulled her hair back into a ponytail, the long curls swaying as she walked. She was a goddamned fantasy, and for once I didn't care that every other guy in the lounge right now was staring at her, because she walked right up to me. And I was the one who got to kiss her.

"Well, that's a fine way to say hello," she said after I finally let my lips leave hers, acting like one of the old-fashioned girls from those old movies.

"You...are dangerous in that outfit, Miss Lennox," I said, tugging on the bottom of the jersey.

"Too much?" she asked, folding her arms a little, shying away over her body. I just pulled her arms back out and held them in front of her.

"Definitely not. You look amazing!" I reached around her and slung her back a bit, kissing her again, and then standing her back up in my arms. "You just make it kinda hard to focus, that's all."

"Ohhhh," she snickered, lowering her eyes and showing her embarrassment from my bold attention.

I held her hand every second she was in the lounge with me, just dragging her around by my side while I introduced my dad to a few people. I hadn't really spent time with her since Christmas Day at my mom's. And the rollercoaster of that day had left us both pretty emotionally spent. I was grateful that my mom had actually heard me when I had it out with her over how she treated Nolan. I knew she wouldn't be able to just flip a switch. But the fact that she even had the smallest hand in Nolan's fellowship award was a good sign—at least I was taking it for one. I grilled Nolan pretty hard about the conversation they had, mostly because her eyes seemed red and swollen when she finally walked out of my mom's office. But she swore to me that my mom hadn't been mean. And she said my mom even told her she respected her, which seemed to mean more to Nolan than being gushed over the way Dylan was, which I guess was just one more reason why I loved Nolan so damned much.

About three hours before game time, Nolan left with my dad to grab a bite to eat before meeting up with the rest of the family to take their seats. They were near our bench this time, only a few rows up. My dad actually turned down box seats to get closer to the action. He was never much for the luxury and high-end side of sporting events. He liked to hear and feel the grit of the game and be close to the field.

The closer we got to kick-off, the more my nerves started to zero in on what was at stake. We weren't contending for the title, just a higher ranking to end the season. But I knew tonight I was out there for evaluation, and how I played meant I ended up third string in Buffalo, riding the bench and freezing my ass off, or with a fighting chance to start someday for a team like San Diego.

I jumped up and down with nervous energy in the tunnel next to Trig. He lived for this kind of stage. And normally, so did I. But I couldn't seem to shake the cloud over my head. I was worried...and that *worried* me. "Yo, Johnson. You ready to show these Buckeyes how it's done?" Trig shouted, bumping fists with me before putting his helmet on his head and kicking off into a sprint to race out onto the field.

My mouth yelled with him, but my head was calculating every aspect of the game. I was thinking about the people in the stands, the people on phones calling stats back to main offices, the lawyers sitting on offers and contracts. My stomach was so sick, I actually ran straight over to the giant trash can behind our bench and hurled everything I had inside me into it.

"What the fuck was that? I'd never lost my head. Not out here?" I thought.

"You alright, Johnson?" I heard one of the coaches shout over my shoulder. I just held my hand up and wiped my mouth with my other arm.

"I'm good. Too much Gatorade. All good, all good," I said, pushing my helmet to my head and begging myself to get a grip on things.

We ended up losing the coin toss, which meant I had to head out onto the field first. I liked having a minute or two to pump myself up, but I wouldn't get that luxury today. I thrust my chest into Trig's and a few of the other guys' as we headed out to the field for the huddle, the special team only getting us to the 23-yard line.

I took my calls, and we ran a few running plays first, gaining only six yards by third down. "Okay, it's game change time, boys. Going audible. Listen up, and hold the pocket," I shouted through my helmet, the roar of the crowd almost deafening.

We got to the line and I shouted, turning side to side for the hard count. "Six-eight-six, green 80, green 80, hut!" I was actually screaming my words as the ball suddenly thrust into my hands. It felt so foreign, like I'd never handled one in my life. Within nano-seconds I was flat on the ground, the turf digging into my teeth while a 300-pound linebacker sat on me, pushing me deeper into the earth, yelling into my ear to "remember what that feels like, motherfucker, cuz you're tasting that shit again!"

My body hurt instantly. I'd been sacked. I'd been sacked plenty of times, but for some reason everything seemed heavier today. Trig reached down and pulled me to my feet, slapping my back as we ran off the field, going three and out.

"Shit. Not a good start," I thought.

I pulled the grass from my mouth and spit out water a few times, spraying some on my face before propping my helmet halfway on my head.

"Come on. Get it together!" I coached myself. I was off my game. Something was wrong. I looked around the stadium, taking in the crowd. I'd played here before. I'd won here before. What the hell was my problem?

The next two outings were pretty much the same, each drive

getting a little deeper. But I couldn't seem to settle into a groove. And I'd eaten turf enough for the day. Finally, in the middle of the second quarter, I got pissed. Sick of it, I started pacing, turning every now and then to look up at the stands. I needed to see Pops. When I finally found him, he was standing with Nolan holding onto one arm, on her tiptoes. Rose was leaning on the other. They both hated to see me take a beating; it always scared them. But my dad's face was different. He was...calm. He noticed me looking and gave me a nod. Just enough. He wasn't worried. Not in the least. Just like I usually was. There was always time, and I always had control.

I channeled his confidence as I ran out to the field, a little renewed energy in my steps. "Okay, how about we don't let those fuckers in this time, huh?" I yelled, pushing at my line's chests. They barked, getting pumped up, everyone ready to get into the game. And I think finally, I was, too.

We broke and got to the line, trying the same audible I had before, only this time I stepped out quicker, my feet knowing right where they needed to be, where I needed to go. Trig was crossing about 15 yards out, and I hit him right on the line as he ran out of bounds. And suddenly there was a shift. We all felt it.

They call it momentum.

We ran the same play four more times, the Buckeyes unable to stop it, and the frustration we were just suffering from finally piled onto their side. Our running backs cut through them as we charged down the field five and 10 yards at a time—finally scoring in a two-minute drive. We were on the board, down by a touchdown, going into the second half, and I was finally ready to get off my ass and fight for this thing that I really wanted.

The second half was a complete 180 from our first half. We dominated the ball, and I even got to air it out a few times, hitting Trig with 30-yard passes for touchdowns. I was feeling it, everything suddenly effortless. I could close my eyes and still see the Harland Motors scoreboard from Coolidge, smell the same grass from home, shut out the crowd—pretend this wasn't the big time. That's how I always did it. I could block it from my mind, but for some reason today I let it in, let it attack me a little. I wouldn't make that mistake again.

It wasn't a blow out, but we won the Rose Bowl 48 to 38, clinching a no. 3 or 4 final for the season. My bones hurt, and I knew I'd be icing some serious bruises and swollen joints for most of the night. I had taken a beating. But I'd also gotten back up. And I hoped that's what the important people watching tonight's game focused on. I wanted to show my toughness, show that I could take anything thrown at me, no matter how hard I got hit.

I wasn't sure where my mother and Sam were sitting for the game, probably in one of the boxes upstairs. And part of me was glad my mom wasn't closer to the field where she could hear the crunch and the sounds of the wind being forced from my lungs. My dad could take it, but she was always convinced that football was going to kill me.

I hung out on the field for about an hour for interviews and the trophy presentations. And I was proud as hell that I'd earned the offensive MVP award. There were times in my life where I'd been on cruise control, just gone through the motions and gotten what I'd wanted because it was easy. But tonight I had to fight, and I was honestly a little surprised that I could fight, and even more that I still came out on top.

I was reveling in my dream; it was all falling into place. I knew I did enough to get the right teams talking. And I knew that Dylan and her father were going to be busy over the next few weeks fielding calls and working on my behalf. I was going to get to have this game in my life, and it was the most amazing feeling in the world. Or at least I thought it was.

When Noles finally made it through the crowd, squeezing through with my dad and brother behind her, pushing and elbowing just to get to me, my football fantasy went black in an instant—all I could see was *her*. I'd give it all up for her. Just like that. Yeah, I'd said that before. But for some reason, right there, right then, I meant it. I knew I would. I'd proven everything I wanted to out there on the field tonight. I was fucking amazing. But none of it mattered if I didn't have her.

When her lips hit mine, it was like morphine, my head going dizzy with relief, and my arms squeezing her to me, suffocating her with my need to not let go. I lifted her off the ground and kissed her for every damn camera in the stadium to capture, finally lowering her and pressing our foreheads together so I could hear her over the frenzy and the buzz.

"You were amazing, Reed! Amazing!" she said, a little teary eyed with her pride. Fuck the trophy. This was all I needed to know my worth.

"It was all for you. All for you," I said, my heart rapid in my chest, and my hands at the side of her face.

"No, this was for you. You deserve it. I'm so proud of you!" she said, kissing me again, and then snuggling into my side, while my dad and Jason came close to congratulate me now. Eventually, everyone made it to the field. And I'm sure being seen with Brent Nichols had the sports world talking. But I wasn't going to worry about it tonight. Or tomorrow. Maybe not ever. I had my girl, and I knew what was important now.

———

The press conference was carried by every sportscast in the Southwest. My dad, of course, had secured all of the clips. "My dad, the press secretary," I mused to myself. I spent the rest of the winter break with my family and Noles. The insurance settlement had finally come in on her parents' house, so it looked like she'd have an actual room to return to for spring break. Of course, her mom had planned to turn it into a library and a guest room, knowing her little girl would probably not be coming back home for good.

School was starting soon, though it all felt like a formality for me now. I'd still finish, even if I had to do some online work or take in a class here and there. Having a college degree was important to my mom, even if I had a multi-million-dollar football contract. Mom had been trying to engage me more about Nolan. Still not the warm and friendly way she was with others, but she was trying, and I could tell. I had to give her the benefit of time.

Nolan was taking me out tonight, some surprise date she said she had planned for months, which sort of surprised me, given the rocky road we'd been on. She invited Sean, Becky, Sienna and Sarah, too, so I wasn't sure how *romantic* this date would be. When I teased her about it, she just elbowed me and lectured me about how we wouldn't see everyone as much in the spring, and that friends were important. She was right, and I'd actually miss the hell out of Sean when he went back to California. But I was really hoping like hell I'd land in San Diego, maybe get to see a lot more of my best friend.

Nolan drove us to some coffee shop in Tempe, right outside ASU's campus. Sarah followed her there with her car loaded with the rest of their stuff, and Sean trailed behind, my ride home. Sarah, Noles and Sienna would be moving back in at campus after tonight, and the thought of not waking up next to Noles like I'd been doing (behind her father's back, which I wasn't very proud of) made me sick. I didn't want to leave her. And I knew that distance was only going to grow.

"Kind of a long drive for coffee, no?" Sean joked as we all climbed out of the cars and headed to the front door.

"We're not here for the coffee, Sean," Nolan hissed back, rolling her eyes a little. She seemed nervous, and it was cute on her. "I have some special people that I want you all to meet."

I almost had it figured out by the time we got to the small front stage set up at the shop. The place was filled with people—most of them couples. I realized they were all parents, and their children, some of them as young as seven or eight, were the people Nolan was talking about.

"Hi, everyone. Are you all ready?" She spoke, and the youthful faces just beamed back at her, nodding. She could evoke confidence, and bravery, and belief in even the smallest creature. She had a gift, and it made the world smile. "Okay, well before we start, I want you all to meet my friends. I thought it might help knowing you had some guaranteed cheerers out here…other than me, of course."

She winked at them when some of them laughed. Others still looked down, shy and nervous, but Nolan gave them each individual attention, lifting them up until they were looking us in the eyes, too. We all went down the line shaking the hands of Nolan's students, each battling their own demon, some disability that tried to make some things impossible. But those demons didn't know who they were dealing with in Nolan. She would win. She always did.

We all settled in our seats just as the lights dimmed, and a small spotlight lit up the tiny stage. Nolan held a microphone in her hand and welcomed everyone.

"Thank you all for coming out. This means a lot to me. I've spent months with the amazing kids up here tonight. And I think they are going to inspire you. I'm really proud of them, and I know you will be, too. Remember, the most important thing we can do is show them how proud we are with our claps and cheers. The sounds you make will echo in their memory, and the next time they face something hard in life, they'll remember," she said, the crowd clapping at her words.

The first child, a small boy in a wheelchair, came to the mic next. He opened a book and read a humorous story he'd written himself about a magic wheelchair that defended the galaxy at night, forcing him to stay awake to pilot it. His mom would always get angry with him when he was tired during the day and roll her eyes when he told her it was because his chair kept him awake. Of course, all revealed itself when the evil overlord kidnapped his mom, and he had to come to her rescue with his magic chair. The kid's story was brilliant, and suddenly I felt inadequate that my only talent was throwing a stupid ball.

Each story, poem or essay was unique and better than the last. The audience cheered loudly, not only out of kindness, but rather genuine awe. Nolan had orchestrated a really special evening, and I was so proud of her. I couldn't wait to tell her. We were on the last performance, and I could tell this one meant the most to Nolan as she sat on the edge of her small stool in the dark corner by the stage, almost as if she was ready to leap into the spotlight to help the young teen now taking the microphone to finish.

Her body jerked constantly as she slid the stool up to the microphone stand, sliding carefully to sit atop it. Her facial tics distracted everyone from what was actually a breathtakingly beautiful face—her blonde hair waving around her chin and cheeks, and her blue eyes full of hope and innocence. She had yet to say a word, and I was already in her corner.

A man, who seemed to be her father, brought a guitar to her and helped her move the strap over her head and shoulder, getting situated and in place. He kissed the top of her head and hopped back down to his seat, grabbing his wife's hand and squeezing it for courage. I knew that move; I'd seen it, and done it myself.

"Hi…uh…I'm…I'm…I'm K-K-Kira," she almost whispered, her nerves already getting the best of her. Nolan just sat there still, nodding and willing her on. "I'm going to…going to…s-s-sing my poem for you."

She just smiled softly, and then looked down, wrapping her crooked fingers around the guitar's neck and body. Somehow, a miracle, she started to strum softly, and the melody was haunting. Beautiful. The room was silent, everyone stunned to silence and afraid all at once. We were all with her, on her team. She wasn't going to fail if we could help it.

Then she started to sing, and her stutter disappeared.

I am not alone. He's with me in my heart.
My brother, he never came. But we've never been apart.
I was supposed to be two, but I only came out one.
The birth, a complication, something done undone.

My baby brother, by a minute, so I've been told.
But he would never come. We would never hold…
His tiny fingers, tiny toes, tiny everything that no one knows.
He wasn't pretend, but real. And something is always hollow.

We were both a surprise. A gift, mom says.
We were wanted, just not planned as…

Most families are.
And there are times, still today, that we all take turns.
We all take the burden, blame and burns.
My fault. Her fault. A punishment, a curse.
But I know it could be worse.

For I am not alone. He lives with me in my heart.
And I could not have even that, and then I'd fall apart.

The entire room stood and cheered and clapped, amazed and buried in our own tears at the power this tiny, struggling girl held over us all. But my eyes were on my girl, her face devastated, and her chest heaving as she struggled to breathe. Kira just found a way to rip away the scars, scars I'd been dancing around, unsure how to deal with myself. And when Nolan bolted from her chair, rushing out the back door, I didn't waste a second and flew after her.

I found her on her knees behind a dumpster, her body shaking uncontrollably, and the whaling sounds of her cries not even trying to be masked. I just wrapped my body around hers, holding her arms down and stopping her from trying to free herself of me. We were in this together, this thing she'd been doing alone. She wasn't ever going to do this alone again.

"Shhhhhhhhh, I'm here. It's okay, baby. I'm here. I know...I know," I whispered, kissing her cheeks and head, and cradling her while I rocked her back-and-forth, my own tears falling uncontrollably now. "I know, and I'm so sorry. God, Nolan. I'm so sorry. But it's okay, I'm here."

She clung to me, her wet face soaking the front of my shirt, her body flat against mine, almost lifeless, but heavy all the same. Her breathing was short and labored. Her shaking not subsiding. "I lost it, Reed. Oh my God!" she started shaking again, her tears coming harder now. I just held on.

"You didn't lose anything. You didn't do anything, you hear me?" I said, begging her to listen to me. "It wasn't right. It wasn't meant to be. Something was wrong, and that's what was supposed to happen. And oh my God, Nolan, I will never forgive myself that you were alone through it all. I'm so sorry, baby. I failed you. God, I'm sorry."

"I didn't tell you. I should have told you! Maybe then…" she started, but I stopped her. She was done blaming herself. She had done that enough.

"No, now listen, Nolan," I held her face a few inches from mine, my hands in her hair, streaks running all along her face. "This had nothing to do with anything you did…or didn't do. You have to stop blaming yourself."

"But what if I can't have children? What if I'm…I'm…done?" she started quaking again.

"You don't know that. Nolan, you need to talk to someone. You don't know anything until you talk to someone about this. Talk to me. And then talk to a doctor. Baby, I know it's scary, but you need to. I love you…so much. But you have to take care of yourself," I was pleading, trying to reach her. She just stared at me, almost through me. For minutes, I looked into her eyes, taking pauses to wipe the tears away.

We sat there completely wrapped in one another's heartbreak, misery, and arms amid piles of trash, and on the cold concrete for minutes. At one point, Sean peered around the corner, worried about where we'd gone. When I caught his attention, I motioned for him to tell the others, and to give us a little more time.

I was finally able to get Nolan to come inside, the parents and her students all long gone. Sarah and Sienna all handled the awkwardness for us, telling people that Nolan had a stomach bug and ran outside ill. Nolan was so upset that she didn't get to talk to Kira, who seemed to be an important student for her, but I seemed to ease her mind during the car ride home, telling her that we could call her mom, and maybe even pay her a visit in a day or two.

I drove Nolan's car to her dorm, and Sean followed us, helping me to carry everything upstairs for her. He and I had already discussed it, and I was not leaving her alone tonight. Sean and Becky would spend the night on Sarah's couch, so they could pick me up in the morning to take me back to my dad's house. I had some important meetings lined up, but not until the late morning. And nothing was more important than being right where I was tonight.

When everyone left us alone, I turned out Nolan's lights and went to her bathroom to turn her shower on. I wanted her to feel comfortable and cared for, so I helped her from her clothes and into the shower. It wasn't about sex or seduction tonight. It was about being there for her, letting her lean on me, in the place I should have been months ago. I washed her hair and soaped her body, washing the makeup stains from her cheeks. I wrapped her in a towel and led her to her bed, sitting her down while I dug through her duffle bag of clothes she'd brought from home. I found the Coolidge football shirt, her favorite, and put it over her head. I pulled a pair of cotton leggings out next and helped her slide those on.

"My hair. It's wet," she sounded so defeated, so melancholy. I pulled the towel from her head slowly and ran my fingers through it. I laid the towel across her pillows and then pulled her big blanket back.

"It'll be okay. Here, just lay on this," I said, easing her back and tucking her under the covers. I pulled my jeans off, and left my boxers and T-shirt on as I slid in next to her and pulled her close. I stroked her face until her eyes finally grew heavy, and I heard the faint hum of her breathing. Tonight was hard. Thinking about it all seemed almost too heavy, and thinking about Nolan working through this alone made me sick to my stomach.

But as hard as tonight was, it was also important. It had to happen, and I couldn't find a way to do it on my own. Kira might have just saved us. I know she saved Nolan. There was only healing from here; I'd make sure of that.

Chapter Twenty-Six

Nolan

"HOW DO you feel about your midterms?" Dr. Ashford asked in her typical soothing voice. It wasn't her fault she was such a stereotype. I suppose her demeanor was just part of the job description. I liked her, actually. Quite a bit. And I think in many ways she was responsible for my academic turnaround this semester. Reed made me promise to talk to someone, even as much as offering to sit with me while I talked to my mom about my miscarriage. But I couldn't bring this to her. Not because I didn't think she could help; I was sure she could. But it would also devastate her. And I wasn't sure I could survive the look on her face, knowing I'd lost a child, her grandchild. I didn't have enough strength left inside to handle that.

"Nolan?" Dr. Ashford asked.

"Hmmmm? Oh, sorry. I was sort of off somewhere," I sat up straight and rolled my shoulders back to attention to listen now. "Midterms. Yes…uh…I feel good. Really good, actually."

"That's good to hear," she nodded, folding her notebook in her lap and clicking her pen closed. "You're heading home for spring break, for the wedding this week, right?"

"Yeah. I get to be a bridesmaid. It's my first wedding. At least, first that I can remember," I smiled faintly, looking down to my locked fingers in my lap.

"And Reed...he gets drafted this week, right?" she asked, as if Reed's draft hadn't been the center of every conversation we'd had for the last month. I just nodded softly in return, holding my breath for a few seconds before letting it out heavily, with a shrug. "What have we learned, Nolan?"

I sighed again. I know she meant well, but sometimes therapy felt a lot like nagging. "That I don't need to waste my positive energy worrying about what ifs," I said, internalizing my worry and masking it from her, afraid I'd be caught in my little act.

She just reached forward before she stood and patted my folded hands. "I know you still worry. It's human, and it would be weird if you didn't. But...you need to try to rationalize with yourself before you let it take over everything. When you recognize your anxiety, remind yourself that nothing has happened to cause it," she said, smiling and standing to her feet in her tall black pumps, towering over me by a good six inches.

I stood and shook her hand, grabbing my bag from the floor and slinging it sideways across my body. I was reaching for her door when she gave me one more piece of advice.

"Oh, and Nolan?" she said. "Try to have a good time. You've earned it."

I nodded and left, wondering if I deserved the good times she says I earned.

———

Buck and Rosie's wedding was going to be late Sunday night out at Winter's Barn. Rosie had made the food herself, prepped it, and hired a few servers to set it up on the wedding day. Everything was country-themed, with a local honky-tonk band and fiddlers for the ceremony, and open fire pits for marshmallow roasting. Sarah, Sienna and I spent the afternoon stringing lights across the barn, and throughout the porch and outdoor dancing area. I couldn't wait to see it at night.

Buck and Reed were in Tucson for several interviews after Friday's draft selection. Reed didn't win the Heisman. But he was selected fourth overall by San Diego, just like Dylan had predicted months ago. I had grown to respect Dylan, though she would never be someone I'd feel comfortable calling a friend. She was smart, and a real advocate for Reed. Her father, however, was unbelievable. I was in awe watching him at Buck's house the days before the draft, fielding call after call, and hanging up on offers he didn't think were worthy of even listening to, only to get call-backs immediately with better terms. A lot of the selection came down to the team's needs and how the players fell in the order. But there still was negotiating to do, especially off the books—about understood resigning agreements, certain playing time guarantees and performance bonuses. It was all kind of shady, but part of the business, I supposed.

I kept reminding myself of Dr. Ashford's warning. Nothing to worry about until there is something to worry about. That was the gist. And I recognized my anxiety. I wore it proudly, carried it around with me. I guess knowing it was there made it more manageable, but I still felt that familiar sickness in my tummy, like trouble was looming.

Reed texted me a few times during the draft, and I recorded everything for him and Buck to see when they finally made it home. He looked so right holding up the blue and gold jersey to his chest. When I closed my eyes, it was like I'd seen him there all along. He was where he was supposed to be; he'd done it. Number 13. My number 13, at least...for now.

I was getting ready with Sienna at Sarah's house, when I finally got his text that they'd made it home.

Hey, we just got in. Dad's getting ready. He's nervous. It's funny.

The thought of Buck feeling nervous made me smile. He'd been married to a strong woman before—Millie. But Rosie was different. I felt like he had finally found his equal.

Well make sure you get him there on time!

I joked, thinking about how pissed Rosie would be if the boys showed up late.

Oh we'll be there, Princess. Can't wait to see you!

His words warmed my insides, and I pushed myself to soak in the now. Tonight, he couldn't wait to see me. That was my reality, and by God I was going to enjoy it.

Sarah braided Sienna and my hair into twists and loops, wrapping it atop our heads. Sienna tackled Sarah's since I was useless when it came to things like this. We all had these cute white shirt-dresses with cowboy boots. Rosie had picked them out, saying she hated the traditional bridesmaid look that got relegated to the back of the closet as soon as the ceremony was over.

Her daughter-in-law was also joining us in the ceremony, and we spent the first hour, long before the boys arrived, taking pictures. It was a little warm outside, which made me even happier to have a light cotton dress on. I was fanning myself with one of the wedding programs when I heard the familiar rumble of Reed's Jeep.

I stood up and shielded my eyes from the setting sun when I heard his whistle.

"Whoa," he said, walking up to me in dark jeans with his boots and a dark gray jacket over his dress shirt. If I didn't know he was a football player, I would have mistaken him for a bull rider. I'd never seen him dressed in his country finest, and I had to admit, it was hot as hell.

"Whoa, yourself. You look hot, Wildcat," I teased, also reaching around him and stuffing my hands in his back pockets to cop a feel of his awesome ass. He jumped a little when I did, which made me giggle. He reached around me and dipped me backwards in his arms, dangling me dangerously close to the ground before he kissed me and pulled me back up to his body, swinging me around.

"Not a Wildcat anymore, remember?" he said, his smile lighting up his face.

"Yeah, but *Charger* just doesn't have the same ring to it. It's not really a pet name. I think I'll still call you Wildcat if that's okay," I joked.

Reed just lifted me in the air again and twirled me around once more. "You can call me whatever you want," he winked, setting me back down gently. He flitted at my skirt a bit while I turned around to let him take the outfit in. "Rosie did good. You look unbelievable. Like I just picked you up from some stage in Nashville."

"Hey, careful, buster. I might start singing," I said, causing Reed to cringe a little and squint one eye. Music didn't run in my veins, and when I tried to sing for real it rarely came out on key.

"Reed! I need some help, son. Pronto!" Buck shouted from a side door in the dressing room area of the barn. Reed just turned to look at me one more time, grabbing my hand and kissing it.

"Looks like I have to give the old man a pep talk," he laughed, and then got a little serious all of a sudden, stepping in closer to me. "I'll see you on the aisle?"

I just nodded and pushed him a bit, urging him to go to help his dad. "Yeah, yeah…you'll see me," I said, gulping a little and pushing down my anxiety that was starting to rear its ugly head.

"Nothing's wrong, we're okay; he's not gone yet." I thought.

The barn was lined with rows of white chairs, and every seat was full when the ceremony finally started. The fiddlers played a beautiful classical tune that I didn't recognize, but it still had a country flavor because of them. I turned the corner of my hallway and met Reed at the door to walk down the aisle together. He reached out his arm and I took it, smiling up at him and just breathing him in.

We walked slowly down the row of seats, and I scanned the

crowd for my family, smiling at them. I found Becky, and Sean, and Calley, too, and they whistled at us like we had just been announced homecoming king and queen. When I turned back to Reed, I realized he was only looking at me, his eyes never leaving my face. I smiled at him, and he returned it, his gaze never wavering. He walked me up the small steps at the front of the barn and leaned in to kiss me softly before we both stepped to our respective sides, whispering in my ear, "I'll see you soon."

The rest of the girls and guys filed in behind us, and both of Rosie's sons walked her down the aisle, hugging their mother and shaking Buck's hand before taking their seats at the front.

The wedding was officiated by an old friend of Buck's, and he told funny stories throughout the ceremony, sometimes embarrassing Buck and leaning in to ask Rosie if she was sure she was making the right move. Everyone would chuckle, and Rosie would always say she was sure. The way she looked at Buck was enviable. It was what I wanted—to know that you had someone. Completely.

When the couple said, "I do," the barn erupted in cheers, guests tossing white rose pedals at Buck and Rosie as they walked back down the aisle. Reed and I were next, and he just grabbed my hand, leading me through the rain of flowers in a jog, laughing and happy. *We were happy. Perhaps our happiest.*

The band started playing almost immediately, firing up the crowd and getting people on the dance floor. Sarah of course had danced with every guy available and was working her way through the girls. Reed, though, never left my side. He swung me around the dance floor, surprisingly good at the country two-step, and held me close for the few slow songs the band played.

We all stood back in a circle when Buck and Rosie took the floor for their dance. The band played a cover of Adele's *Make You Feel My Love*, and watching Buck whisper in his bride's ear, kiss her cheek, and hold her adoringly, made my knees weak and put tears in the eyes of a lot of the other women at the party.

Reed just stood behind me throughout the entire thing, his arms locked solidly around my body, and his chin resting on my shoulder, while he leaned down to be at my level. Each time I'd turn to look at

him, I'd catch his eyes already on me, and he would take the opportunity to kiss me softly.

It was quickly becoming the most amazing night of my life.
After a little while, we all found our way to the tables under the
twinkling white lights the girls and I had strung. The effect only
added to the stars that shown bright above, the full moon out for
display, too. Rosie's food was devoured, and soon after our plates
were cleared, the servers started passing out the champagne. I took
my glass and tasted a tiny sip, peeking at Reed and making a
funny face.

"Don't like it?" he scrunched his face, asking me.

"It's okay. I never really cared for champagne," I said, taking
one more tiny sip and reevaluating my opinion a bit. "Well…actu-
ally, this is kinda good."

He poked my side a little and kissed my neck. "Slow down there.
I don't need you getting all bold and tipsy and taking my dad's
clients to the pool tables down the road and hustling them out
of cash."

I was about to dish it right back to him when we were interrupted with the clanking of glasses and spoons, Buck getting our
attention. A few people in the audience groaned, an inside joke
about Buck's long speeches.

"Yeah, yeah. It's my wedding, and I'll talk if I want to," he
teased back, belly laughing. When the room finally quieted, Buck
took a deep breath and turned to Rosie before looking back out at
the guests seated before him. "Thank you all, so much, for coming
on out here tonight. I hope you're having a good time. Chuck?
Don? Great music boys!" Buck said, holding his glass up to toast
the band.

"Tonight's a big deal for me. Now, I know what you're thinking.
'But Buck, we've been to your weddings before'…and yeah, you
have. I have a shitload of toasters, so thanks for those," he laughed,
getting even more chuckles from the crowd.

"But tonight's different. You see, this one?" he said, leaning over
to kiss Rosie's head. "This one's forever. She's seen me at my worst.
Hell, she's taped me up and put me back together more times than

my own mother. She's yelled at me for being stupid, forced me to eat right, forgiven me for sneaking gallons of ice cream, and didn't judge me when I told her I had young girlfriends because I was afraid of dying."

The crowd was quiet at his words, his face full of love and affection as he turned to Rosie and spoke his words right to her. "Rose, my love. It took me years…way too many, I know…to get my head on straight. But it's on there now, straight as an arrow. And I am so happy that I get to spend the rest of my years making up for lost time with you. I love you, my heart, and my soul. And thanks for picking me right back."

Rosie stood at his words and grabbed both sides of Buck's face, kissing him on the lips and causing a renewed round of cheers and whistles from the crowd. Everyone lifted their glasses in the air and took a drink in their honor. I was setting mine on the table when my napkin slipped from my lap and I bent down under the table to pick it up. Just then, I saw Reed's boots step up on top of the seat next to me and heard the clanking of his spoon on the glass again.

"Sorry…almost done," he said, his voice so similar to his father's now. "I'm the best man, and it's sort of tradition that best men say something at these things. I'd know…I've done this before, right Pops?" Everyone laughed at Reed's joke, picking on his dad's marriages. His father just wadded up his napkin and threw it at his son.

"I'm kidding, I'm kidding. I love you Pops, you know that. And Rosie, you've been family to me my entire life. Tonight? Well, that's just a formality for me. It makes it official." Reed gulped a little, looking down, his eyes wide and concentrating.

"It's funny, I do this a lot. Talk in front of crowds. But sometimes I get nervous. Phew, I'm a little nervous now," he reached down to take another sip from his glass. I felt bad, I almost wanted to rescue him. I knew he didn't really like attention. He tolerated it, played his part when he had to, whatever it took to get back out on the football field. I squeezed his hand at his side, and he looked down, his eyes intent on me, and his smile faint and thoughtful. He left his gaze on me when he continued to talk, and I hoped it would help calm his nerves.

"So, I'm supposed to say something wise—something meaningful, and deep—about love. But everything I know about love you taught me, Pops. So it just doesn't seem right passing on any words of wisdom to you here," he spoke, his eyes still trained on mine as he lifted one side of his mouth into a half smile, his irresistible dimple punctuating his words. That dimple. I was done the first time I'd seen it.

"I'm not going to give you any advice. At least, not anything you don't already know. But I would like to tell you what I've learned, what you've taught me. I've learned that sometimes love is hard. Life makes love hard, constantly pushing against you and finding things to throw in your way. And sometimes those things knock you down. No…they knock the shit out of you, knock you on your ass, isn't that what you said, Pops?"

"Sure is, son. Sure is," Buck piped in, leaning back in his chair, his face proud, and his head nodding. I looked back at Reed, his eyes never once leaving me. My heart was starting to race from his attention.

"Right. It knocks you on your ass. But then you get up. You get up, because that person, the one you love more than anything on earth…well, putting it bluntly, like my father taught me, they make getting your ass knocked down worth the trouble," Reed said. He was speaking to me, and I knew it. My hands were sweating from the attention, but my heart was swelling for the love from this man, the fact that he was washing away my insecurities right here, in front of everyone.

Reed stepped back down from his chair to the ground and everyone reached for their glasses, getting ready to toast. Only Reed didn't reach for a glass. Instead, he pushed his hand in his pocket and pulled out a tiny antique box, holding it for a few brief seconds in his giant hand before slipping down to one knee in front of me. I heard the gasps and a few whimpers from my friends just before the entire scene folded in on me, my ears drowning out everything but Reed. "Oh my God!" my mind screamed.

"Nolan. From the moment I met you, I knew you were different. You were tough, and honest, and smart, and funny, and beautiful. But you also fit me, like nothing else in my entire life had ever fit before. You are all of my missing pieces," he spoke, shaking his head a little as he laughed to himself softly, his eyes returning back to mine. "You are the good in me. What drives me, what motivates me. Yeah…I love football. But what I leave out there on that field, it's all for you. And I'd give that all up in a second if I had to. Because you…well, you've knocked me on my ass. But you're worth all the trouble."

Reed flipped the box open, revealing an antique ring with small swirls of diamonds and a pearl at the center. It was beautiful and perfect. It was old, and told a story, like our love. I couldn't blink, but rather could only sit frozen in my chair while Reed knelt before me. I managed to look up briefly at my mother, her eyes teary and a smile on her face. Reed followed my gaze and looked back at me, grinning mischievously. "Oh, they know all about this," he said, reaching into the box while the crowd snickered a little at my surprise. I was shaking now, my arms covered in goose bumps.

"Nolan Lynn Lennox. I've got a plan, and I hope you'll be on board with it. You see, I have to leave soon for San Diego. And I'm going to be far. And I'm going to be busy. And I'm not going to get to come see you anytime I want. And it sucks, and I hate it, and I'm so sorry it makes you sad. But I'd like to make you a deal," his voice so warm and gentle, his words making my eyes water and my hands shake. He reached down to wipe away a tear, leaving his hand on my cheek for a second just to touch me.

"You wear this ring and promise me you'll love me forever, and when you're done with your fellowship next year, we'll get married. That's it. No more ups. No more downs. Just me and you—and our forever," he said, pulling the ring from the box and holding it in front of me. Forever. Reed wanted me…forever.

My fingers tingled, and my eyes zeroed in on Reed's, the smile still there on his face. It never left, not once all night. Through the shock, I managed to stretch my lips into a smile, and I reached to touch his hands, nodding *yes*.

"Yes? Is that yes?" he asked, our foreheads touching while he slid the ring on my finger. It was a perfect fit, and I'd wear it for always.

"Yes," I choked, the tears falling a bit now. "Yes, I'll marry you Reed Johnson. You're worth the trouble, too."

He stood and lifted me with him, swinging me around and knocking into the table a little, neither of us caring. "That's a yes, everyone," Reed shouted. "Drink up! She said yes!"

Sarah was the first to whistle, her fingers in her mouth so it carried loudly through the desert air. Everyone else joined in after, but all I heard were Reed's words in my ear.

"You have no idea how happy you've just made me, and I'm going to spend the rest of my life trying to make you just as happy," he said, kissing me long and hard, his hands holding my chin and face.

"You already do," I said, happy tears falling now.

"God I love you," he whispered, hugging me tightly to his chest.

"I knew you did," I said, holding my breath and staring into the eyes I'd just made a promise to love forever. He smiled at my words, the same ones he had said to me the first time we uttered those words to one another. He just held me tighter then, and never let go.

Epilogue

Reed

MY BODY FELT like it had been carried under a freight train. I'd taken beatings in college ball, and I thought practices had toughened me up enough, but I'd never been hit like I was out on that field today. I stood there like nothing was wrong, though. I'd keep it to myself until I got home, and Nolan forced me to soak in ice. Part of me thought she kind of liked torturing me with the freezing ice baths.

I'd finally gotten my shot at starting. Four long years as the number two, with a play or two here and there, but this year the starting gig was finally mine. I played well today. We won, and I threw two passes to the end zone. But that one interception was going to plague me. I caught Nolan's eyes as she stood to the side on the field, waiting with my dad. She knew I'd be replaying the interception all day, too. She just gave me a thumb's up and mouthed, "You were awesome," her attempt for me to shrug off my error. I wish I could; it just wasn't in me.

The San Diego media had been hounding me all week leading up to the game. The team was mine this year, and I was going to sink or swim. Today, at least, I'd get to live to another Sunday. I gave Nolan the sign for a few more minutes while one of the camera guys clipped a microphone to the front of my jersey. One more interview. I could do this.

The questions were always the same: What did you learn under Sampson? Do you feel ready? What do you need to work on? I rattled off my answers by rote, changing a word around here and there, just to make it seem as if I was saying something fascinating and new.

The reporter was just getting in the groove of his questioning, when I looked over and realized Nolan was gone. My dad was still there, so I wondered what had happened. I knew I was irritating the reporter, because I was so damned distracted, but I couldn't help but search for her. I usually met her in the family area, because the field was pretty crowded after the game.

"I'm sorry. Can I just take a short pause? I just need to check on something. I'm all yours in just a sec. I promise," I said, unclipping the mic and handing it to the camera guy while I slid through the crowd of reporters to my dad. "Hey. Where's Noles?"

My dad just shrugged me off as I walked up. "She's fine, she's fine. It's probably just that thing they get…what is it?" my dad was typing on his phone while he was talking to me, driving me nuts. "Morning sickness. Probably just morning sick…"

He looked up, realizing his mistake, his face breaking out into an unmistakable smile. My breath stopped, and I started scanning the field, looking for my girl. I finally saw her walking back onto the grass from one of the tunnels, and I took off into a sprint. She just dropped her purse and sank her head down, shaking it.

"Oh no! Was she crying? Not again. Please God, not again!" I prayed.

As I got closer to her, I realized she was laughing. And when I reached for her hands, she just looked at me and smiled. "I knew your dad would blow it," she said, her lips forming a tight, confident smile. I looked down at her belly and then back up at her.

"Are you…are you sure?" I asked. She just nodded big.

"Oh, I'm sure. It's about six weeks according to the doctor," she said, laughing a little at my stunned face.

"We're...pregnant?" I said, placing my hands on her stomach now and staring at it again. I'd never felt something so important before. So fragile. Nolan was giggling, and I looked up at her, my mouth unable to do anything but smile.

"Uh, I'm pretty sure I'm the one that's pregnant. You get to be a dad, yeah. But I don't see you throwing up your damn breakfast in a stadium bathroom," she said, her hands on her hips. I laughed out loud, half because she was right, and it was funny, and half because I'd never been happier than I was in this exact moment.

I got down on my knees and hugged her waist, just listening to her like I could hear something. I knew it was ridiculous, but suddenly I couldn't wait to get her home to touch her belly and talk about names and Google whatever the hell it was we were supposed to do.

"Hey, I'm having a baby!" I shouted to the reporters standing and staring now. They started to walk over, taking pictures of us together. Suddenly, my interviews got a whole lot more interesting, and Nolan fielded a few questions, too. When she started to look tired, I held up a hand and apologized to the few reporters left. My girl was running out of steam, and I had to get her home.

"Sorry guys. Just give me a call and we'll talk. I gotta get my family home," I smiled. Family. I was going to have a family.

I took Nolan's purse from her and tucked it under my arm. "I can hold my purse. You look silly," she sassed. I refused to give it back, though. If I had my way, she wouldn't carry anything for the next nine months. "Fine, if you insist. I'm going to start bringing the heavier one, though, just to torture you," she said, crinkling her nose at me. I just crinkled mine back and leaned in to kiss her quickly.

I held her hand as we walked through the family area and down to the garage. Suddenly, I felt guilty making her climb up into a lifted Jeep. I was going to get a new car tomorrow. Hell, I might just go get one tonight.

We drove home through the hills and pulled onto our private

street. I was waiting for the gates to swing open when Nolan broke the silence.

"Peyton," she said.

"I'm sorry?" I asked, a little confused.

"Our baby. I'd like to name him Peyton," she smiled, looking straight ahead as I drove through the gates to our house.

"Him, huh? You feeling a boy?" I said, my male instincts kicking in with pride at the thought of having a son.

"Either way," she shrugged.

"Either way what?" I asked, then realized. "Oh, yeah. Either way. I'm happy whatever we have."

Nolan just laughed to herself, rubbing her hands over her sleepy eyes. "No, silly. Either way. We're naming our baby Peyton either way."

Peyton, just like Nolan. I loved it with all my heart, instantly. Just like my girl.

"Yeah, Peyton. I like it," I said, falling in love with her all over again.

~THE END~

Acknowledgments

**updated: As with Waiting on the Sidelines, I've decided to keep my original words in here. It's been longer than a year now. It feels like just yesterday, too. :) **

Last year, I began a journey. I finally dedicated myself to finishing something I started, something deeply personal and that meant more to me than anything I'd ever done before professionally. When *Waiting on the Sidelines* went live for the world to read in April 2013, I wanted to pass out—both from the thrill of it being done and real and tangible (at least, as tangible as an e-book can be) and from the panic that no one would care it was there.

Thankfully, my panic was misguided. To see this story embraced by readers around the world is so special to me. I have carried Nolan Lennox in my head for years, and to see others love her as much as I do is the best affirmation that I'm really doing something I'm supposed to be doing when I string words together into stories.

I knew when I finished *Waiting on the Sidelines* that I wanted Reed and Nolan's story to continue. But I had to make sure others wanted it to as well. And bless you, readers, for not being shy. It's because of you that *Going Long* is here. And I hope I have met your expectations.

Just as with *Waiting on the Sidelines*, *Going Long* has a wonderful support team of friends and family that helped it move from my MacBook to e-reader. Thank you, Team Ginger—you girls are my heart and soul (my super-ultra battery in the Arizona desert). Mom, dad, Phil and family—thanks for knowing I could do this. My sweet husband, thanks for giving me a real fairytale of my very own (I'm one of the lucky ones, don't I know it!) And Carter, thank you for always checking to make sure mommy had enough sports in the book. I promise, someday we will write the story together about the boy who learns to play baseball with magic shoes and Bryce Harper's bat (honestly, my son has some great ideas).

Thank you, Lesley and Jayne, for being such amazing artistic geniuses and sharing your time and talent with me. You make things look so dang good. And thank you, Billi Joy Carson, the best editor this side of the Mississippi (and perhaps the other side, too…I haven't travelled east in quite some time).

But most importantly, thank you readers and bloggers. You have taken time from your lives to tell your friends, blog, Tweet and Facebook your passion for Reed and Nolan's story. And I know that you are the reason for any success my stories may find. You are amazing, and I love each and every one of you!

If you enjoyed *Waiting on the Sidelines* and *Going Long*, I would love it if you would share your thoughts with others. Please consider posting a review, lending both books or recommending it. If you do post a review, please let me know so I can thank you and share your review on my websites. You can find me on Goodreads or at www.authorgingerscott.com or www.littlemisswrite.com. Please also consider liking my facebook page at www.facebook.com/Ginger-ScottAuthor and following me on Twitter @TheGingerScott. And if you'd just like to drop me a line, I'd love to hear from you. I love email (I do a happy dance; honestly, I do!).

About the author…

Ginger Scott is a journalist and writer from Peoria, Arizona. An Arizona native, Scott infused a lot of her home state into *Waiting on the Sidelines* and its sequel, *Going Long*. Scott is a graduate and associate faculty member of Arizona State University's Cronkite

School of Journalism. When she's not tapping furiously on her MacBook during the wee hours or reading in the dark on her iPad, she's probably at a baseball diamond somewhere watching her son or her favorite team, the Arizona Diamondbacks, take the field.

In addition to *Waiting on the Sidelines* and *Going Long,* Scott is working on an entirely new story. For the latest on her upcoming new-adult romance, follow her on Facebook or visit her online.

Also by Ginger Scott

The Waiting Series

Waiting on the Sidelines

Going Long

coming in January 2019

The Hail Mary

Like Us Duet

A Boy Like You

A Girl Like Me

The Falling Series

This Is Falling

You And Everything After The

Girl I Was Before In Your

Dreams

The Harper Boys

Wild Reckless

Wicked Restless

Standalone Reads

Cry Baby

The Hard Count

Memphis

Hold My Breath

How We Deal With Gravity

Blindness

About the Author

Ginger Scott is an Amazon-bestselling and Goodreads Choice Award-nominated author from Peoria, Arizona. She is the author of several young and new adult romances, including bestsellers Cry Baby, The Hard Count, A Boy Like You, This Is Falling and Wild Reckless.

A sucker for a good romance, Ginger's other passion is sports, and she often blends the two in her stories. When she's not writing, the odds are high that she's somewhere near a baseball diamond, either watching her son field pop flies like Bryce Harper or cheering on her favorite baseball team, the Arizona Diamondbacks. Ginger lives in Arizona and is married to her college sweetheart whom she met at ASU (fork 'em, Devils).

FIND GINGER ONLINE: www.littlemisswrite.com

Made in the USA
Las Vegas, NV
07 January 2021